PURSUIT OF THE JADE EMPRESS

A DAVID BLAISE MYSTERY

Also by MB Dabney

An Untidy Affair
A Deadly Game

Short Stories

Black on Black in Black
Anthology: The Fish That Got Away

Miss Hattie Mae's Secret
Anthology: Decades of Dirt: Murder, Mystery and Mayhem from the Crossroads of Crime

Killing Santa Claus
Anthology: Homicide for the Holidays

Callipygian
Anthology: The Fine Art of Murder

Maribeth: The Trophy Wife
Anthology: Center City Crime

The Missing Medallion
Anthology: Hoosier Hoops and Hijinks

Death — In 9 Innings
Anthology: Scenic and Sinister: Landmarks of Indiana

Editor

Decades of Dirt: Murder, Mystery and Mayhem from the Crossroads of Crime
Co-editor with Barbara Swander Miller

MURDER 20/20
Co-editor with Lillie Evans and Shari Held

Scenic and Sinister: Landmarks of Indiana
Co-edited with Janet E. Williams

PURSUIT OF THE JADE EMPRESS

A DAVID BLAISE MYSTERY

MB DABNEY

Pursuit of the Jade Empress
A David Blaise Mystery

Published by Per Bastet Publications LLC, P.O. Box 3023
Corydon, IN 47112

Cover by T. Lee Harris

ISBN 978-1-942166-96-2

Available in trade paperback and DRM-free ebook formats

PURSUIT OF THE JADE EMPRESS

A DAVID BLAISE MYSTERY

To Angela, my love.

Let’s do Paris — again.

Praise For An Untidy Affair

MB Dabney delivers . . . an emotional roller coaster with twists and usually surprising turns.

~~ Sharyn Flanagan, the *Philadelphia Tribune*

Praise For A Deadly Game

The story hits many of the beats of a traditional (albeit enthralling) detective story, from deceitful clients to David (Blaise) getting roughed up. It's the nuanced character of David himself who truly elevates this tale. A charismatic private eye electrifies this absorbing murder mystery.

~~ Kirkus Review

MB Dabney takes us on a twisty whodunit ride with a clever, ethical detective who's dodging knives while solving more than one intricate puzzle at a time.

~~ Sandy Lender, fantasy author of the *Choices Meant for Gods* series.

A Deadly Game has more twists and turns than East River Drive along the Schuylkill River in Philadelphia, and will keep you on the edge of your seat.

~~ Diana Catt, award-winning author of *Death Map*

ACKNOWLEDGEMENTS

In addition to two of my brothers, Eric and David, I need to thank Iris Martin, the late Pam Moran, and a host of the usual suspects — Janis Thornton, Diana Catt, Joel Hennessy, and Robin Lovelace — for their help, advice, and suggestions, or for reading early drafts of this book. I also need to thank Rea Best, Janice Mimms, Jennifer and Howard Scott, the late Jackie Spurlock, Warren Spurlock, Jody Spurlock Harris, David Norwood, Sharyn Flanagan, former police officers (and twins) Wendy Otto and Cindy Fox, Curtis Strother, Angela Brown, Eric Mychaels, Kim Hennessy, Nicole Taylor, and Seth Bengelsdorf for their help and moral support, often at times when they were unaware that I needed the support the most.

As always, this book wouldn't be possible without the help of Marian Allen and her team at Per Bastet Publications. Thank you, yet again.

CHAPTER I

"Grammy Taylor's had a heart attack!"

I looked at my watch — it was nearly half-past noon — and I wondered, for the one-millionth time, if I had it right. I reminded myself, however, that the information was good. Solid. The exchange would be Saturday. At noon. In Fairmount Park. In a parking lot off of Memorial Drive, just past the Sculpture Gardens.

That meant they were late.

It also meant I'd probably be late for my law school study group on constitutional law. And the final was only days away.

"You gonna have to pay me extra for this, David. They late. It's my day off and I be doin' this as a favor. I got better things to do than just sittin' here on ah Saturday in Fairmount Park," said Mae. "I got shoppin' to do. Bonwit's having ah sale."

Bonwit Teller is struggling as far as I could tell, so they're always having a sale, I wanted to say but didn't, though I, too, was tired of sitting around, waiting. The contact said noon in the park and they were positive.

"Just a little longer. Okay? Please," I responded, shifting my weight from one hip to the other as I sat on a picnic blanket under a tree on a small hill across the road from the parking lot. It was the perfect vantage point and cover for surveillance, which is partly what I do.

My name is David Blaise and I'm a private detective.

Mabelene Washington is my secretary and though I occasionally use her for research outside the office, such as checking public records in City Hall, I rarely use her for field work. I don't like to potentially put her in harm's way. But the opportunity for this surveillance came up suddenly late on Friday and I had few options. Besides, I wasn't expecting any trouble.

I faintly heard what sounded like an engine on the verge of a misfire and glanced to my right. About a thousand feet down the road was a van, just the sort of vehicle I was told to expect. I got up and then noticed in the opposite direction a fast-moving, full-sized, dirty white sedan that had seen better days. It appeared headed for the parking lot.

"Here they come. Get ready. Let's go," I said.

Mae, who can best be described as a shapely woman, struggled a little getting up because she was wearing such tight-fitting jeans. Yet she shrugged off any help. In addition to the jeans, she wore a white V-neck T-shirt, a black-and-white houndstooth jacket, and peep-toe shoes.

If anyone noticed — and I hoped they wouldn't — she looked like a pretty woman on an outing in the park having some sexy pictures taken.

I first positioned myself in front of her with my back to the parking lot. Through the camera lens, I viewed Mae next to a tree on which I had hung a bunch of black and white balloons. They moved about in a gentle breeze. With any luck, none would pop and draw attention to us.

I could hear both vehicles pull into the lot. I pretended to take pictures.

"Let me know when they're getting out of the cars and we'll switch positions," I said, "just as we talked about."

"I hope you're gettin' some of this, cause I'm lookin' good," Mae said, striking a pose.

"Only a couple when we finish, Mae. You know I'll be focused on what they're doing back there."

"They gettin' out."

"Okay, quick. Switch positions. And take the jacket off and throw it over your shoulder," I instructed. I shouldn't have been surprised that her T-shirt was as tight as the jeans.

Now I was facing the parking lot. I quickly focused the camera to get clear shots across the way. The vehicles were side by side with the van on the right, and as luck would have it, the backs of the vehicles were facing me.

With Mae's out-of-focus body in the foreground, I started taking pictures, trying to keep track of the number of shots. The camera had film with thirty-six exposures, but I didn't want to take the time to switch to a backup camera and perhaps miss something important.

Click, click, click.

As I expected, a thin, tall, white guy got out of the driver's side of the van and walked to the back, while a beefier Black guy from the van's passenger side came around to the back. From the other vehicle, I was surprised when a casually dressed woman, who had been driving, got out and moved to the back of her car with a medium-build Black guy, who had been in the front passenger seat.

I hadn't expected a woman to be part of what apparently is a growing fencing operation in the Philadelphia area. But I quickly reminded myself to keep an open mind.

"The camera loves you, baby," I joked to Mae as if I was a hotshot fashion photographer, all the while focusing on taking pictures of the woman and the tall van driver. I wanted to get their faces as best I could as they shook hands. But getting clear shots of the tall van driver was the most important thing my client needed.

Click, click, click.

Mae turned and posed with her hip cocked, her back arched, and her butt protruding in my direction. "I know you like this pose. You just want some shots of my ass," she said with alluring sweetness. "You know you do, Daddy."

Click, click, click.

She was right, at least in part. She possessed the callipygian assets that Black men so love in their women, and she knew how to best flaunt them. We first met more than a year-and-a-half ago when, due to a toxic mixture of overwork, loneliness and bad judgment, I visited a Center City gentleman's club where she worked as a hooker.

A ho, as she'd say without reservation or any hint of embarrassment. As she told me once, she'd been called worse.

That night after our romp in the hay, Mae, who went by the playful name of Baby Cakes, told me she was a secretarial school graduate. I hated doing clerical work in my small, one-man detective agency office, so I gave her one of the last business cards I carried in my wallet. I told her to call someday if she was serious, though I doubted I'd ever hear from her or see her again.

I had no plans to return to the gentleman's club.

Therefore, imagine my surprise when, several days later, she contacted me, saying she was looking for a job and for a way out of "this business," the euphemism she used for prostitution. The night before, Mae had said, she and all the other ladies in the gentleman's club were robbed at gunpoint.

Against my better judgment, I hired her — and it's proven to be an excellent decision. Mae is hard-working, possesses excellent administrative and management skills, and exhibits just the right amount of irreverence to keep me on my toes.

Despite how we first met, our professional working relationship — in addition to both our individual choices — required that we never have sex again. That did not, however, stop her from being flirty, from time to time, as it's one of her major character traits. I often found her flirtatiousness amusing, though at other times I found it irritating.

Today was one of those times.

"They look like Calvin Klein boxes, I think. Can't tell," I said, staring hard through the camera lens. "I'll look closer later. Now turn back to face me and put the jacket back on and pose again."

Click, click, click.

After all the boxes were taken from the van and placed in the car, the Black guy pulled out a knife, cut open one of the boxes, and looked inside. Satisfied, he acknowledged as much to the woman. She then handed a white envelope to the tall van driver, who looked inside and then nodded to the woman.

Click, click, click.

After shaking hands, they closed the backs of their vehicles, got inside, and drove off. And I took one last set of pictures. I looked down at the camera and noted that I had taken thirty-two pictures and still had four exposures left.

"I can take a couple pictures of you now, Mae, if you want."

"You know I do," she said cheerfully. I smiled and took the last four pictures.

The pictures weren't a chore. The camera did love her.

Mae, who was roughly my age, just hitting her mid-thirties — she wouldn't exactly tell her age, which is one of her vanities — was an attractive woman, but years of working in the world's oldest profession had somewhat hardened her. She was brassy, often spoke her mind when she shouldn't but was straight-forward, generally honest, protective, dependable, and steadfastly loyal.

Once we were finished, I packed my equipment, folded the blanket, and took down the balloons.

Walking back to my car parked behind a small building more than a quarter mile away, Mae struggled along the uneven ground. "You should have worn more comfortable shoes," I said.

"And you can keep yo 'pinions on that to yo-self," she snapped back, though nearly falling twice and needing my arm to steady herself.

I let her comment go.

"I'm just amazed they were so brazen that they made such an exchange out in the open in Fairmount Park."

"What was in the boxes, you know?" she asked.

We reached my car, I unlocked the front door for Mae and deposited the cameras and lens in the back seat before going around to the driver's side. The interior of the car, a new 1986 Honda Accord I had just purchased, was warmed under the springtime sun, which enhanced the new-car smell inside.

Mae turned on the radio. The channel was set for WDAS and soon the sound of Anita Baker singing "Caught up in the Rapture" filled the car.

"One of the boxes definitely contains ladies' activewear. Maybe swimsuits. It could be worth several thousand dollars," I said, steering the car out of the park and toward Center City to drop Mae off at Bonwit's at Seventeenth and Chestnut. "Not sure of the other boxes. Clothing, though, I'm sure."

"I can get knockoff swimsuits on the street, probably behind Bonwit's," she said. "I could get you a nice one for Marie as a surprise."

As I headed down West River Drive, with the houses of Boathouse Row on the opposite side of the Schuylkill River and downtown Philly looming ahead, I briefly took my eyes off the road to stare at Mae. "Do not tell me I'm working my butt off to help catch thieves and you're going to go buy from them."

She held up her hands and broke into a smile. "Just joshin', David."

"That better be all."

After dropping Mae off downtown, I took Walnut and headed back into West Philly to the Penn campus and the law school library, arriving just in time for a three-and-a-half-hour session with my study group. They were all younger than me, most by nearly a decade. Maturity and cynicism had yet to kill their youthful confidence that, with law degrees, they were going to change the world. I had been working long enough to no longer have such confidence.

"We're going for burgers and beer down at Al's on 40th, Street," said Maurice, the leader of our group, after we finished studying. "You wanna come along?"

"Nah," I said. "I've got to drop off some film to be developed for work on Monday and then check on one or two things in the office before I head home. I'll just have a pizza when I get there. You guys go ahead."

Back in the car, I headed to 52nd Street and parked at the McDonald's at Chestnut, unconcerned that it might get towed for staying more than one hour. The free, off-street parking was a privilege I enjoyed for the occasional security work I did for the manager of the restaurant.

After parking, I walked across the street to drop off the film at a Kodak store to be developed and then headed to my office.

David Blaise Investigations was in a two-room office suite on the second floor in a corner building owned by my brother-in-law's company, the Stuart Thomas Management and Development Company. I got the office space for only a dollar a month, which greatly contributed to my healthier financial situation over the past year.

Thanks, Stuart. You're a mensch.

"Yo, yo, yo. It's the private dick," said Mookie, a snitch and street vendor who stood beside a table with cartons of cigarettes, gold and silver chains, and necklaces, sunglasses, and cassette tapes. There were a few assorted clothing items in a box beside the table.

In all likelihood, Mookie would one day end up with some of the stolen merchandise I saw earlier in the day. He was a malnourished, dark-skinned man, with thinning uncombed hair, and the hard look of the streets. Word was that Mookie, whose real first name was Sterling — how he came to be called Mookie was a mystery in itself — had once been a promising art student until drugs and poverty left him to hustle for basic survival on the street.

"How's it hangin', Mook," I said breezily as I was passing. My office was only a half-a-block away.

"Iz got sum information for ya," he managed to say in a loud whisper through some missing front teeth.

For some unknown reason, I slowed and finally, as curiosity got the better of me, I stopped and turned back to him. "What sort of information?"

"I hear somethin's big goin' down 'bout some old jewelry. A necklace," Mookie said and held out his weather-beaten, calloused, dark-skinned hand, as if for a payment for his flimsy tip. "Youz knowz how we work."

I shook my head and continued to my office. "That's not even a bread crumb, Mookie."

I doubted if he was crestfallen, though I didn't turn back to see. Mookie got lots of negative reactions every day. This one wouldn't even rate.

I unlocked the front door to the corner office building and entered, relocking the door afterwards. Needing the exercise, I walked up to the second floor and down the hall to my office suite. A plaque on the wall beside the door read: David Blaise Investigations.

As it was a Saturday, and no one was in the office, the only light was from the outside through the windows but it was just enough for me to be able to see.

On my desk was a file I'd left out the previous day before I rushed off to my final class session of the semester. Grabbing the file now, I noticed lights blinking on my answering machine, meaning I had messages, which was odd because it was the weekend. I punched the play button before walking over to a filing cabinet.

The first message was left at 12:45 in the afternoon.

"Davey, it's Allen," my brother said in a rush of nervous energy. "Call me as soon as you get this."

That was odd. Why would Allen call me in the office on a Saturday?

There were two other incoming calls before 3:30. In the first call of the two, "It's Eli, man. Call me," abruptly demanded my other younger brother. There was no voice message from the second call.

Then came the message at 4:15 from my sister, Valerie. She sounded like she was crying.

"I've called and called and left you messages at your apartment and at the office all afternoon. We've been trying to reach you," she said, stopping, I think, to wipe her nose. I could hear her tears. "We're in the ER. At Temple," she said, pausing just slightly to, perhaps, ensure the message was clear. "The new Temple University Hospital emergency room."

The next thing she said nearly caused my knees to buckle. I don't remember what I did with the file I held in my hand.

"Grammy Taylor's had a heart attack."

~*~

Stunned into inaction at first, without thinking I somehow managed to pick up the telephone and call all three siblings but got no answers. My consciousness was flooded with a cacophony of thoughts and images that blurred my vision.

I recalled random conversations with Grammy Taylor and bits of her wisdom and information from years earlier. She often recounted family stories, some dating back scores of years.

~*~

It was a cool, overcast day in Atlanta on April 28, 1905. But the sun eventually burned away the clouds by the afternoon, just in time for a baby to come into the world in a second-floor bedroom in a well-kept house in Brownsville, an economically thriving middle-class Black section south of downtown. Though the parents — Elijah and Cora Anderson, who were born in bondage more than four decades earlier — had every reason to believe it was a boy, a girl was born, the mother's sixth birth and the only female. Though she was seemingly healthy, they prayed throughout that day and into the night for the girl's survival. Two of the earlier five had died in either childbirth or in their infancy.

As the day and time of her birth were late on a Friday afternoon and county offices were closed over the weekend, news of Georgia Marie Anderson's arrival wasn't officially recorded until the following Monday, and thus her official birthday is listed as May 1.

Upon seeing her, the midwife, who was an aunt, dubbed her Georgie Mae, a nickname which stuck with family and friends until one day, after she married, she was addressed as Mama, then Mama Taylor and then, eventually, as Grammy Taylor.

~*~

"It's me," I said in a call to my on-again, off-again love interest who was spending the weekend with her parents in West Chester.

"David, where have you been? Everyone's been trying to reach you all afternoon. They rushed Grammy Taylor to the hospital," said Marie Toussaint. "She's had a heart attack."

"How do you know? I was just calling to tell you," I said. "My sister left me a message on my office phone. I tried to reach her or my brothers and haven't gotten an answer."

"They're probably at the hospital. You still in the office?"

"Yes. I was about to head out. Where are you?"

In another reality, the question would have been humorous or at least ironic. I was, after all, the one who called her. I should know where I called. But for some reason, that obvious fact escaped me before I asked, which raised red flags for Marie.

"Are you all right, David? You seem lost," Marie said, concern evident in her voice. "Do you need me to go with you to the hospital? I can borrow my parents' car and come get you."

I desperately longed for her at that moment, and for her physical and emotional support. But what I needed was to get to the hospital as quickly as possible. Before it was too late.

"No, but thank you. I'm heading over there now. I'll call you as soon as I know anything," I said, adding, "I promise."

"Okay, but I'm here if you need me."

"Thanks. I appreciate that. I'll call you later tonight and come pick you up tomorrow."

"I love you, Boo."

"Love you, too," I honestly replied.

~*~

Love, in general, and love of family, especially, were cornerstones of Grammy Taylor's life from early on. And love was more than just the greatest commandment of her jealous God, whom she said especially favored Baptists.

For Georgie Mae, that love was a requirement hatched out of tragedy.

The event that came to shape her personality and her viewpoint of familial love occurred in September 1906, when she was only eighteen months old and, thus, was too young to actually remember it.

I was in my car speeding down Chestnut Street on the way to North Philadelphia as Grammy Taylor's retelling of the Atlanta Race Massacre filled my head. The massacre left a void in her household that her parents were never able to completely fill.

At the time, with the memory of the hardships of the Civil War fading, though not its long-term hatreds, whites in Atlanta were resentful of Black economic success and feared their growing political power. Spurred on by unconfirmed reports that a couple of white women had been raped, presumably by Blacks, mobs of white men and boys descended on Black businesses and homes, smashing windows and setting properties on fire. They also randomly and viciously attacked Black people, male or female, that they encountered on the streets or on trolley cars as Black folk tried to escape the violence.

Elijah Jr. and his younger brother, King David, were working as shoeshine boys in a prominent Black barber shop on Decatur Street in Atlanta when a mob attacked the store, I remembered Grammy Taylor's retelling of the story, now embedded in our family's oral history.

Elijah pushed his brother out a side door, allowing him to escape as Elijah fought off a group of white men. King David safely made the two-mile journey home, unharmed. But Elijah's love and sacrifice cost him his life. His battered and broken body was discovered the next day in the debris of the barber shop, which was burned to the ground.

Growing up, Georgie Mae's parents reminded her of Elijah's love for his brother and his sacrifice and death, much like that of Jesus of Nazareth.

As a reminder of that love, my youngest brother, Elijah, was named after his long-dead great uncle who was murdered in Atlanta more than a half-century before Eli was born. And me? My full legal name, though unknown to most people and rarely ever spoken aloud even within the family, is King-David Anderson Blaise.

~*~

Arriving in North Philly, I parked across the street and ran to the entrance of the newly constructed nine-story hospital. Inside, I approached the front desk in the lobby where a middle-aged Black woman wearing all white answered the telephone and the questions for the people who came up to her. She looked up at me over the top of her glasses with tired eyes that conveyed, "Don't come up in here actin' a fool. I'm near the end of my shift and my feet hurt."

But what she said was, "Can I help you?"

"My grandmother was brought to the hospital this afternoon. I think they may have admitted her," I said, too afraid to contemplate what it meant if she was transported here and NOT admitted to the hospital.

"Let me see. I'll check with the operator. What's the patient's name?"

"Taylor. Georgia Marie Taylor," I replied with a touch too much impatience.

She picked up the phone, dialed and spoke to God-knows-who. I tried not to display my nervousness until I noticed I was unconsciously tapping my fingers on the counter in front of her. To her credit, she didn't appear to notice and was still impassive when she hung up the telephone to address me, her eyes again viewing me over the top of her glasses. "She's in the cardiac critical care unit. Fifth floor. Room 5107. The elevators are down this hallway," she said, raising her arm and pointing left, "to the first corridor on the right. Fifth floor."

She then said something unexpected as I hurried off. "Good luck, sir."

It took a while for the elevator to arrive, which always seems the case in hospitals. But I went up with only one stop on the way to the fifth floor. Exiting the elevator, I looked for any sign indicating the direction to Room 5107. Rooms 5101 to 5120 were to the left and I headed in that direction.

There are women in my life who mean the world to me. Marie, of course, my sister Val, even my secretary Mae. But the one who holds my life together — the person who is my strength, my Rock of Gibraltar — is Grammy Taylor.

During my years in Naval intelligence, I faced extremely dangerous situations many times. And as a private eye, I stared down the barrel of a gun more than once.

But as I reached for the door handle to Room 5107 at Temple University Hospital, I realized I had never been more terrified in my life.

CHAPTER II

"I can't tell you how sorry I am about your grandmother."

Like other large East Coast cities, such as New York or Boston, Philadelphia is a city with a lot of old Protestant wealth — or, in Philly's case, old Quaker wealth. And few retail establishments catered to that old Quaker wealth better than the Strawbridge and Clothier department store. Its flagship store in Center City at Eighth and Market streets housed floors of the finest merchandise money could buy. From women's high fashion to men's formal wear; from the latest ladies' shoes to the finest jewelry and watches; and from highest quality men's shirts, ties, suits and accessories to the best home goods, china, and bedding — it was all at Strawbridge's.

Despite changing times and consumer habits, the store was doing well, so well that the store's top executives — mostly descendants of the nineteenth century founders Justus C. Strawbridge and Isaac H. Clothier — were constantly fending off hostile takeover bids by Wall Street power brokers.

As I got off the elevator on an upper floor, I became aware of the ambient music quietly piped through hidden speakers that accompanied my walk through the home goods department to a far corner of the retail floor. The music was so quiet, calming, and peaceful that I was sure shoppers rarely noticed it.

Down a short, stark white hallway at the back of the floor, I approached a set of frosted glass doors. Over the top it read: Executive Offices.

Earlier in the morning, before I left home, I debated what to wear to this appointment. Generally, I wear jeans, sneakers, and a sports shirt — and occasionally a dress shirt without a tie

— under a blazer or jacket. I like blazers because they can be dressed up or down but, more practically, because they add at least four more pockets in which to carry things, such as spare pens and notebooks for taking notes.

Though I was up late — it was well past midnight before I went to bed — I rose early, and showered, shaved and ate before ironing a white dress shirt. I put on my best red paisley tie — from S&C, of course — a Navy blue blazer, tan slacks, and oxblood red loafers. Close enough to Sunday-go-to-meeting attire that even Grammy Taylor, the all-knowing guardian angel of appropriate church apparel, would undoubtedly approve. I knew that if I was going to quietly walk the halls of this elegant bastion of old Quaker wealth, I needed to at least dress the part.

I opened the door to the Executive Offices and walked through, and immediately felt like Dorothy must have in The Wizard of Oz when she opened the door of her black-and-white Kansas farmhouse to the full color of the Munchkin city in the Merry Old Land of Oz. This corridor was markedly different from the previously stark white hallway, though in keeping with the simplicity of its founders.

The décor of the S&C Executive Offices was warm and comforting, the carpeting a charcoal gray and the walls a warm cream. The lighting was less harsh compared to the brightness of the store's retail floors.

And there was no music.

The walls leading to the reception desk were lined with pictures displaying the department store's famed past and framed posters of old newspaper ads of the store. One advertisement caught my attention and I stopped to view it. It was a Christmas ad from 1938, featuring a number of items, including a woman's full-length fur coat for only $125.

I was sure that now, nearly five decades later in 1986, a Strawbridge customer couldn't get a fur coat for only one-and-a-quarter. But I made a mental note to ask.

"How may I help you?" politely asked the young, dark-haired receptionist, the gatekeeper to this inner sanctum.

"I have an appointment with Raymond Dawson at ten." I looked at my watch. I was precisely on time.

"And your name?"

"David Blaise."

"If you'll have a seat, I'll let him know you're here," she said pleasantly, indicating a couple of chairs, separated by a small table with flowers, that were up against the wall. On the wall behind the chairs was a picture of the store from the 1920s.

I didn't have to wait long before Raymond came down the hall. His long strides made him appear taller than his five-foot-seven height and displayed both confidence and purpose. Raymond was always a snappy dresser, so being an executive in a major retail department store was a good fit.

He wore a classic, two-button, fitted suit in beige, with a blue, button-down dress shirt, and a blue and beige tie. He looked like he was about to model a department store ad for men's suits.

I rose as he approached.

"David, good of you to come down," he said, extending a hand, which I shook. Looking at the large envelope in my other hand, he said, "Is that it?"

"Yes," I replied.

"Good. Come on down to my office," Raymond said, turning to head back in the direction from which he came. While I quickly surmised it wasn't in the direction of the offices of the store's highest-ranking executives, many of whom had Strawbridge as a surname, it was nonetheless impressive. The plaque outside his office door read: Raymond Dawson, Senior Vice President, Fashion Merchandising.

For some reason, I thought, "Movin' on up, to the east side," the opening lyrics to the television program, The Jeffersons.

"Sorry for the mess," he said, closing the door and removing his jacket, placing it on a wooden hanger and then the hanger on a hook on the back of the door. "Work, work, work. It's never done. Let's sit at this table."

His desk was neat as a pin but the table was littered with fabric swatches of plaids and tweeds, and cottons in solids and various color patterns. An assortment of women's fall fashions was on a rack against a wall next to another table on which lay V- and crew-neck cashmere sweaters in colors of red, yellow, tan, cream, navy, gray, and black.

"I'm meeting with a couple of the gals in ladies' sportswear right after I finish with you to make a few of the final merchandising decisions for Fall and Christmas delivery. One of the men's sportswear buyers is stopping by after that," Raymond said. "Thanks for coming in."

I pulled up a chair to the table and sat, then handed the photo envelope to Raymond. He took it but seemed decidedly uncomfortable and, of course, I knew why. For more than thirty-six hours, since Saturday night after I got to the hospital, I had wrestled with what to say to him at this moment. But in the end, he spoke first.

"David, I'm so sorry. I can't tell you how sorry I am about your grandmother. I would never do anything to harm her. You know that," he said rapidly, almost as if he was pleading for mercy.

"Of course not, Ray. No one's blaming you."

"I just didn't know," he said, nervously running his hand over his short black hair, which was styled from front to back.

I reassured him again. "How could you have? None of us knew. It was a total surprise."

"How's she doing?"

"Fine. Just fine. Doctors closely monitored her Saturday night, and all day yesterday and last night. I didn't head home from the hospital until late."

"And Val?" he asked.

When Ray and I were in high school together, my younger sister Valerie had a huge crush on him. Though surely the crush had long since died a quiet death, Ray has always tried not to show how flattered he was by it or how much he enjoyed it.

"She was there, too, of course," I said. "And my brothers."

"And what's his name? Stuart? Was he there?"

I smiled. Raymond knew full well what the man's name was. He had attended their wedding and probably bought them a gift.

"Nope. He was off taking care of the twins while Valerie, me and my brothers spent the day at the hospital," I said. "Allen and his wife Renee . . . they live in the house now with her . . . they're on the third floor . . . Allen and Renee are supposed to pick her up and take her home this afternoon when she gets released. Valerie just got a promotion to assistant vice president at the bank, so she's not stopping by the house 'til she gets off work later.

"When she gets old, I'm sure she'll be just like Grammy," I added, amused at the thought.

Raymond didn't speak or make eye contact. He didn't seem to know what to say next.

"And it was all because, for her birthday, I gave her some. . . ."

"Chamomile tea, yes. Or so it seems. It's what the doctors say probably caused the, uh, anna-fla-lacks-tics reaction . . . or however you pronounce that."

Raymond was generally easy-going and full of good humor, so it was a relief to finally witness a smile making an appearance on the man's face for the first time in this meeting.

"Anaphylactic reaction. I can't believe you got admitted into an Ivy League law school and you can't pronounce anaphylactic," he joked, seemingly relieved and at least a little relaxed.

"Hardy-har-har," I replied, also joking, holding hands out in an open gesture. "Anaphylactic. You happy now?"

"Exceedingly," he said, his eyebrows rising a bit. But then he turned serious again. "I've always loved Grammy Taylor. Back in the olden days when you and I were in high school, she made me feel so welcome, like I was a part of the family. You remember? And I thought for her birthday it would be nice if I got her some of our best chamomile tea. We have the very best stuff here, you know."

I leaned back in the chair, composed and relaxed. "She prefers coffee but does sometimes drink herbal tea. The doctors said the kind she's been drinking occasionally over the years was probably so weak that she never noticed an allergic reaction to it. Plus, now she's older . . . bodies do change with age . . . and what you gave her was good, expensive stuff. She wasn't used to that," I said.

He picked up the envelope containing photographs and looked inside without taking out any of the pictures. Then he got up and took the envelope to his desk. As he turned to face me, leaning back against his desk with his arms crossed over his chest, I could tell Ray was stalling. And he looked worried, unsure of himself.

Walking over to the other table, Raymond picked up a gray V-neck cashmere sweater and unfolded it. Holding it up, he looked at me. "What do you think? Would you buy this sweater? How much would you be willing to pay?"

I was totally caught off-guard. "Um, I don't know, Ray. I just don't know. How much is it?"

"When we get a shipment in, it'll retail in the Fall for about eighty dollars. It's a good sweater, two-ply, made locally in the U.S.," he said, refolding the sweater and putting it back on the table. "We'll put it in the Christmas catalogue for about sixty bucks but we'll still be making money on it even at that price point."

He was running out of places to hide in our talk and, as I had things to do, I couldn't afford the time to let him meander as he mustered up his courage.

"Raymond," I said sternly. He got the hint and sat down again to face me.

"I gave it to her more than a week ago. How did it . . . happen? Was she by herself? Alone?"

"No, Renee was in the house, upstairs. I don't know how much she drank but the reaction on Saturday was extreme," I said. "Renee said she heard a commotion. A porcelain teapot falling and breaking, followed by the thud of Grammy Taylor hitting the floor. She rushed downstairs and Grammy was unconscious."

"Oh, my God," Raymond exclaimed.

"She displayed all the symptoms of a heart attack. Rapid heart rate, difficulty breathing, faint, paleness, and they rushed her to the hospital and started calling everybody. But I didn't get the calls . . . I was busy on your case and didn't know they were calling me. And later in the afternoon I went to the law library to study."

"But how did they know it was an allergic reaction?"

"Anaphylactic reaction," I corrected.

"Yes, I know that," he said, apparently unfazed that I corrected him, "but how did they know?"

"She was conscious by the time the ambulance came to take her to Temple and at the hospital they immediately ran tests for cardiac issues but they were all negative. Her heart is fine. Then, they thought it might be an allergic reaction. Some of her symptoms were similar to food allergies. They asked Valerie if she had any allergies and she said she didn't know. And of course, my brothers had no idea. But doctors decided to test her and also give her a shot of epinephrine. She was better in ten minutes."

"Epinephrine, huh? That you can say," he said.

I ignored the ribbing.

"I hadn't reached anyone on the phone before I got to the hospital. When I walked into the room, I was expecting the worst. But . . . and you won't believe this, Ray . . . when I walked in, she was sitting up in bed playing bid whist with Valerie, Allen and Eli. The four of them." I laughed.

Raymond laughed, too. "The good, church-going lady plays cards? Blasphemy."

"What can I say? She's played whist for years, probably since college. Because of the meds, she was still a little loopy when I got there so they were letting her win."

"I'm just glad she's okay."

"Yeah, me too. I don't know what I'd do without her," I said and then brought us back to the business at hand. "You gonna look at the pictures or what? I'm billing you for them . . . and for the hours . . . either way."

"Ah, yeah, the pictures," he said, going back to his desk for the photo envelope and looking inside. As he flipped through the photographs, I considered my relationship with Raymond.

Ray and I had met in high school and formed a strong friendship, in part because he had easy access to a car for us to get around. Also I was shy, and hanging with Ray, whose good-looks and out-going, charming nature were a magnet for girls, meant I had more opportunities to meet cute girls than if I was alone. In fact, I rarely got a date until I started cruising with Raymond.

We were socially active in high school — it was Ray who convinced me to pursue law as a career — and in college, always looking for ways to correct some injustice. But the hard realities of life struck in the spring before college graduation. Looking to become a civil rights attorney, I was accepted to Penn law school but lacked the money to go. I chose the Navy instead, reasoning I could enter law school after a tour of duty in the military.

But by joining the Navy, Raymond said I was selling out

to The Man. Numerous times I wanted to point out that he, Raymond Dawson, was selling out to the capitalist system by running off to Rutgers to get an MBA.

I never voiced that to him.

The distance between us grew in the decade after college until some maturity, and Raymond becoming a father, somehow helped us re-connect.

"Snoopy, these are great pictures. You got some good shots," said Raymond, calling me by my college fraternity name since we were in private and behind a closed door. He came back to the table and sat down across from me.

"Just the sort of thing we need to catch that son-of-a-bitch and send his thieving ass to jail. Jerk's an assistant buyer, though I didn't hire him. He was here before me."

There was a soft rap at the door and someone entered before Raymond had a chance to invite them in. He rose from his chair and I followed suit as a tall, thin, white guy entered.

If Ray's fitted suit looked good but off the rack, this guy's suit looked fantastic and tailor-made. He was in his mid-forties, with just a touch of gray at the temples, and moved with confidence as if he owned the place.

Which, in part, he did.

"Andrew, come on in. Glad you could make it. I wanted to introduce you to David Blaise," Raymond said to the new man. Turning to me, he said, "David, this is my boss, Andrew Strawbridge. He's the store's Senior Executive Vice President for Retail Operations, Fashion Merchandising, and Advertising, Marketing and Promotions."

"Wow," I said, extending my hand. "That covers a lot."

"Pretty much everything but finance, personnel and legal," Raymond chimed in.

"Yes, well, it's a job, I guess. But you guys, sit down," Andrew said, leaning back onto Raymond's desk so as to demonstrate his superior position. "Are those the pictures? Let me see them."

Raymond handed over the packet of pictures and Andrew extracted a pair of glasses from an inside jacket pocket and placed them on his long, sharp nose. We were quiet as he examined the photographs. Andrew grunted several times as he flipped through one-by-one. "These are good pictures, Mr. Blaise. Photography is a hobby of mine. But I'm just an amateur," he said, letting me know it was more than just an idle hobby to him.

Finally, he plopped down the photos on the desk and continued to address me.

"What kind of equipment did you use?"

"Thirty-five millimeter Canon SLR with a telephoto zoom lens," I said. "As you see from the photos, it provided excellent resolution and clarity at that distance."

"Impressive," he said. "What was the distance? And they never saw or noticed you?"

"I don't think so," I answered. "I engaged an assistant . . . had her taking certain poses or holding up an object . . . to distract anyone who might notice. It was from about fifty to sixty yards. We were under a tree and slightly elevated on a hill, so that also worked to my advantage."

Andrew looked quickly at his gold Longines watch and turned to grab the pictures again as he stood up. "Mind if I take a couple of these with me? I'm having lunch at noon with Peter and the Old Man, and I wanted to show them. Decide on what we want to do and when."

"Yes, of course," said Raymond, standing again.

"And I want you there when we do it, of course. Either today or tomorrow, at the latest," said Andrew. "Keep your calendar fairly flexible until we meet with Stephenson."

"Yes. I think I should be there," Raymond said. "I haven't told his boss yet."

"No," Andrew said suddenly, sounding somewhat alarmed. "Don't do that until just before we handle Stephenson. Which buyer is his boss?"

"Toni Benson, ladies' sportswear and activewear."

Andrew was quiet for a moment, lost in his own thoughts as he took off his glasses and put them back in his jacket pocket.

"Maybe we should get rid of Benson, too. Fire her. No arrest, of course, like with Stephenson. He's her assistant," he said. "She's not involved, is she?"

"Don't think so," Raymond said.

"But if she's managing her buys so poorly that she didn't notice we were paying for more merchandise than we apparently were receiving, she's doing a pissant job. Stephenson was stealing right under her nose."

"Andy, let me handle that, okay? Firing her is probably not necessary. And firing her for something she didn't directly do could put us in legal jeopardy."

Andrew nodded agreement but said, "Then maybe a demotion. I could transfer her to one of the stores. An assistant store manager. That way, if she doesn't just resign, she'll have closer supervision."

Ray said nothing and Andrew turned back to me.

"Raymond says you do good work, and judging from these," Andrew said, "I'd say he's right. I need your discretion. Can't talk about this outside this office."

"It's confidential, of course," I answered.

"Good," he said.

"I don't think our vetting process is currently working well enough. That's the responsibility of another of my cousins," he said in a tone which indicated he disapproved of their failings. Eyeing me closely, he said, "This case, Mr. Blaise, shows we could use your resources more."

I nodded but Raymond spoke up first. "I can draw up a proposal and present it to you and the executive group later this week for consideration."

Andrew shook my hand again and left, closing the door behind him.

"That's a Strawbridge, huh?"

Raymond walked around his desk and sat down. He looked very serious again, as if the weight of his job and being under the microscope in a building full of Strawbridges was once again catching up to him.

"Yep. You can't walk down the hall without bumping into one. And I'm sure there are some closet Clothiers around, too. But mostly, it's Strawbridges. And the whole lot of them on edge because of Ronald Baron."

"They fought back his bid to buy the store, right?"

Raymond swept his hand across his desk as if to rid it of small specks of dust. But the desk was highly polished and dust free. "But for how long?"

I opted again to get the topic back on track. "What's going to happen with Stephenson?"

"We've been watching him closely for a couple of weeks and I did what you suggested. We contacted that police detective you mentioned, Thompson, and they're looking into it, too," he said. "We'll confront Stephenson, who will deny everything, of course, but we'll fire him anyway and hand over all the evidence, including your pictures, to the cops." He patted the envelope with the photographs. "They'll conduct their own investigation. Then they'll probably arrest him."

"I thought you said something bigger is going on," I said.

"So I did. I did, indeed," Raymond said, smiling again. "It's what the cops and the Feds think, or at least what they've alluded to." He stopped, a pregnant pause, you might say, to then drive home a point. "And it's all your fault, apparently."

Shocked, I moved forward in my chair to hover over Raymond's desk. "What? Are you kiddin' me? What have I got to do with anything?"

Raymond, now clearly enjoying himself, said, "As you know, I talked to your cop detective-slash-friend as we were looking into what we suspected Stephenson was doing. Thompson told me it may be part of a growing fencing operation of stolen items here in the city. Some quite valuable. And it's activity the FBI seems interested in, too."

I shook my head, confused with where he was going. "But what's all that got to do with me?"

"Two years ago, you helped break up a turf war between a couple of rival Italian mobsters. You stopped the bloodshed and helped send a whole bunch of guys to federal prison," said Raymond. "They probably still hate you down in South Philly for that."

"Yeah, I know. I was called to testify at several federal trials last year. So what?"

"Things quieted down but not everything changed. Once those major players were no longer on the scene . . . and they were no longer on the scene in large measure because of you . . . once they were gone, there was a power vacuum that *you* helped to create. And that vacuum, that void, is now slowly being filled, as power always fills a void."

"What are you saying?" I asked.

"You're smart. You figure it out."

I contemplated that for a moment then pushed the chair back and got up. I looked around the office and walked back over to the table with the cashmere sweaters, although I didn't touch them. I stuffed my hands into my pants pockets and turned around to face my friend, who returned a look with searching intensity.

It was time to change the subject. Glancing down at the sweaters again and back to Raymond, I said, "They obviously think highly of you here at the store."

"Andrew personally recruited me and offered me lots of money and promised me independence," he said as he got up and walked over. He took a chair near the table but I remained standing. "They're all pretty hands on and this is my first Fall season. Lots of pressure here," Raymond said and sighed. "I'm reminded everywhere that this department store has been around for a hundred years and I had better not screw it up."

He offered a dry chuckle. I inadvertently changed that in a hurry.

"How's Dorothy Grace?" I asked and took a chair near him.

At the mention of his two-year old's name, a genuine smile as bright as the midday sun appeared on his face. Raymond leaned back in his chair and patted his chest, relaxing in the thought of her.

It was a pleasure to see.

"Man, she's a trip. So adorable. Looks a lot like my mom before she passed. I know we spoil her, Audrey and me, but I don't care. She's just so adorable." Raymond beamed. "It's a joy to go home every day after the chaos and stress of this place. If I don't get home too late, I read to her at night before bed."

"That sounds great. Fatherhood is doing you well. Where you livin'?" I asked.

"Not far. A short walk. I can get to work in less than ten minutes. Glad I don't have to drive 'cause my place is so pricey and having to pay to park on the regular would kill me," he said. "I'm on Washington Square West, across the street from the park. And the park is great. Love takin' the kid over there to play. It's a lot less crowded than Rittenhouse Square."

I chuckled. "It's a long way from where we grew up in North Philly."

"Yeah, well, Andrew helped me secure the loan. They wanted me to be close to the store and," he started and stopped, before adding, "part of the deal in hiring me is that Audrey and I get married. They're really family-oriented here, as you might imagine. The deal was that I had six months, but I asked for a three-month extension, which gets me to this fall. I'm sure they won't extend it again."

"What's the problem? You love her, don't you? You're gettin' along."

"Yeah, I do. But marriage. I don't know," he said, then

changed the subject, targeting me. And I knew in an instant that I made a mistake bringing up Audrey.

"What about you and your lady?" Raymond said.

I uncomfortably shifted my weight in the chair and scratched my head in an area that didn't itch. "Marie and I aren't in that place right now. She's about to graduate from Textiles and is looking for a job. She does fashion design."

"Maybe there's a job here at Strawbridge's," Raymond said hopefully.

I stood up, ready to leave. "I don't know. I think she's focused on getting something in New York. But I'll ask if she's interested and let you know," I said as I reached across to shake his hand. "Anywho, I've got to run. Got a little free time and I gotta study for a final."

We shook. "Working on that law degree," he said.

"At night. And it's tough."

"You always knew it would be. But I'm proud of you."

"I'm proud of us both," I said as we headed for the door and the walk down the hallway to the reception desk.

"You up for some ball on Saturday? You won't be working a case, will you?" Raymond asked.

"Uh, probably free. What time?"

"Around one, I guess."

"Where? And don't say those courts over in Fairmount Park off of Belmont. Those courts are a mess. Stuff growin' out of cracks in the broken pavement," I said.

"Naw, Snoopy, I'm, uh. . . ." he stumbled with hesitation and sounded a tad self-conscious, "I'm in a club now. The building's down near the Bourse building, a block and a half off of Independence Mall. Got basketball and racquetball courts, a pool, a full gym, and a running track upstairs. It's real cool."

I halted and touched his sleeve. We were alone in the hallway and still out of ear shot of the receptionist. "So, you're all fancy now. Next thing you'll tell me is you're in the Union League up on Broad."

Raymond gave me a look of haughty resignation. "Keep your voice down," he said and started us walking again. "I'll have to reserve us a court. Won't be difficult. It's mostly white dudes in there and they play racquetball. One o'clock. And Randall's coming, too, so it'll be two-on-two, if you have a fourth."

I thought quickly and a name came to mind. "I think I can find a partner to play against you two," I said light-heartedly, just as we reached the reception desk.

"Iris," Raymond said to the pretty, young, dark-haired receptionist, "that package I left with you."

"Yes, sir. It's right here," the woman said as she reached down to pick up a box beautifully wrapped in an ancient rose pattern with a dark rose-colored ribbon. Raymond handed me the package.

"Ray, what's this?" I asked.

"It's just my way of apologizing to Grammy Taylor for the tea."

"I told you, Ray, you don't have to do anything. Everyone understands, especially my grandmother."

"I insist."

I also understood, and accepted the gift. As I turned to leave, he said, "It's a serving pot for coffee with a traditional rose pattern. No tea. If she wants that, she's on her own."

CHAPTER III

"Elijah."

I was getting just a little sticky under my arms as I made the short walk from my car to the office. The sun was beating down hard and, though only in early May, the temperature at noon was already well above 80. But I wasn't too concerned. I planned to spend most of the day inside my air-conditioned office.

"Good morning, Mae . . . um, afternoon now, I guess," I said cheerfully. She was on a telephone call and apparently it was so important that she barely looked up at me.

"Afternoon, boss," she said hurriedly, then shielded her lips and the phone's mouthpiece from me to say, "I said I'll get it."

Though curious as to who she was talking to, I didn't stop to ask and continued into my office.

I took off my tie and jacket and threw both onto the couch situated against the wall opposite my desk. Once seated, I thought yet again that I needed to shop for a more comfortable desk chair than the old wooden thing I was using. It was already past its prime when I picked it up at a garage sale more than three years ago. But since I hated office work and tried to be in the field as much as possible, a new chair was never a priority, at least not until I sat down again.

What was always a priority was finding paying gigs, and getting paid for them once I was finished. Marketing myself and searching for paying work was the hardest and most time-consuming part of my job, and it was also the part that made me the most uncomfortable.

I reached for pen and paper so I could write the invoice that Mae would type up to bill Strawbridge's for the surveillance and the pictures.

Next, I turned my attention to the classified section of the day's Inquirer, which was open in the in-box tray on my desk. As she did every day, Mae read through the section and circled in red any item I might be interested in pursuing.

I had just started looking through the section when I heard Mae get off the phone and she appeared at my open door with a couple of pink telephone memos in hand.

"You got these calls this morning before you got in but they ain't nothin', if you asks me," she said. Dropping one on the desk, she said, "This here's from a Xerox salesman."

I picked it up and noticed the return phone number and read the name with no interest. I didn't need a new copy machine and this was just a cold call. Looking back up at Mae, I said, "And the other?"

She dropped the other pink slip on the desk. "This one's from some lady who wants to come in to assess your office needs. It's all bullshit, if you asks me."

I agreed with her but didn't offer a comment. However, I did notice her shoes as she turned to leave the office.

"Those new? They look nice."

They looked conservative compared to what she used to wear to work. Being employed in a regular nine-to-five office job was having an effect on her daytime apparel choices. In the early days of her employment with me, Mae's attire was so . . . uh, provocative . . . uh, edgy . . . that in another context seeing her dressed like that would require paying a cover charge.

But times had changed.

"Got them at Bonwit's on Saturday after you dropped me off. Told you they be havin' ah sale," she said, modeling the four-inch black-pattern leather pumps with satin red bow. "Got them for ah steal."

"Good for you," I said but switched to the subject that held my curiosity. "Who were you talking to on the phone just now?"

She evaded. "Ah, it's nothin'. Um, personal, really."

I wanted to pursue it and would have except that at that moment I heard someone enter the outer office. Mae heard it, too, and was heading out to greet them when I heard a male voice I instantly recognized.

"Is King-David in?" he said. "I'm his brother, Eli."

I shot out of my seat as if from a cannon, rushed around my desk, and hurried past Mae to the outer office to see my younger brother standing there. He looked around, taking in the space, as if he was seeing the office for the first time, which, as it turned out, was the case. No one in my family, not even Grammy Taylor or my sister Valerie, had ever set foot in my office. And as far as I could tell or remember, Stuart, who owned the building, had only been to my office once, and that was two years ago when I signed the one-dollar-a-month lease and he personally handed me the keys.

"Elijah. What are you doing here?" I asked as I rushed past Mae, who looked confused as to how Eli had referred to me.

I gave him A Look and he caught on quickly.

"I came to see my Big Brother," he said. But looking closely at me again and seeing the unspoken skepticism, Eli backed up to include his true purpose. "David, I'm here because I need help. Your help. I want to hire you as a detective."

~*~

In all families, relationships between individual members can be both complicated and ever-changing. That is certainly the case in my family. I'm close to my grandmother, of course, and my sister. But with my brothers, not so much. Or, more accurately stated, the effort between the male members of my family, psychologically speaking, takes a lot and, in many ways, that effort is generally more than we want to make.

Despite that, however, Elijah and I hold a special bond that was originally forged decades before either of us was born. And in our own ways, we know it, thanks in part to our grandmother bringing it up.

My parents had barely had the money for my tuition at Temple and certainly not enough left over for me to live on-campus. Plus, they wouldn't have paid for me to stay in a dorm — despite my protestations — because our house in North Philadelphia was closer to many of my classes on the Temple campus than were some of the dormitory buildings. Therefore, I walked to school.

Eli was still in elementary school when I started college and thus our lives were in totally different places. However, he looked up to me with an air of hopeful adoration that I, as an insecure teenager just starting college, wasn't emotionally prepared for, nor entirely comfortable with.

But little things in one's life can have a huge impact on the life of another. It was certainly the case with Elijah and me.

One day when I was between classes and had access to my dad's car, Eli begged and begged me to take him to get a thirty-cent cheeseburger at a newly opened McDonald's restaurant on Broad Street. Despite needing to get back on campus for my next class, I relented. And the little guy was thrilled as we drove to the restaurant, which was less than a mile away, and went inside to order. I then drove him back home and prepared to immediately head out.

Sitting in the living room about to watch some TV, Eli opened the wrapper of his cheeseburger and discovered that not only was it not hot, it didn't have any cheese. Eli was hurt but I was livid. The kid had been cheated out of something so simple that he badly wanted and that, in fact, we had paid for. At a minimum, it's what we expected.

Yet, I was in a bind. Do I take it back and demand a hot cheeseburger? Or do I let him accept the situation, sorry as it was, and head to class so as not to be late?

In the end, it was no decision at all. I took it back to the restaurant and demanded a new burger. I wanted it hot and I wanted it with cheese.

Needless to say, I got to the class late.

However, that simple act for my brother more than fifteen years ago had a profound impact on our younger-brother/older-brother relationship. So much so, I still hear him occasionally talk about the incident with friends when he talks about his big brother.

He did NOT mention it when he arrived in my office, thankfully. It probably wasn't even on his mind. Yet I instantly knew this request for my help could turn out to be another cheeseburger moment.

Thus, where else would we go but to the McDonald's on the corner of 52nd and Chestnut to talk about what he wanted to hire me to do.

We settled into a booth near the front window after we ordered and got our food. They got the orders right and the food was hot. But still this was a peculiar situation for me, and not because I paid for the food. I have never had a relative for a client, with the exception of Stuart, but he's only a relative by marriage.

That doesn't count, I told myself.

Stuart's case did work out, of course. I saved his hide, his business and his family, and I got a good deal on office space.

I reserved some judgment on whether to take Eli's case, or at least that's what I told myself.

"Okay, then. What's this all about?" I said as I added some ketchup to my French fries.

"It's about Kareem Adams."

The name sounded familiar, though I couldn't immediately put my finger on it. Uncertainty must have showed on my face because Eli jumped in with some context and background.

"He's the guy police thought killed that white girl in Center City last month as she was walking to her car in a parking lot outside a Wawa on 21st Street. Mary Ann Tolk. The cops were looking for him," he said.

"Ah, yes," I said. "And by the time they caught up with him up in North Philly and raided the house where he was hiding, he had killed himself. They said it was a drug overdose."

Elijah flinched and paused while reaching for his soda. I apparently had struck a nerve. He looked me squarely in the face with a seriousness I had rarely seen in him. "I'm not convinced all that's true. Lots of people are skeptical. Someone's lying."

Now I looked at him with that same skepticism. "What makes you say that?"

"It's the facts. They just don't add up."

"What facts? From what I remember seeing in the papers, he was an ex-con with a violent streak, and was a drug addict. He overdosed."

"You can't believe everything that you read, and you know that," he admonished, though not too harshly. "It's why I want you to investigate what happened to him." He stopped again and took a breath. "A group of us have raised some money and I can pay you. How much do you charge?"

"Eli, it's not the money that's the issue."

"What, then?" he asked.

"I don't normally take cases from a family member. The emotional ties could cloud my judgment."

"You took that case involving Stuart a couple of years back. Why not my case?"

I was caught off guard. No one was supposed to know about that. Certainly, no one in the family. "How do you know about Stuart?"

"We all know about it. Well, I guess Valerie probably doesn't know, thank the Lord, but everybody else does."

I pushed my tray of food to the side and sat back in the booth as I contemplated that bit of information. I had only half-eaten my sandwich. Deep in thought, I didn't notice the manager of the McDonald's coming up. He stopped and surveyed the table with a smile on his face.

"I saw you come in when I was working back on the grill. Is everything good? The food's good? The service?" Rhys said, smiling, his hands on his hips. "You haven't finished. Can I get you anything?"

"Um, no, thanks. Everything's great," I said, then added, "This is my brother, Elijah. And Eli, this is Rhys Davies. He manages here."

They exchanged pleasantries, as one does in a civil society. Before Rhys headed off, he said to Eli, "Nice to meet someone in David's family. Only person who comes around is his secretary, who always comes in for coffee. But I like her, if you know what I mean," he said with a sly smile. As it happened there was nothing between them but sly smiles and free cups of coffee.

But to me, he continued, "Let me know if you need anything. And thanks for all your help, David. It's been a great benefit to the place in terms of security." I didn't do much, just made sure he knew about the most up-to-date and reliable monitoring systems, and checked the perimeter after hours on busy weekend nights.

And with that, Rhys walked off.

Eli smiled at me like a cat who had just caught the kitchen mouse and was bringing it to the master of the house.

"A *great benefit*? I see," he started. "You hide out here in West Philadelphia to get away from the family in North Philly. But we all know the *great benefit* you are to others, and not just because you grace us with your presence on Sunday nights for dinner at Grammy's house. We hear things." He stopped to let that sink in as he picked at his food, putting a stray piece of shredded lettuce in his mouth. Then, with his dark brown eyes boring into me, Eli added, "I need your help, Davey. This is important and I didn't know where else to turn. I don't think what we're hearing about Kareem is what happened."

I resigned myself to the inevitability of this cheeseburger moment.

"Tell me what you need."

"I need you to look up around Girard and find out what really happened with Kareem, for a starter," he said, sounding relieved, leaning back on the seat.

"I'm gonna need you to come up there with me, at least to start."

"No problem. When you want to go?"

I looked at my watch and made the decision. "Now."

CHAPTER IV

"Pastor Pat know him. He know everybody 'round here."

"How'd you get caught up in all this, Eli," I asked as I drove across the Chestnut Street Bridge over the Schuylkill and into Center City.

"How do you mean?" he said.

"Come on, Eli. Don't be evasive," I said, taking quick glances at him in the passenger seat. "You know what I mean."

He took a deep breath and exhaled, apparently resigning himself to having to come up with an answer.

"I've always looked up to you, wanted to be like you," he said. "Your heart has always been in pursuing justice, social justice. That's why, when I went to Clark Atlanta . . . on the advice of our grandmother, you know, because Clark is where she went to college . . . I majored in social work."

"I didn't remember that was your major," I chimed in, surprised. "I thought it was business. Or maybe music."

"Oh, pleeeze. Music? Huh," he coughed. "If I was going for music, then I would have tried for the Curtis Institute here in Philly, and we all know who Grammy wanted to go there."

I let the comment sit in the air unanswered until Eli continued.

"No. Social work. And, like you, I had to get away from the family. They were smothering me," Eli said. "I only lived on the third floor of Grammy's house for a few months once I was out of school and was looking for a job. When I got the gig at the Justice Consortium in South Philly and I saved up enough money, I got an apartment. It's on Christian. It's a dump but it's all I can afford on a social worker's salary."

"And it's near the social scene on South Street," I said pointedly. "Lots happenin' down there and you're young and single. I totally understand the allure."

It was Eli's turn to stay silent, so I changed the subject. "The Justice Consortium?"

"Yeah. We try to fight the good fight, just like you, I guess," Eli said. "People . . . little people, everyday people, mostly poor people . . . come to us looking for help in finding justice or in finding peace in the unjust circumstances of their daily lives."

"And Kareem?" I ventured.

"One of the guys in the office . . . same position as me, a street case worker . . . had been working up in North Philly and had heard of some anti-drug activities Kareem had been doing."

I took a left onto 22nd Street, drove past Ben Franklin Parkway and over to Pennsylvania Street, and took another left. We continued onward to 29th and hung a right. Two blocks later we were at Girard Avenue. I pulled over to park just shy of the intersection, one of the busiest in the area, where the far reaches of Center City meet the edges of both North and West Philly.

For a few minutes we sat and plotted our next move.

"Where was it that Adams was stayin'?" I asked.

"The papers said Stiles, a street up ahead of us on the other side of Girard. His block was off of 30th, which is to the left," said Eli.

"You know this area? It's a bit far afield for you, isn't it?"

"I'm at least partially familiar here," he said.

"Okay, but why don't you just follow my lead. I do this all the time," I said, reaching for the door handle with one hand and pointing to the right with the other. "Why don't we ask down that way first? This is the busiest corner in the neighborhood. Somebody's bound to know something about Adams."

The sidewalks along Girard were teeming with people just struggling to make it through the day. Other than a small branch of First Pennsylvania Bank, the area was crowded with discount retail shops. Some sold cheap clothes, shoes, and accessories, while others sold inexpensive hair products and extensions. For those without a banking account, in the middle of the block was a check cashing business that legitimately robbed the poor, but still appeared to have more customers than First Pennsy on the corner.

Filling out the area were a couple of takeout-only Chinese food joints, and several tiny restaurants that sold Malt-40s and specialized in artery-clogging fried foods — fried chicken, fried fish, French fried potatoes — cooked in oils made from animal fat.

We picked different sides of the street, entering establishments or just talking to people who passed on the street. We canvassed the area for more than an hour and weren't getting very far. Everyone had heard of the police raid and they blamed poor Kareem's death on the cops. But no one was willing to say they knew him personally.

That is, not until I stumbled upon a thin older man who looked and sounded like he was high on something, or a lot of somethings.

The man, who identified himself simply as Joey, was sitting at a small table outside a takeout restaurant, using a plastic fork to eat beef fried rice from a white container. A Malt-40 was next to his right elbow, always at the ready. Despite the cold drink, beads of sweat dotted his forehead below a receding hairline.

He was sitting on the side of the street facing the blazing sun.

In most social environments, including this one, good manners are a show of respect. I asked if I could take a seat and ask a couple of questions. Joey, his mouth full of rice, nodded and I took the empty chair across the table as he reached for his beer.

"You know this guy, right?" I asked, showing Joey a mug shot of Adams from an earlier arrest. Eli had provided me with the picture before we left West Philly.

"Yeah," Joey said, taking a swig of the beer. Some of it ran down his chin and added another stain to his already stained shirt. "Why you care? You ain't with the po-leese."

He had a gravelly voice, as if someone had spent decades dragging sandpaper over his vocal cords. It made him sound much older than he appeared to be, though he still appeared older than he probably was.

I didn't answer his question nor did I ask how he knew I wasn't a cop. I just pressed on. "How'd you know him? Because he was dealing and using drugs?" I said.

"No," Joey said vehemently, his mouth so full of rice he spit out a piece or two as he spoke. "He don't do no drugs."

Thinking I misheard, I asked Joey to repeat himself. "He don't do no drugs?"

Puzzled, I looked up at Eli, who had come over from across the street when I sat down and was standing next to me.

Before we drove over to this part of town, Eli showed me the news article with the police news release that stated that Adams, an apparent junkie, died of a massive, self-induced heroin overdose. Drug paraphernalia was found on or near his body, including a needle found in his left arm, according to police.

"People who are new to drugs don't go on a massive binge for a day and a half. People ease into drug addiction. They smoke some pot or take pills, and then may slip into harder and harder drugs. Cocaine, heroin. What have you. They don't start off mainlining heroin for thirty-six hours straight.

"If Joey here is right, Adams wouldn't have had that much in his system when he was found. Either the papers are wrong or the police lied or decided once they had their man, there was no need to dig deeper," I concluded.

"I'm sure the police lied," Eli said.

"It's only a possibility," I cautioned. Turning back to Joey, I asked, "You know of anybody else who might know about Kareem Adams?"

"Pastor Pat know him. He know everybody 'round here."

"Who's Pastor Pat?" I asked Joey.

"He got dat church down the block. The big one. He live 'round the corner."

I looked down the street at the large stone church on the next corner down, near 28th Street. Like every other building in the area, it was old, probably dating back to the late nineteenth century, and was in need of some tender loving care.

As we were leaving, Joey grabbed my arm from across the table. "I helped you. Could ya spare me a little change or a SEPTA token so I can get home?"

Before I reacted, Eli reached into his pocket, pulled out a couple of ones and handed them over. Then we both headed up the street.

~*~

The church was only a block away, so we walked. It was a massive stone structure roughly a hundred-and-thirty years old and built by German Protestants, judging from the church's original name etched into the stone across the front — Deutsch Evangelisch-Lutherische Kirche. The neighborhood had changed substantially since the late nineteenth century and long gone were all the descendants of the original Germans who had worshiped in the church for decades.

A set of wooden double doors painted a bright red welcomed people to the Joy to the World Community Church. A sign hanging on the side of the building announced that Bible Study was on Sunday at 9:30 a.m., followed by morning services at 10:30 a.m. The Rev. Dr. Killian Patrick O'Neil, pastor.

"No wonder he goes by Patrick. With a first name like that . . . how do you pronounce it? Killy-lee-ann? . . . Whooo, what a mouthful," Eli commented as we approached the door.

The stained-glass windows, which were tilted outward, were well above street level, which meant the main part of the interior of the church was at least up a half a flight of stairs. From the outside, it didn't appear as if any lights were on inside.

The heavy doors were unlocked and we entered cautiously. After the darkness, the first thing I noticed was a stifling heat. The church, or at least this part, was not air-conditioned and, unfortunately, keeping the windows open did little to move around the already superheated air.

Inside the vestibule, stairs led either up toward the darkened sanctuary or down toward a Fellowship Hall. Eli was looking upstairs but called downstairs. "Hello. Is anyone here?"

"Yes, yes, I'm down here. May I help you?" returned a disembodied voice from below.

We headed downstairs, grateful that the parishioners could afford air-conditioning — and lights — in the lower-level Fellowship Hall. On one wall was a map of the world that indicated foreign lands where Christian missionaries toiled, two boards with what appeared to be announcements and two large posters extolling the virtues of remaining drug-free.

The man striding toward us was not who I would have expected to see, though he wore a black shirt with the collar of a clergyman.

The Rev. O'Neil was a tall, imposing, middle-aged man, with large beefy hands, a rugged, muscular body, and broad shoulders. Twenty years earlier, it would be easy to see him playing as a defensive back in college, though probably not for a Division One school. He had a thick head of reddish hair that looked like he rarely combed it. His skin was a pale white, as if he rarely got any sun and would burn easily if he did.

His character lines suggested he smiled a lot, although he

wore a cautious look as he approached us two strangers.

"Gentlemen, what can I do for you?" he said, his hand outstretched. I took it.

"My name is David Blaise. I'm a private investigator, and this is . . ." I paused, uncertain at first as to how to proceed. But Eli stepped in.

"I'm Elijah Blaise. We're partners in a small family-run agency," he said. I glanced sideways at him but didn't correct him.

"Ahh, good Biblical names. David, the one whom God loved. And Elijah, a mighty prophet sent by God to turn Israel from her evil ways. Interesting," he said thoughtfully. "Good to meet you. I'm Reverend Patrick O'Neil but folks 'round these parts just call me Pastor Pat. What brings you two to my door?"

"We've been going through the neighborhood, trying to get a picture of Kareem Adams, who I assume you know was recently found dead in a house a couple of blocks from here," I said. "He apparently was wanted by the police in the stabbing death of a young woman downtown nearly two weeks ago."

Pastor Pat sighed at the mention of Kareem's name.

"I beg your pardon," I said.

"He had such promise. A promise wasted," Pastor Pat said. Sorrow was obvious in his voice. "Kareem. When he was young, he attended church here regularly. Many poor families to the north either come to worship here or stop by on the days that we have food distribution. It's part of our ministry outreach.

"But Kareem . . . I'm not sure he had fully repented for his sins before he died. I pray every day for his eternal soul, and for the souls of young men and women like him. A Day of Reckoning will come."

"For him, it already has," Eli said.

"Here on earth, yes. But what I was referring to is the Day of Reckoning before our Lord and Savior, Jesus Christ."

I could see Pastor Pat was growing comfortable with our conversation, so I risked taking out a notebook and pencil.

"You mind if I jot down some things as we talk?" I asked. "Just to keep things straight."

Pastor Pat didn't immediately answer but finally gave a short nod of his head.

"I don't know what I can tell you. But why don't you come into the office?"

CHAPTER V

"He's a southpaw."

Pastor Pat led us down a short hallway to a small, windowless room. It was crammed with books and papers, a lectern made of a light-colored wood, a desk and chair, one other chair and a well-worn sofa with one cushion that apparently was more heavily used than the others. A large floor fan was just outside the doorway blowing cooler air from the hallway into the office.

I took the couch and sank into it further than I expected. Eli took the chair and almost immediately looked at his watch. Pastor Pat sat at the chair at his desk but rolled it toward the sofa.

"You know, David," Eli said, rising from the chair, "I've just remembered a meeting I have at the Justice Consortium this afternoon. If I don't rush, I'll be late."

Pastor Pat perked up upon hearing The Consortium. "It's a good place. They have a conscience, a moral compass, and they act on it."

I looked at Eli, puzzled. "How are you going to get down there in time? I drove us up here and, frankly, I still have a number of questions to ask the pastor."

"I'll take the Girard trolley downtown and catch a cab from there."

"I guess I'll catch up with you later," I said, still confused as to why Eli felt the need to leave so soon.

"Let me show you out," Pastor Pat said to Eli. To me, he said, "I'll be right back."

Pastor Pat escorted Eli to the front door. I couldn't hear them talking but heard the large wooden front doors close again once Eli had left. Moments later, Pastor Pat returned.

"Now, what can I help you with?"

"For starters, tell me about Kareem," I said.

Pastor Pat leaned back in his chair, his feet planted squarely on the floor, his arms folded across his chest. He studied me seriously. The expression on his face was unreadable but I withstood the examination without speaking or making a sound. Pastor Pat must have satisfied himself, because his posture finally relaxed and he moved forward in his seat again.

"The newspapers are quick to demonize Black men," Pastor Pat started.

It was my turn to examine him. I sat back on the couch before saying, "Perhaps. But Kareem Adams, from what I've read and heard, certainly was no angel. He was on parole for armed robbery at the time of that murder. And he was the prime suspect . . . the only suspect. Reports place him outside or near the convenience store where she was killed. And don't forget, the weapon used in the shooting was found in his house. That's a lot of evidence to indicate guilt."

As I laid that out, I was glad Elijah had decided to leave early. He was much more emotionally caught up in the case, while I was merely searching for facts to prove what had happened and find some peace for all concerned.

Pastor Pat seemed to have a more balanced view.

"And it's all circumstantial," he said. "Mary Ann Tolk's murder was a tragedy in every sense of the word. I can only imagine what her family is going through. And if Kareem had anything to do with it, he should have been brought to justice. I'm making no excuses for him. But his family is suffering, too, and through no fault of their own. They didn't cause any of this. All I'm saying is that Kareem was more than the monster he was portrayed to be on television and in the papers."

Pastor Pat rose from his chair. "Come with me. I want to show you something."

We walked out of his office and into the Fellowship Hall, headed to a wall which contained numerous pictures of church members and church activities.

"I've been here for fifteen years and I remember Kareem from the very first week. He was a young boy back then, eight, nine, maybe ten. His mother would drop him off at church for Sunday School and quickly leave before anyone had a chance to ask her to stay for Bible Study.

"Look at this picture," Pastor Pat said. "That's Kareem, second from the right on the front row."

The picture showed two rows of boys in dark blue basketball jerseys. Though Kareem could only have been ten or twelve, I instantly recognized him from pictures Eli had showed me.

Kareem was sitting, staring directly at the camera with a big smile on his face. He was a skinny kid with a thin face. He had a mop of thick, nappy hair on his head that appeared as if he hadn't combed it in days, hadn't washed it in weeks and hadn't had it cut in months.

"We put a basketball team together, and played in a small inter-church league. Just a number of churches on this side of town. We weren't very good but that wasn't the point. We kept those kids busy and off the streets. And we tried to reach them for Christ," Pastor Pat said.

"What happened?"

"After a couple of years, the grant money for the league ran out and we couldn't keep it going," Pastor Pat said.

"Was Kareem any good?" I asked.

"Not bad. And over here, look at these." There were numerous pictures of church activities, including some from inside the church and others outside, such as at a church picnic and the like. "That's him there, at a picnic, eating with his mother. I think that's her. And this here, playing softball. That's him pitching the ball."

"Good picture," I said, studying it a bit. "He's a southpaw."

Looking closely at the picture as if noticing for the first time, he said, "Yes. I guess he was. I didn't remember that."

Across the room was a long, wooden table, a little rough around the edges but extremely sturdy in appearance. It was next to a row of glass block windows which let in natural light from outside. On the table were a stack of Bibles, some pamphlets and other religious literature, all free for the taking, except the Bibles.

"Kareem had little guidance at home and was beginning to hang with a bad crowd. That was about ten years ago. One summer I had him and a couple of other boys who attended church help me build this table. Mostly, however, it was me and Kareem."

"Nice job," I commented.

Pastor Pat thanked me absentmindedly then shook his head and ran his fingers through his hair. He appeared to recall a memory but the moment quickly passed.

"In his teens, when his mother exercised even less control over him, Kareem started to come to church less frequently, although he never stopped coming altogether. And he started doing drugs. First pot, then the hard stuff," the pastor said.

We returned to his office. Pastor Pat sat before he resumed. Even this brief walk down memory lane seemed to tire the pastor, as if he carried a weight he never put down. His eyes were sad.

I took notes, which didn't seem to disturb him.

"He got caught up in an armed robbery with a couple of guys right after he turned eighteen. With no lawyer and no money, he got time. I went up to visit him in a prison near Williamsport about twice a month. I was the only one who visited regularly. Not even his mother, but I couldn't blame her. She had to work, which was barely enough for just her to survive. Kareem got out after a couple of years but prison had changed him, hardened him. He was a child when he went in. A mostly innocent child. He was a man when he came out. But he would come to see me. He wouldn't come to church on Sundays but he'd visit me, here in my office."

"When was that?"

"A couple of years ago, after he was out," Pastor Pat said. "But then he got on at Amtrak. A porter on long-haul trips. He traveled a lot. He'd go away and be gone for some time. I think he once said out West. California, maybe up in the Northwest around Seattle. But I know he was out in LA sometimes. I just hoped and prayed it wasn't drugs or trafficking."

I was taking all this information down.

"What makes you think it was trafficking?"

"All that travel, being away for long periods," the pastor said. "I don't know. Hate that my mind would go there."

"However, you said he started using drugs in his teens. The hard stuff, you said. Wouldn't be a major leap," I said. "Was that when . . . in his teens . . . when he started on heroin?"

A look that could have been anger flashed on the pastor's face but was quickly replaced with surprise.

"Heroin? Kareem never used heroin. Said he'd never touch the stuff. Saw what it did to guys in prison," Pastor Pat said.

I backtracked, flipping through my notebook until I found what I was looking for.

"The Philadelphia medical examiner's report said Kareem Adams died of a heroin overdose," I said, looking down at notes. "It said he injected it into his arm."

"I don't know about that. But Kareem said numerous times he hated needles and that heroin lays waste to people and their lives. His drug of choice, back then, before prison, was crack. Bad enough, I suppose. But that's what he said."

Turning his chair around to face his desk, the pastor rolled back over to it.

I pulled a large, wing-backed chair closer to the pastor's desk. There was an open Bible and next to it was a yellow legal pad with a series of notes he had been taking. He wrote in small letters.

"Your sermon?" I asked.

"For Sunday, yes. I'm still working on it. But look here," he said, reaching over for a large photo album. On the spine it was labeled *drug war*.

Inside were street picture after street picture, shots of cars slowly passing street corners. In some shots the drivers of the cars were clearly visible. But in others, just the cars and license plates were discernible. The pictures were taken at different times during the day, at different angles and with differing levels of clarity.

"After prison, Kareem was different. Poor, uneducated, desperate, searching."

"For what?"

Pastor Pat's facial expression turned decidedly more serious. His next questions came slowly, tentatively. "Do you attend church?"

"No," I replied, maybe too quickly.

"But you used to. When you were younger, perhaps?"

"Yes, as a child, I went to church all the time. With my grandmother, especially."

"Where did you go?"

"To a Baptist church up off of Diamond and 19th. My grandmother played there sometimes."

He looked away from me for a second, as if in thought, then returned to face me. "But you stopped for some reason. When you were old enough to make the decision for yourself, probably, and weren't forced to go as a child."

He was silent and contemplative for a moment. Then he continued.

"When people, as adults, start attending church again, they're searching for something, though they may be unaware of it. They're searching for answers. Kareem hadn't reached that point yet but he came here a lot . . . to this office . . . to talk. And the church door was always open," Pastor Pat said. "You may not know it to look at him but he had a moral center . . . and he used it to help me.

"He cared about his mother, I could tell, and about the neighborhood. The community. He saw what drugs were doing to people. And he abhorred it. It's why he helped me organize groups of volunteers to stand out on certain corners where there was a lot of drug activity. The drug dealers saw the people taking pictures and it affected what was going on at that corner. The dealers could be threatening but, ultimately, they'd move to another corner."

"You took pictures of people in cars buying drugs," I said, again looking at the photographs. "Amazing."

"Yes, that area near 29th Street and Girard, 30th and Girard and on the side streets close to the expressway. Young businessmen from downtown could pull off the highway, ride only a few blocks, pick up something and head back to the highway. Quick and easy. And they didn't have to drive deep into North Philly to get it."

I looked closely at some of the pictures and the cars and license numbers.

"You show these to the police?" I asked.

"Yes, but they said they couldn't do anything . . . about the cars or the people in them. But the drug trafficking on those corners dropped dramatically," Pastor Pat said. "And it was in part thanks to Kareem Adams."

Before I left, I asked the pastor whether I could take of couple of the pictures with me, though profusely promising to return them. He agreed and I handed him my business card as a bit of added assurance.

I still left the church more puzzled about Kareem than I was when Eli first approached me. What was clear to me, however, was that something wasn't right, though I wasn't sure what.

CHAPTER VI

"Hey there, handsome. What's your name?"

Walking back to my car, I was perplexed. Was Kareem Adams a cold-hearted young man who would mug a woman on the street and kill her for little more than a few dollars that, in fact, he didn't get? Or was he a troubled young man, a former convict, who himself was a victim of some other monstrous crime?

He could be neither. He could be both.

Available street parking is difficult to find during the best of times in most of Center City and I ended up driving around the block three times close to my destination before I found a parking spot on South Street, just around the corner from The Philadelphia Tribune on 16th.

The paper was located in one of the oldest parts of Philadelphia, which started to see large growth in the late eighteenth and early nineteenth centuries. And while the current Tribune building isn't nearly that old, many of the surrounding streets are. Since there was parking on both sides of the street in front, there was room for only one lane of traffic heading north. The streets on either side of the Tribune building are narrow and brick-paved, and more appropriately could be described as alleys.

I hadn't called ahead and hoped the trip wasn't in vain. But when my source wasn't at his desk, he was known to frequent a certain drinking hole on 15th Street, only a few blocks away in the direction of City Hall.

As I approached the building, I saw two young women standing around near a bench in front, apparently taking a break. Talking, they enjoyed a hearty laugh at something just before one of them turned and noticed me approach.

"Hey there, handsome," the shorter of the two said flirtatiously as I passed on the way to a series of steps to the entrance of the building. "I'm Lynn. What's your name?"

She was perhaps twenty years old, all of five feet tall, if that, and as cute as could be. *Must be a college intern at the paper*, I thought, judging by her casual attire of jeans, sneakers, and a deep-red Temple University polo shirt. The owner of the paper believed in formality and generally enforced a fairly strict dress code, especially if he was in the building.

The young woman held a captivating smile, and briefly had me wishing I was back in school at Temple.

I halted the thought. *You're working*, I reminded myself. *And you have a girlfriend!*

Sorta.

I answered her with a question of my own. "Is Randolph Williams in?" I said as I slowed but continued my trek to the door.

The other woman, the taller of the two by seven or eight inches, was a couple of years older, very soft on the eyes, and possessed the statuesque figure that would have made the Greek goddess Aphrodite jealous.

She spoke up.

"He's at his desk but he's on deadline," she said in a mellifluous voice. "Probably can't talk."

I returned her smile. "I'll chance it."

Once inside, the receptionist directed me to the newsroom on the third floor, and I took the stairs.

The walls in the newsroom were a muted gray, a color so neutral and bland that they sparked neither attention nor distraction. And they probably had grown duller with age. The room was divided into rows of four desks, side-by-side, facing four side-by-side desks opposite them.

There were windows at one end of the room facing east,

out the front and onto 16th Street below. However, the largest and most dominant windows faced south, though the view outside was nothing to crow about. They faced the red brick wall of the building on the other side of a narrow side street.

The room was warm, because it was hot outside, and smelled of old newsprint, which wasn't surprising, given the stacks of old editions lining one wall.

There was little conversation going on, just the rhythmic peck on computer keyboards as reporters worked to finish stories on deadline, although one reporter was on the telephone interviewing someone. Other than the occasional traffic outside, the only other noise came from two teletype machines in the corner — one for United Press International, the other for the Associated Press — churning out hard copies of their wire service stories.

In his many years of toiling away in one of the country's oldest, largest, and most successful Black newspapers, Randolph Williams had seen it all, and had written about most of it. He was a short man, likable, congenial, and curious, and was a dogged, tenacious reporter who passed those traits onto young reporters he mentored.

As he was the paper's senior reporter, Randolph's desk was the first I encountered upon entering the newsroom, though his back was to me. His desk, which held his computer, and the surrounding area was a jumbled mess piled high with old newspapers, used reporter's notebooks, and papers of all sorts. Looking at the chaos of it all, one wondered how he managed to find anything or get any work done.

His black fedora, a constant companion, was perched atop a stack of old Tribunes, within easy arm's reach in case he needed to grab it quickly to rush off to a breaking story or to merely wander outside to satisfy his nicotine habit.

The chair to the desk next to Randolph's was empty — I assumed the reporter was out — and I took the seat. Randolph turned, surprised.

"Blaise, what are you doing up here?" he asked, looking around the newsroom suspiciously. Then, his attention settled back on me. "Oh, yeah, the boss man is away this week. Otherwise, you would have needed a papal dispensation to be up in the newsroom."

"You busy? On deadline?" I asked, pausing ever-so-briefly for an answer before rushing ahead without hearing one. "I needed to ask you about some things."

The stale aroma of cigarettes permeated the area around Randolph, and the tips of several of the fingers on his right hand were yellowed from the filter-less brand of smokes he loved.

"No. Not on deadline," he said, pushing himself back from his computer keyboard. "Just finished a profile on the new police commissioner, Kevin Tucker. He's the first commissioner named from outside the department in sixty years, for all the good it'll do him. Can't see how he'll be able to reform that behemoth." Eyeing me closely again, he asked, "But, what can I do you for?"

"What do you know about the Kareem Adams incident . . . his death, I mean . . . and the murder of that girl . . . young woman . . . Mary Ann Tolk?"

"I know the pieces of puzzle don't fit. Or at least not what law enforcement has been saying," he said, scratching the gray stubble on his left cheek.

At that moment, the two women from outside walked into the newsroom. The taller of the two, whose name I learned later was Leanita, went to a desk on the far right of the room, while the young woman who had introduced herself to me as Lynn took a seat at the desk directly facing Randolph.

"Hello again, handsome," she said cheerfully to me over the top of her computer screen. The screen was so high and her seat was so low, I could hardly see more of her than her eyes, which sparkled with youthful, good-natured mischief.

Randolph looked over to the young woman and said, "Lynn, why don't you bring a chair over and talk. This is my friend David Blaise. He's a PI." Turning back to me, he continued, "David, this is Lynn McCullough. She's a promising young intern from over at Temple. Doin' a bang-up job, too. Sorry to see her leave at the end of the week, now that the semester's over."

Lynn pulled a chair over to sit right next to Randolph and facing me, partly blocking the aisle.

Randolph first addressed his intern. "David, here, is on the same trail that we're on. Looking into the death of Kareem Adams."

And with that, Lynn's expressive face changed. Gone were the cute dimples and the sparkle in her brown eyes, replaced by a furrowed brow and a serious countenance. Though she said not a word, clearly the subject had an impact on her professionally and, perhaps, even personally.

Since she was young and inexperienced, she probably hadn't developed much of a cynical exterior that would help emotionally shield her from many of the heartbreaking stories she'd have to cover. If this was a career she planned to pursue, she would need to develop that cynical exterior — or she'd either burn out or go insane.

"Lynn has been helping with this story," Randolph said to me, then, turning to his young intern, he added with a disapproving voice, "And she went up there, alone, against my wishes, to question people about the incident. But I told her not to do that. Alone."

"But I got some valuable information and I found his mother," she said until Randolph interrupted.

"Who slammed a door in your face and told you to never come back," he said. "I told you not to go there alone. You don't know that area."

Lynn was about to say something but just sighed and held her peace.

"Someone just today asked me to look into this and I need some background so I'll know where to focus my attention," I said. "That's why I've come to you."

Randolph took a deep breath. "Back in mid-April, Mary Ann Tolk was coming out of a Wawa convenience store over off of 21st Street near where she lived with her boyfriend who apparently works in City Hall for some powerful politician. But she was approached by a guy in a black, hooded sweatshirt on the sidewalk. All that was on a security camera outside the store. He must have demanded her purse which she had on her shoulder. He grabbed for it and she resisted. When she didn't give up the purse, he stabbed her in the chest and ran off. She was rushed to Hahneman Hospital where she died."

"Could the attacker be identified from the camera footage?" I asked.

"It took a lot to get the police to release it," Randolph said, "but no, you can't determine who it was, or even if he was Black or white. He was wearing a hood and knew how to cover up any distinguishing features. Looked like it could have been a pro."

Silence filled the air for a few moments. Lynn fidgeted while Randolph ran his hand over his head that was sparsely covered in short graying hair. "Now that's the question, isn't it? How they laser focused on a single individual so quickly."

"I assume the mayor and the new police commissioner were under tremendous pressure . . . public pressure . . . to find someone since it was such a brazen attack on a young Caucasian woman," I said, trying to gauge their reaction.

Randolph looked at Lynn then back to me. "There was that, of course, because they needed to solve it fast."

"But from what we've been able to tell, Kareem Adams's name just dropped in on them out of the blue one day and they ran with it. And once they did, how convenient it was that he was dead from a supposed drug overdose by the time they caught up with him," Lynn said with more than a hint of sadness in her voice.

"I have some contacts on the police force. Maybe that's where I'll start."

"Be careful, Blaise. This case smells fishy and if you start blaming cops, you're gonna get stonewalled," Randolph said.

"Thanks for the advice." I said, then asked, "What did you find out about the mother, Lynn? You clearly got her address, though she shut you out."

"She works at Strawbridge and Clothier's out at the Plymouth Meeting Mall."

"Strawbridge's?" I really perked up upon hearing that. "You sure?"

She nodded yes.

"She goes by her maiden name. Sheree Jackson," Randolph said. "It's how she stayed out of the spotlight after her son was accused of murder. She'd have gotten death threats."

"I want to write a story about HER," Lynn started but Randolph stopped her.

"It's not the time yet. We're trying to run some things down . . . other sources . . . before we write anything that directly includes her, out of fear for her safety and privacy," he said.

I was thinking of taking a trip up to Plymouth Meeting but I didn't mention that. The Tribune may not have gotten anything out of the mother but that didn't mean I couldn't try. I just had to find the right approach.

I decided to redirect their thinking in case Randolph could be reading my thoughts. He did know me well.

"I was over in the Girard area in North Philly just now. Before I head back over that way, I'll see what other avenues I can track down first," I said as I got up. I shook Randolph's hand, though he remained seated, but Lynn got up. Her cheerfulness had returned.

"I'll walk you downstairs," she said.

I reached for her hand to shake it. It was small and surprisingly soft, although I had no reason to find that surprising.

"That really won't be necessary. I'm sure I can find my way. But thank you all the same."

And with that, I made a hasty retreat.

~*~

It was getting late and before I ended my workday, I had one more stop I wanted to make. At the corner of 16th and South, I saw a public telephone and was glad I had a quarter to make the call.

Marie answered before the second ring.

"Hey. Where have you been? I couldn't reach you. Mae merely said you were out."

"You've been trying to reach me? Is everything okay?

"Yeah. Sure. I was just checkin' to see that *you're* okay."

This made me happy. I shifted my weight from one foot to the other, and leaned into the small telephone enclosure. "I'm good. Busy. After my morning meeting, Eli stopped by the office and asked me to take a case. Look into something."

"Eli? You mean your brother?" she said, letting the question hang. "You took a case from him?"

"I know, I know. Family. But he sounded desperate," I said. "I've been checking on things and looking for leads all day. I'm at a payphone down in Center City now."

Then she asked the question that was often on her mind when I took a new case but I could always tell she was reluctant to ask it.

"Is it . . . a dangerous case?"

"I don't think so," I said, trying to sound reassuring. I could tell she was relieved.

"Where you going now?" Marie asked.

"Up to North Philly. I won't be there long. You want to stop by later? I haven't called the house yet today but I'm sure Grammy Taylor should be back home by now."

There was a pause on the line. I wasn't sure what it meant. "Naw. I think I'll stay in and prepare for my interview in New York."

So, there's the rub. She was looking for a job out of the city and wasn't ready to discuss what her moving to New York — or somewhere else — would mean for her or for us. And she definitely didn't want to do it with me on a payphone as I stood on a street corner.

Even I realized this wasn't the best time.

"Okay."

"Don't sound so dejected," Marie said. "I do love you. You know that, Boo."

"Yes, I know. I'll call you when I get home before jumping in the sack."

~*~

Twenty minutes after my call to Marie I was on the steps to Grammy Taylor's house and could hear the people inside moving about. I knocked softly at the door, which was answered by Valerie. She welcomed me with a hug, nearly causing me to drop Raymond's apology gift, and pulled me into the house.

"What's that?" she asked, closing the door and not waiting for an answer. "We're all in here back in the kitchen getting dinner together for Grammy and trying to get her to sit down," she said.

"Good luck with that," I said.

Renee and Val were cooking and fussing over my grandmother, who reminded everyone that it was her house and her kitchen, and she didn't need anyone's help. Allen was setting the dining room table with an everyday setting, which was a little less formal than the setting used on Sundays. Stuart was out in the tiny backyard playing games with the twins, Cora and Cody, to keep them from rippin' and runnin' through the house.

The warm, welcoming aroma of baked chicken greeted me as I entered the kitchen. My grandmother turned and reached up to me. The embrace was heartfelt.

"Come with me," I said to her as I took her hand to lead her back into the living room where I had left the gift.

"What is this?" she said with a puzzled expression as I handed it over.

"It's from Raymond. He wanted to apologize for the tea."

"Oh, that dear boy. He didn't need to do that. I'm fine," she said. She attempted to give it back to me but I pulled away.

Eli arrived just before dinner was placed on the table. The meal was as delicious as ever, the atmosphere was pleasant and loving, and it all came to an end much too soon. Quietly, as I helped with cleaning up the kitchen, Valerie pulled me aside and gave me my marching orders regarding stopping by to see my grandmother in the morning before work. Yet even without her forceful *suggestion*, it was something I already planned to do.

"I'll be over at around eight-thirty in the morning to check in on you before I head to the office," I said to my grandmother as I headed toward the door.

"It's not necessary to come over all that way. I'll be just fine," she protested, but I waved it off.

"No matter. I'll still be here," I said. I hugged her one last time and bid everyone good-night. And then stepped out the door into an unseasonably warm spring evening.

CHAPTER VII

I did a B-flat major scale as a tribute to Monk

I slept restlessly, tossing and turning, and once had to get up to change my t-shirt because it was drenched in sweat because of the heat.

I thought about stolen department store merchandise and how it ended up on street corners to be sold by the likes of Mookie. I also thought about Kareem Adams, wondering how an ex-con who was helping his community rid street corners of drug trafficking could end up being the main suspect in the stabbing death of a woman in Center City and, eventually, dying of a drug overdose in North Philly.

They were new mysteries in my life.

Normally, I welcomed such mysteries as distractions from the banality of my normal cases. But my intuition told me these were different, though I didn't know actually how.

And then there was Marie, who was complicating my personal life.

Those concerns swirled around in my head, obscuring my view and testing my judgment. It was very late before I totally fell asleep, and morning came too quickly.

~*~

I got to my grandmother's house and let myself in just as Allen and his wife were heading out to work. I was dragging for more reasons than just a lack of food and morning caffeine. And I didn't need ribbing from my brother.

"I got some news for you about Clara. Your ex," Allen teased playfully as he descended the stairs from the second floor.

He worked as a police officer at the city transit authority, where Clara Perry, my ex, was the head of the security department, and thus was Allen's boss. She had been leery at first about even interviewing him but she did and he got the job and, after nine months, it appeared to be working out.

"I don't care to hear about it," I said, sternly, leaving no doubt to my meaning.

"You sure?" he said, clearly amused, as Renee grabbed his arm and moved him, reluctantly, toward the front door. "It's juicy."

"Yes, I'm sure," I snapped. "I've moved on. I'm sure she has, too."

Allen's eyes widened. "Oh, yeah, she sure has," he teased even more.

"Allen, leave Davey alone," Renee said to her husband, still guiding him toward the front door. "Come on or you'll be late to work." Turning back to me, she added, "It's okay, David. He doesn't mean anything by it."

"Okay," Allen said as he adjusted his uniform and checked his pocket to ensure he had his SEPTA badge. "Have it your way."

And with that, they both walked out the door and I sighed in relief.

I walked to the back of the house where Grammy was sitting at a table in a small kitchen nook. She was reading the morning paper and drinking coffee but got up as I approached.

"You want some coffee? Go sit down. Since you're here, let me get you something to eat."

I breakfasted on fried eggs, bacon, toast with homemade jam, orange juice, and coffee. I didn't talk much and let Grammy Taylor chortle on about subjects that did not hold my interest. She didn't appear to notice I wasn't talking until I finished eating.

"It was good of you to bring Marie by the hospital on

Sunday. She is such a joy!" she said.

"Yes, she is," I responded cautiously, afraid of where this was going. "But we're at a complicated place at the moment, with her graduating and deciding what to pursue . . . and where. Here in the city or perhaps in New York."

Grammy started to respond but I shook my head and stopped her. And she, amazingly, took the hint.

"You haven't said much since you got here," she said as she stood up and wiped her hands on her apron. "Something's on your mind. Is it about work? You want to talk to me about it?"

"No, I don't care to talk about it. I just need to figure some things out. Professional things, of course, but also some personal."

It was a difficult time for Marie and me. Shapely, smart, sexy, and incredibly intuitive, Marie would be my girlfriend except that she wasn't. Not any longer, at least, though my family said it was hard to tell the difference. Often times, it was hard for me to tell the difference, too.

We started dating while I was investigating a murder case a year ago, only to place her life in danger before I identified the killer. But that incident drew us both closer together.

She was my lover and chief sounding board; and I was her rock, supporter, and mentor. Marie helped me decide to rent the house where I now live, and I suggested she could save money by moving in with several girls instead of living alone. The new Canon camera I have for surveillance was a Christmas gift from Marie, and she helped me pick out the best accessories to utilize the camera to the utmost.

My Christmas gift to her was a replica of an antique pendant on a silver chain. And I paid a pretty penny for it at a Center City store on Jeweler's Row on Sansom Street.

The strain of my job, however, and the stress of her final year in college were too much. We had parted officially as a couple several months ago, though we speak on the phone nearly every day and still have dinner together once or twice a week. I hadn't dated another woman since, although Mae said my celibacy was causing me to be crabby in the office.

I was deep in thought when my grandmother said, "Come with me to the living room." I must have looked confused and she persisted, "Come on, let's go."

We walked into the small, claustrophobic living room, filled with old furniture and decades-old knick-knacks collected during a life well lived. The air was stale and stuffy, due to poor ventilation, but there wasn't a speck of dust anywhere.

As soon as we entered the room, I knew — and regretted — where we were headed. Situated along the wall next to a fireplace mantle was a dark-colored upright piano with a matching stool. There was sheet music on the stand.

"Come on, let's play. It's been ages since we've played together," Grammy said.

I was quite aware of that fact because, while Sundays aren't the only days I stop by, they are the days I stay the longest. And me playing piano, especially with my grandmother on a Sunday, has long been a source of friction in the family. I wasn't the only one in the family who played an instrument, but I was the one who displayed the most talent and, as the oldest of four siblings, I was the one who was encouraged and nurtured the most.

In everyone else's eyes, the piano signified my position as my grandmother's favorite. And in ways both subtle and blatant, my siblings reminded me of it. It wasn't just that I was the oldest. I was also named after Georgie Mae's closest brother. They shared a bond that had lasted until his death five years ago.

Great-uncle David had also played the piano, perhaps even this one.

When I was a child, Grammy Taylor had tutored me on the piano and I spent many hours practicing. But I didn't mind. I loved spending time with her because she was kind and she spoiled me. There were always cookies and milk, or a slice of cake, after practice, even as my parents discouraged it. But Grammy Taylor ignored them anyway.

"You have to practice if you're going to be a great pianist one day," she would say. "I know you will. And you'll go to the Curtis Institute downtown. They'll have to admit you."

It didn't matter that, by the time I reached high school, my career goals completely changed from music to social justice. After all, the Curtis Institute got hundreds and hundreds of applications each year from people who wanted a career in music. I did not.

Grammy Taylor was heartbroken when I announced that I planned to attend Temple and then law school to become a civil rights attorney.

Also, to tell the truth, I was good but not *that good.* I wasn't a prodigy, though I was comfortable on the keyboard and could get lost in thought when I played, especially when I played alone.

It had been more than a year, perhaps eighteen months, since I last played. But to please my grandmother, I obediently walked over to the piano, pulled out the bench and sat. I scooted over to the right to make space for her to join me on my left. I stretched my fingers, cracked my knuckles, and raised the lip to the keyboard to stare down at eighty-eight keys of ebony and ivory.

I first did a series of exercises to wake up my fingers and reacquaint them to their proper positions on the keys. I played a C-major scale — just the ivory keys — from left to right, from the lowest pitch keys to the highest, and then back down again. And to liven things up, I did a B-flat major scale as a tribute to Monk, who created some of his greatest music in B-flat.

After staring down at my fingers and the piano keys as I practiced, I finally looked up at the sheet music in the stand, and I smiled. Simple and lively, it was Little Rhapsody on Hungarian Themes and, not surprisingly, was a duet played by two people on a piano.

Had no one played this piano since I had last tickled the ivories? Or, knowing I'd be over this morning, had my grandmother placed that sheet music on the stand for me to discover?

I let that thought occupy my mind just before I signaled my readiness and we started to play.

Given I was on the right, I played Primo, the higher notes, and she was Secondo, playing the lower notes. I focused on the notes on the page with my fingers hitting the correct keys at the right moment. It got easier as we played and I got lost in the music. It's a short piece, played in under two minutes, but once my grandmother finished the final two notes, I continued, improvising and jazzing up the music.

I barely noticed that Grammy wasn't playing as I continued, engulfed in the sound that reverberated around the room. And at that moment, there was nothing else, only the sound of music. There was no stolen merchandise from Strawbridge and Clothier, no longer the deaths of Mary Ann Tolk and Kareem Adams, no constitutional law, and not even Marie moving away.

The music cleared my mind as I experienced the sheer joy of playing and hearing the magic I created. And in doing so, much of the chaos of the recent past cleared and I knew what to do next.

I was playing a melody in a minor key but ended on a major chord. The ending: Perfect.

I turned to my grandmother, who sat silently, smiling at me. "Thank you for having me play," I said, and leaned over to give her a peck on the cheek.

She accompanied me to the front door and we shared a final hug. I stepped livelier when I left.

~*~

I stopped by the office just as Mae arrived but didn't stay long. After we exchanged pleasantries and I instructed her on what needed to be accomplished while I was gone, I grabbed what I needed — notes and a couple of pictures — and rushed out.

My best boots-on-the-ground source in the police department was Detective John Thompson, a man of medium height with a fairly easy-going personality, though he approached police work with steadfast seriousness. He had his ear to the ground and his finger on the pulse of the city, so he was generally up-to-date on most major law enforcement investigations. Thompson occasionally shared some of that information with me, if I asked nicely, or at least he steered me in the right direction, as long as it also benefited the police department.

But as with all good things, he came with a liability — his partner, Sergeant Ryan Gregory.

Gregory was as by-the-book as a cop could be. Tall, imposing, and stern in expression and personality, he sported a crew cut, a hairstyle that went out of fashion two decades ago. And as you might expect, Gregory saw the world in stark black and white. No gray areas. In his view, there were good guys and bad guys, and since he wore a police badge, he was, by definition, one of the good guys.

In the year since I'd first met him, Gregory had only spoken kindly to me once — and then just barely. I wasn't expecting it again any time soon.

Gregory could barely contain his contempt for all private detectives, and me in particular, while Thompson, who often found my presence tiresome, grudgingly accepted my usefulness — to a degree.

In the past year, the two officers had moved from a precinct in South Philadelphia to one in West Philly. The station had a grungy look about it. The walls were a nondescript greenish-gray paint that was just on the verge of peeling. The station itself was old, much like the surrounding neighborhood, and the furniture was uncomfortable, as if the city had decided that providing a more modern environment might also suggest that downtown officials truly cared about the inhabitants of the station or of the community it served.

Blessedly, Gregory was out when I wandered over to Thompson's desk and took a seat beside it. He was busy on the telephone and just looked at me through his reading glasses, a new development in the past year.

"What are you doing here, Blaise, and what do you want?" he said as soon as he hung up and tried to look busy straightening papers and opening and closing desk drawers as if he was urgently looking for something important.

I didn't answer immediately, just tried to settle comfortably in an otherwise uncomfortable chair, and pulled out my notebook. Glancing through it quickly, I looked back up to him. "There are a couple of things you might help me with."

"I was afraid of that as soon as I saw you. I'm a public employee, not a part of your operation," Thompson said.

"And you also know I'm a private citizen who's helped you solve a couple of cases," I retorted.

Thompson couldn't argue with that, and merely exhaled heavily and repeated himself impatiently, "What do you want, Blaise?"

"I'm looking into the death of Kareem Adams," I said. "There are people in the community who are questioning how he died."

"The *community* is wrong," said Gregory, who came up from behind me carrying two cups of coffee. He placed one on Thompson's desk, while glaring at me, and placed the other on his own desk, though he remained standing. "Adams was a drug addict and a killer. He died of an overdose. End of story. And you can tell *that* to the . . . community."

"But there are still questions," I said, refusing to be intimidated by his dominant standing position.

Gregory was about to speak but merely crossed his arms over his chest as Thompson broke in first. "Like what?" he said, though he also sounded skeptical.

"How was Adams first identified as a suspect?" I said.

"We got a tip," Gregory chimed in confidently.

"You guys get lots of tips, all day and all the time. And undoubtedly even more this time, given the high profile of the case."

Thompson put up a finger to stop Gregory from replying. "The department got a tip from a reliable source about a week after the stabbing. We investigated . . . and I was part of that investigation . . . and it was found to be credible, so an arrest warrant was issued. By then we knew where he was staying before the warrant was served." He paused before adding, "Blaise, I was there right behind the SWAT team when it was served. Everything was done properly . . . by the book. I saw the body. He was on a bed in a second-floor bedroom which contained a lot of drugs and drug paraphernalia. He died of a heroin overdose."

"Was an autopsy done?"

"Yes," Gregory said curtly.

"Standard procedure in this sort of case. The results were released to the public," Thompson said. "Overdose."

"That was the cause of death . . . an overdose, yes . . . but not the manner of death," I corrected. "It could have been an accident, or a suicide, or a murder." Gregory huffed but I continued. "And was there any other evidence linking Adams to Tolk's murder?"

By then, Gregory had had enough. "He was a fuckin' junkie," he said, raising his voice enough to get the attention of others in the squad room. "What other evidence is needed? We have it on video tape from the murder scene. He killed her. Plain and simple. And for what? Nothing! I just wish we had arrested the son-of-a-bitch, and tried and convicted him of first-degree murder. Then the needle that went into his arm to end his miserable life would have been deliberate and not a mistake he made."

Gregory took a sip of his coffee, then slammed it down on his desk, spilling some on his papers. "It's cold," he growled. "And I don't have to stand here and listen to your crap."

I watched in silence as he stormed off.

"He has a daughter her age . . . Mary Ann Tolk's age," Thompson said of his partner. "Her name's Katie and she's living over across the Walt Whitman in Bellmawr . . . safe, or so he thinks . . . but still he's a touch sensitive about the murder of a woman that age."

"I hope it doesn't cloud his judgment in terms of his police work here in Philly," I said. "And besides, it's not as if there's no crime in Jersey. Crime, even violent crime, can happen anywhere."

"I know that," he said. "But in any event, I'm keeping an eye on him."

Wanting to keep the conversation cool and calm, I waited a couple of heartbeats and quickly contemplated why the police department would purchase such hard, uncomfortable chairs for its squad rooms.

I did not voice that question with Thompson.

"Detective, I didn't come here to piss you off or anyone else. I'm just looking for some answers to questions that I know you've heard people around the city asking."

"Like what?" he asked, leaning onto his desk and making a steeple with his fingers.

"Everyone I've spoken to who knew him said he had used drugs before he went to prison but not since. Well, a little pot, but that's it. And he never used heroin. Ever. A pastor up that way said he was helping in an anti-drug effort in the area."

Thompson sat back and reached into a drawer and pulled out an envelope, handing it to me. "You mean this?"

I looked inside and there were pictures, similar to what Pastor Pat showed me, of cars stopping at street corners all the way up Girard to the Philadelphia Zoo at 34th Street. The pictures caught faces and license plates.

"You already know about all this," I said. His fingers were steepled again. "And about the possible retribution for those anti-drug activities."

He nodded and leaned forward, then looked in the direction that his partner had taken. "You cannot breathe a word of this to anyone, you understand. Nobody," Thompson said, looking again to make sure Gregory wasn't coming back. "We've been trying to keep this quiet. The case is officially closed, which makes the politicians happy, but there are still questions, as you pointed out, regarding the manner of his death. Those questions need answering. There's no doubt it was an overdose, most likely self-inflicted."

Thompson paused and surveyed his desk without his gaze settling on anything in particular. "It's possible the scene was just made to look that way."

"It could be murder," I said.

"Yes, it's possible." And he sat back in his chair.

"What. . . ." I started but he shook his head to stop me.

"That's all I can say," Thompson said.

And with that, he said no more. Unmoving, I stared at him and he stared back, unmoving and unmoved. In the time I had known Thompson, I had learned he was fair and open-minded, but when he had made up his mind, that was generally it.

Therefore, I was the one who blinked first and I changed subjects. "Do me a favor."

Thompson still looked skeptical. "Now what?" he said in a flat tone.

"Check your police reports on the crime scene for when Kareem was found," I said, and I reached inside my jacket for the pictures from the church. "Then check out these pictures, especially the top one."

Thompson accepted the pictures, all the while trying to read my face as to what he should be looking for. I just shook my head "no" and was about to stand up when I remembered that Kareem Adams wasn't the only reason I stopped in.

When I didn't go, Thompson said, "There's more?" Then, showing some frustration, he asked, to no one in particular, "Can this day get any worse?"

"I'll be easy on you, John," I said, reaching into my jacket pocket again. "I've got more pictures. But first, what can you tell me about fencing stolen merchandise in the city?"

A curious calm, like a veil, settled once again over him. Thompson leaned back in his chair, relaxed. "You workin' a case?"

"Somewhat. I have a client . . . in a retail store . . . who has expressed some concern over stolen items. I'm checking out some things."

"Your client over at Strawbridge and Clothier? We've been talking to an executive over there for several weeks. Dawson's his name," Thompson said.

"Raymond Dawson, VP of fashion merchandising. I've known him for years. We went to high school and college together. He's a frat brother, too," I said.

Thompson nodded, taking in the information. "He said he knew you and that you suggested that he call me."

"Glad to be of service," I said with a bit of sarcasm.

"Fencing, yes, there's been a major uptick in the last couple years, and not just here in the Philadelphia area. There are channels that stretch over a number of states," he said. "It's not just in department store merchandise. We're looking into all sorts of stolen items, including jewelry, artwork, high-end items. Things a collector might be willing to obtain through illegal means, and pay a hefty price for them."

He stopped to consider his next words.

"There appears to be a major connection here in Philadelphia that we've been trying to nail down. We've been looking into your street friend up on 52nd . . . " the detective said as I interrupted.

"Mookie."

"Yeah, that's him."

"But Mookie's only on the street level. He's not a major player," I said.

"Yeah. We know that. But he's a great source for information. He gave us a tip that something big is going down."

"He say what?" I asked, and checked my watch.

"We've been trying to get more information out of him . . . and others . . . regarding who's behind this fencing operation, especially the hot, expensive stuff. You got any information for me?" Thompson asked.

"Not much. But have you ever seen any of these people before?" I said as I handed Thompson pictures from my Saturday surveillance job.

Thompson looked at several pictures and sat forward in his chair, seemingly focusing hard on one person in the photos. He turned one picture towards me. It was the one where the woman was shaking hands with Stephenson at the conclusion of the exchange.

"Her? You kiddin' me, right?"

"No," I said, a little tension creeping up my spine.

"When was it taken?"

"Last Saturday in Fairmount Park. I was on a hill across the street from the parking lot where the exchange took place. I was working on the Strawbridge case. Why do you ask?"

His expression was stern and serious. “This woman here, shaking hands with the guy after accepting the stolen merchandise. That’s Darcy Hayes. She’s with the FBI.”

CHAPTER VIII

But I did the stupid thing anyway.

I spent Wednesday morning in the office, catching up on paperwork, writing up additional notes on my Kareem Adams inquiry, and having Mae, who — surprise, surprise — arrived early, sort through files and discard obsolete material. I don't care for administrative work and, if left to my own devices, my files would be a mess, which means Mae's work as my administrative assistant and secretary is essential to my small operation.

She finds a place for everything and keeps everything in its place, despite my attempts at maintaining the chaos.

Sometimes, I wonder how I managed before I hired her.

I contemplated what the involvement of the FBI might mean in the Strawbridge case. Did Raymond reach out to them, in addition to the city cops, but failed to mention it to me? Or was there more going on than what Raymond knew, which was more likely the case?

In any event, it was something to explore later. As for now, it was final exam day.

At noon, I headed out to the Penn law library for a final session with my study group. I had one of the nation's top constitutional scholars in Professor Timothy Caldwell Robertson. A former federal judge, Professor Robertson was renowned for his encyclopedic knowledge of obscure and arcane legal theories, which kept the class on its toes. Though I already felt as prepared as I could be, I accepted the group's invitation for one last get together before the final from 5:30 to 9:30 that evening.

Afterwards, I felt drained but also relieved that the semester was finally over. However, instead of going out for beer with the group, I headed back to the office for a little more work and to consider this new element — the involvement of the FBI in the case of S&C's stolen merchandise.

When I reached the office and walked in, I was surprised to see the lights were still on. Mae is my only full-time employee — I outsourced any other work I needed — and it was well past her office hours. She was also surprised when I arrived.

"Mae, what are you still doing here?"

She shuffled some papers around, slammed closed a desk drawer, and mumbled a reply.

"Ahh, thought I'd . . . ah . . . catch up on some paperwork," she said. "Thought you were gone. You said you were headed home after your test."

In all the time I had known her, Mae had only directly lied to me once — until tonight. I just looked at her for a second but let it pass. I was tired and decided I'd address the issue with her on another day.

"I'll be in my office," I said but stopped and turned around as I stood in the open doorway. "How long will you be here? I may be a bit. I have some catching up to do, too. You wanta order some Chinese? The place down the block is still open. Or maybe I could pick up a pizza. I'm payin'."

Mae gave me a smile, though a sad one. "No, it's okay. I'm not hungry," she said, timidly. At that moment, it was hard for me to judge her emotional state, but it was curious. She rarely turned down free food. "And, ah, I think I'll head out soon."

"As you wish," I said and entered my office, leaving the door open as was generally my practice when I don't have a client in there or have a confidential telephone conversation. The open door made communication between us easier, and I'm all about ease at work in the office.

After I sat behind my desk, I took out a notebook I carried and flipped through some other observations on the Strawbridge job, which I had not written up yet for Mae. I liked to write my reports in longhand and have Mae type up three copies — one for the client, one for me and one for her files. I reached into the top drawer on the right, picked up my gun and placed it on my desk, and then pulled out the yellow legal pad that had been lying under the gun.

It was nearly 10 o'clock and I could hear her moving around, seemingly straightening up and preparing to leave, when the office door opened and someone entered. I couldn't see who.

"Okay, now, Baby Cakes, you got it?" said a deep baritone voice at a normal volume. I pushed back from my desk and rose from my chair just as I heard Mae say, "Hush. Not so loud."

I walked to my doorway and saw a giant of a man. Six-foot-five, 250-plus pounds. His shoulder and arm muscles strained the fabric of his brown suit jacket, probably because it was tailored for a smaller man. The palms of his large hands were flat on Mae's desk and he looked menacingly down at her, only to turn his menacing countenance to me at the doorway.

He stood up to face me directly. His arms were about an inch and a half too long for his jacket, and his pant legs were also too short. This man needed a better tailor, but he was six inches taller and more than fifty pounds heavier than me, so I wasn't going to bring it up.

In addition, his jacket hung poorly on the right side and his pocket bulged somewhat. He raised his hand up slightly but didn't reach into the pocket for his gun.

"What you want, muthafucka? This don't involve you," the man growled. He moved one step toward me and stopped.

I didn't move. "Everything that happens in my office involves me," I countered.

Mae was quickly out of her seat and moved between us. She was facing the man and raised a hand to his chest but looked back toward me as she said, "It's okay, David. I can handle this."

"Yeah, *David.* You go back in yo bum-ass office before I have to teach yo bum ass a painful lesson," the man said, more harshly than before. And this time, his hand did move toward his jacket pocket.

At that point, I had few options and none were good. I was facing a hostile man who was much, much bigger than me and who was about to pull a piece. And my own gun was behind me on my desk.

But I did the stupid thing anyway.

"And you listen to me, you asshole. Get the fuck out of my office now and don't you ever come back," I said as I stepped back through the doorway and slammed the door so hard it must have rattled the building.

The man made an unintelligible sound and must have shoved Mae hard to the side. I didn't see it but didn't have time to worry about Mae. I knew what was about to happen and had little time to prepare as I ducked to the left — out of the line of fire — and then toward my desk.

Three shots rang out, shattering the frosted glass on the upper half of my door. On the floor but back around my desk, I reached up for my weapon just as the giant kicked open the door and stepped in.

That's when I fired. Twice.

"*Ahhh,*" the giant of a man screamed and went down, dropping his gun to grab his left knee. He was rolling around on the floor just inside my office, grimacing in pain. "You shot me, you, muthafucka. I'm gonna kill your muthafuckin' ass."

"Maybe," I said as I rose and kicked his gun out of his reach. "But not today." To Mae, who had just rushed into the room, I said, "Call an ambulance and the cops."

~*~

"Another disgruntled client?" mocked police Sgt. Gregory, who was facing me and taking down some notes. I was leaning back onto Mae's desk.

"Hardly." I wasn't going to let him get to me.

The paramedics had cut the man's pant leg from the cuff to the hip to get to the wound, which they bandaged before placing him on a stretcher. Strapped down to keep him from falling — or from escaping — they wheeled him down the hallway to the elevator to the first floor and to a waiting ambulance on the street.

I had looked out the window and noticed a crowd had gathered outside. The spectators were undoubtedly whispering and gossiping about what was happening on the second floor. Some might have tried to venture inside except that uniformed officers kept them back.

Thompson scratched his head as if doing so would provide clarity to his thinking. I was standing and Mae was seated behind her desk. Other uniformed officers were going over my office. The police had both my gun and the wounded man's gun.

"You say neither you nor your secretary know this man or why he was here or what he wanted?" Thompson said, holding a small, black notebook in his left hand.

"That's right," I answered for both Mae and myself.

"David, you expect me to believe that?" Thompson said in a slightly softer tone, as he might to a close colleague or perhaps to a friend.

"Yes, detective, I do," I replied, keeping it professional.

"Maybe we should just take them downtown for questioning," Gregory said with a certain glee. "Sit them in the cooler for a night. Should loosen them up a bit."

Mae looked scared and was about to speak when I interrupted, addressing my response to Gregory. "You have no reason to hold us. We haven't done anything wrong."

"You just shot a man," Gregory said. "At the very least, that's a weapons offense and endangering the welfare of others. And that's just the beginning."

"He fired at me first," I countered. "I have a permit for the gun and I used it to protect myself and my employee from a violent intruder who was in *my* office."

Thompson, the senior of the two police detectives, closed his notebook and signaled to Gregory that they were leaving. To me, he said, "Okay. We've been over this all before, you know. Don't leave town. After we question the suspect, we may have more questions for you. And, David," he said more softly, again, "you have my number in case you remember something."

This time I responded in kind. "I'll call it, thanks."

"Yeah, right. I'm sure you will," Thompson said with a dry chuckle, clearly not believing me.

Once everyone was gone, I pulled up a chair to Mae's desk to face her directly. "Mabelene, what's going on? Who was that guy and what the hell did he want?"

She avoided eye contact. "I can't say. Really," she said, finally looking into my face, "I can't say."

"Are you in some sorta trouble?"

"Not anymore."

"Why not?" I asked.

"Really, David, I can't say now."

I wasn't getting anywhere and didn't expect to get any more tonight. I put the chair back in its place against the wall next to a filing cabinet across from Mae's desk. "Let's go," I said.

Mae got up and looked at the broken glass to my door and then beyond that to my office and the bullet holes in the window to the outside. I guessed her thoughts.

"Insurance will cover it," I said as we turned out the lights and closed the door to lock up the office. "I'll have you file the claim papers tomorrow."

"And what about your brother-in-law?" Mae asked.

Stuart, my landlord. The guy I'd likely see in four days'

time during the weekly family dinner on Sunday evening at my grandmother's house.

"Not to worry," I said as we walked down the hallway. "I'll re-enlist in the Navy. With any luck, they'll ship me out before Sunday."

CHAPTER IX

It was a teardrop pendant with a large jade stone in a silver setting.

"Oh, David! Are you all right? Why didn't you call me earlier?"

Marie punched me hard in the shoulder as we stood in the living room of the apartment in the Fairmount section of the city that she shared with a gaggle of girls. Then, she threw her arms around me and pulled me into a tight hug. "You worry me so much."

I had given her the basics of the evening but without going into any details, especially that I had been shot at. No need to worry her needlessly since he was in the hospital and no way capable of doing me harm.

"It was all okay. I wasn't worried," I said, but added to myself, *much.*

"Is Mae okay, too? She wasn't hurt or anything, was she?"

"No, Mabelene's fine. Just a little unsettled at first. But she was better by the time we left the office."

"Why was she even there so late?" she asked.

I shrugged and let that suffice for a response.

Had the night's events not happened, I had planned to bring up Raymond's offer for Marie to consider a fashion job at Strawbridge's. But today, I decided it would wait. Or, perhaps, I would never bring it up at all. Ever. With a degree in fashion design, Marie's eyes were set on a career in New York. What kinda selfish jerk would try to stand in the way of that?

"If I get a job in Manhattan, you could move and start a detective agency there," she had said to me in my bed after we had celebrated Valentine's Day together three months ago. "You could transfer your license to New York State. You have the experience behind you."

"It's not that easy," I said, sitting up in bed. "It's taken me ten years to just get to the point where I'm not working hand-to-mouth. If I moved to New York, I'd have to start all over again. From scratch."

Marie propped up on her right elbow, facing me.

"David, you could work for someone else for a change. Perhaps change careers altogether after you get your law degree," she said. She didn't look at me as she spoke her next words. "Maybe there's another reason you can't leave Philadelphia."

"Like what?"

"Your family."

"That's not true," I argued, although the comment did sting.

"Really? They're an anchor holding you in place," she said.

"I don't even live in the same part of town as most of my family."

"But you do live in the *SAME* city. And you call or visit Grammy Taylor several times a week in addition to having dinner there religiously every Sunday."

"Not every Sunday," I protested.

"Yeah, right. When was the last time you missed a Sunday dinner there?" she said, adding, "Can't remember, can you?"

"I thought you liked my grandmother," I said, trying to re-direct the conversation just a little.

"I do. I love Grammy Taylor. And that's the point. You haven't . . . you can't pull away from them, any of them. Not even from your brothers, despite the fact that you're barely speaking to them most of the time," she said and got out of bed, reaching for her clothes so she could get dressed. "I love you for your dedication to family. But for me, an outsider, it can be smothering."

That night, she had left and I didn't try to stop her. And though neither of us made a complete break, the strain was still there. We continued to talk or see each other regularly. And it's why I offered to drive her to 30th Street Station to take Amtrak to Manhattan for her job interview.

"Why didn't you call me last night after it happened?" said Marie, who was wearing her best interview outfit — a black wool jacket and a straight black skirt.

"And what for? What could you have done? Besides, the invasion was over," I said.

Going to stand in front of the mirror over her dresser, she picked up a necklace I had bought for her. It was to bring her good luck. "Fasten this in the back, please."

The necklace was the replica antique I got for her months ago — a teardrop pendant with a large jade-like stone in a silver setting, with smaller stones that looked like little diamonds but were actually cubic zirconia.

"It's beautiful, David. Thank you so much," she had said when I gave it to her at Christmas.

I fastened the pendant around her neck. She was wearing a white, V-neck blouse with a pleated front that would draw attention to the fashionable accessory without it being a distraction.

Beside the dresser was a black leather Ann Klein portfolio, a graduation gift from me. I got it at Strawbridge's at a deep discount, thanks to Raymond. I grabbed it and we headed out to my car. She lived only a block from Eastern State Penitentiary, a massive nineteenth century prison that had been finally closed for good only fifteen years ago. I opened the car door for her and tried not to glance too much at her legs. But she noticed and smiled. I said nothing and walked around to the other side of the car to get in.

The drive to the Amtrak station was short but we covered some ground, though nothing about our personal relationship.

I pulled up to the curb at the station and got out but left the engine running. I walked around the car to open her door. We hugged warmly when she got out and I handed her the portfolio.

"Good luck, babe. I know you'll do fine. You have everything they need. You just need to sell it. And I know you can do that."

"Thanks," she said. We kissed. I wanted to hold her longer, as if letting go meant letting go forever. But I let go. I wouldn't be the one responsible for her missing the train.

"I hope you get the job," I said, surprised that I actually meant it, despite what it might mean for us.

"I do, too. And when I do, we'll work things out. I promise."

Marie turned to wave to me one last time before going through the revolving door into the station. "I love you, Boo."

I waved and headed back to the car.

CHAPTER X

"Mr. Charlie say he'd kill you. He be very serious. I believed him."

Other than a "Good Morning" we exchanged when I arrived at the office, Mae and I barely spoke. It was okay. I wasn't ready for an emotional tug of war over the events of last night and I had reports to write up for three clients so that Mae could do the billing. By mid-morning, a glass repairman arrived to replace the glass in my office door and board up the outside window until a replacement arrived.

As I worked on my legal pad, the sound of Mae's electric typewriter and the scraping of metal as she opened file cabinet doors in the next office let me know she was busy on something.

Just before noon, Mae walked into my office and dropped a folder with a stack of black-and-white photos inside.

"I'm going to lunch now," she said. "That okay?"

"Yeah, but take your office key with you. I may be gone by the time you get back. I'll leave you a note as to where I should be."

She nodded, said nothing, and returned to her domain in the outer office.

I watched as she left.

A year ago, Mae had lived on Osage Avenue down the block from the MOVE house. And, like sixty other neighborhood homes, her house was destroyed in the fire caused after police firebombed the MOVE house, killing eleven of the thirteen people inside, including five who were children.

The city had rebuilt her house, along with the others, but she promptly sold it and moved into a nice, brick apartment building on Pine, only a four-block walk from work. To save money, she often walked home for lunch when the weather was nice, as it was today.

I wanted some answers from the police before I spoke to her about last night. But my relationship with the police was like that of many marriages — some good times and some bad times. When I found an open parking space on Walnut Street, only a block from the police station, I hoped this would be one of the good times.

~*~

"I need some information on that guy from my office last night," I said as I walked up to Thompson's desk.

"Back again, I see. And somehow, I'm not surprised. I see you more than I see my wife and kids . . . and I like them a lot more," Thompson said, taking off his glasses and placing them on some papers on his desk. "You ready to come clean about last night?"

Taking a chair, I resigned myself to the inevitable. I didn't know much but I knew I'd have to come up with something. "And you'll tell me what you have on the guy?" I said, bargaining what little I could.

Thompson didn't move a muscle, though I could tell we had an understanding. But I'd have to be the one to start.

"I finished a law school exam at Penn last night and instead of heading home, though I was exhausted, I went back to the office. Had some paperwork to finish. Mae, who should have already left hours earlier, was there. Not sure why," I said. "She didn't say much and seemed in a hurry to leave."

"What time was that?" he said. He picked up his glasses and cleaned them with his tie, but didn't put them on.

"Around 9:30, thereabouts," I said, stopping to see if he had another question. There wasn't and I continued. "So, I'm in my office and this big guy comes into the outer office, apparently to see Mae. He must not have known I was there. I wasn't supposed to be, originally. She would have been alone."

I stopped again but he hadn't made a move to take any notes. "Go on, Blaise."

"From my office, I hear him call her Baby Cakes, which caught my attention, you know, because of her past."

"Isn't that. . . ."

"The name she used as a prostitute? Yes, it was."

"Is she in the trade again?" Oddly, he seemed embarrassed to ask, as if he was bringing up a sensitive subject about a family member.

"I don't think she's done any jobs since last year, when she *promised* me she had totally stopped."

"Then what could it be?" he asked.

"No idea. He demanded she give him something. I'm not sure what. But he was serious and sounded threatening. I got up and went to my door. We had words and I told him to get his ass out of my office."

Thompson looked amused. "That was dumb, you know. I thought you were smarter than that."

"Apparently not. I was operating on instinct," I said, trying to sound more confident than I was at the time. "That's when he started for his gun. I quickly got back into my office and he fired through the door, then busted his way in. I had my gun by then and fired twice. Mae called you guys and the ambulance and that's it. All I know."

"And what about your secretary? What's she know?" Thompson said. "So far, you haven't told me anything that I didn't know or assume last night."

I shook my head. "No idea what she knows. She hasn't been willing to talk and I haven't pressed her yet. I wanted to learn a little more about the big guy from you before I asked her again."

My back was to him and I didn't see Gregory approach me from behind.

"My, my. If it isn't the irritating private eye . . . nosing around. What you doin' here, Blaise?" Gregory asked as he walked up to a desk adjacent to Thompson's. He placed a cup of coffee in front of his partner and one on his desk before he sat down.

"And a howdy doody to you, too, Sergeant Gregory."

There was an awkward silence that Thompson blessedly ended.

"What is it you want to know, David?" Thompson said. He probably used my first name as a way to ease the tension between Gregory and me.

"Name and condition of the guy," I said.

Thompson picked up his coffee and took a sip before he addressed me. "Small time muscle man but likely with some big-time connections. Name's Benjamin Floyd. Got a rap sheet with priors. Did a little time a few years ago for armed robbery. Mostly, he busts up people, but last year there was an assault with a deadly weapon. Until last night, he was out on bail pending trial."

"Not anymore," Gregory said through a mouthful of jelly donut.

"What's his condition?" I asked.

"Stable. He's down at Presbyterian. Those were really good shots you gave him to the knee and thigh," Thompson said, sounding impressed.

"Lucky shots," Gregory said with a smirk. "But Floyd'll walk with a limp from now on."

"You talk to him last night?" I said.

"This morning," Thompson answered, "But he ain't saying anything. I told him, though, we're going to up the charges against him."

I asked why.

Gregory took another sip of coffee to wash down some donut in his mouth. "Cause one of his shots went through your office window and across the street. Hit an old guy, who's in serious condition at Pennsylvania Hospital."

"What's the word on the street?" I asked.

Thompson looked at Gregory as if for guidance and then back to me. "We have a source up your way. . . ."

"Yes, yes, Mookie. I know that," I said, frustrated that they were trying to be coy. Gregory looked at me as if I had just revealed the secret of the Shroud of Turin. "Hey, he's a police informant. Everybody knows that," I added.

Gregory looked at Thompson, who gave a nearly imperceptible nod. "He says someone hired Floyd to shake down people regarding a piece of stolen property that's missing. A watch, jewelry, something like that," Gregory said.

"And he thinks Mae has it or knows where to find it?"

"We're not sure what to make of it until he or your secretary talks," Gregory said impatiently. "Any chance of that happenin' anytime soon?"

"I'll see what I can do," I said and started to get up.

"You do that, Blaise," Gregory said.

I didn't bring up the FBI while talking to Thompson at the police station because I didn't want to hear any comments from Gregory.

~*~

Mae was at her desk when I arrived back at the office and I immediately pulled up a chair.

"The man I shot last night is Benjamin Floyd. How do you know him? Was he someone from your past?"

She started to get up. "David. . . ."

"Sit down, Mae. You're not going anywhere until I get some answers. And if you don't talk and give me some, I'm sure the police will come knocking," I said. "Floyd's somebody's muscle, I know that. But whose? And what did he want from you?"

Sorrow seemed to descend over Mae's entire body. She moved some papers around on her desk and straightened a pen-and-pencil set I gave her for her birthday last fall. She was delaying and I just had to wait for it to play out.

"He knows me. Could've been a john from before but I don't remember him. I didn't know him." As Mae quieted down, she stopped fidgeting and looked directly at me. "I gotta call a while ago . . . about ah week . . . from some guy who knew me from . . . from before, when I was workin' in this business."

"Who was he? He have a name?"

"I don't remember his name . . . his real name . . . if he give it to me ever," she said. "I just called him Mr. Charlie."

Mr. Charlie, I laughed to myself. Not sure if she caught the humor in that, even when I asked the next question. "So I guess he's white?"

"No. He's Negro."

Then I was surprised, given the use of the expression Mr. Charlie as a pejorative expression in the Black community. Much like Uncle Tom.

But I let it go. "Did he ever come here, himself?"

"No. He say he'd send somebody. In a couple of days. It was the guy you shot. You just said his name's Floyd."

"Floyd's boss . . . the guy who sent him . . . what's he look like?" I asked.

"Little guy. He was kinda fancy, puttin' on airs, like he's all about sumthin' and he ain't 'bout nuthin'.

"Describe him."

"Like I said, he be small. Nothin' to look at, really. Probably my daddy's age. And he wear a Process."

"A Process?" I interrupted. *Wow. Old School.*

"Yeah," she continued, barely acknowledging the question. "Big nose. Nice lips, though. He like to kiss me. I didn't let him at first but did later. Nice fancy clothes . . . suit jacket and tie . . . and he drop some cash. Could tell he be some kinda petty hustler but I didn't know what. He just come in, ask for me, we do our thing, and he tip me good."

"This was at the gentleman's club where I met you? Rita's place?"

"Yes."

I thought about this for a minute and Mae was squirming again. I could tell the questions were getting a little uncomfortable for her, as if the life she thought she left behind was catching up with her again. I decided to make it quick. I still needed answers because I really didn't have much to go on. But from the sound of it, he was definitely Old School. And that was a start.

"You know anything else about him?"

"No, not really," was the reply. "He didn't have on a weddin' ring but I think he be married."

"When was the last time you saw him? How long ago?"

"Don't know. Last year, couple of weeks . . . a month . . . before I met you and started workin' here. I don't remember for sure."

"How'd he know you work for me now?"

Mae shook her head as I considered the possible answers. At some point I thought I'd have to talk to Mae's former employer.

"But it wasn't me he really wanted," Mae said.

"Then who?" I asked.

"You."

I leaned back in my chair. Puzzled, I asked. "Me? Why me? Before last night, I hadn't seen that guy . . . Floyd . . . before. I have no idea who he's working for."

This time she did get up, straightened her dress as if smoothing out some wrinkles, and walked to my office door. The window hadn't been repaired yet. "The window guy will be here between two and four to fix the window." I was about to interrupt and redirect the conversation when she turned back to face me.

"Mr. Charlie first called me, he say there was sumthin' he wanted that you got or you know about. He tracked it to you. It was stolen . . . some stolen property. Said it was extremely valuable and he wanted it back, otherwise . . ." she said and stopped, letting the words hang in the air. "Otherwise, he threatened to kill you."

"What? I don't have anything of his. Stolen or otherwise. What was it he wanted?" I asked.

"I told him I'd talk to you and get it back, if you had what he wanted. There was no need for violence or for him to hurt you," she said, ignoring my questions. "I told him I needed a little more time. I was supposed to have 'til next week but he called me yesterday and said time's up. Said he be sendin' a guy over last night. I knew you'd be out of the office, so I thought I could reason with him first. It's why I was surprised when you showed up."

"Mabelene, what are you talking about?"

Mae walked to her desk but didn't sit down. "I think it's the necklace you gave Marie a couple of months ago. You told me you bought it a while back," she said.

"That replica antique necklace with the green pendant? That wasn't stolen. I got it from a jewelry store down on Samsom. Paid one-hundred fifty bucks for it."

"Apparently, it's worth a lot more than that. He said it's been missing for a couple of years and whoever wanted it tracked it down to where you bought it . . . and then to you," Mae said, coming to stand over me, her voice shaky. "Mr. Charlie say he'd kill you . . . if I didn't get it back and give it to him. Then he'd kill me. He be very serious. And I believed him."

I walked back into my office. And suddenly, a thought rushed into my head. Turning back, I said, "Mae, is Marie in any danger?"

"I don't think so, as long as I get the necklace back."

She's wearing the damned thing today, I thought. *But she's staying with a friend in New York until early next week. That's good. But I've got to reach her.*

"You should have told me this, Mae."

"I know, I know. But after all the things you've done for me, I wanted to take care of it for you," she rambled on. "Didn't want you in danger."

I sat and rested my elbows on my desk as I rubbed my temples. "Danger is part of my job. You know that. It's why I have a gun. You should've trusted me . . . come to me. You would've had to, eventually," I said, looking up and exhaling deeply. "But with this guy in custody we may have a little time to sort out some things first."

I reached into my desk for my gun, forgetting that the police had taken it last night as evidence. Once it was returned, I knew I'd have to start carrying it all the time until this necklace issue was resolved.

I looked at my wristwatch and made a decision that had been in the back of my mind for the better part of the day. "It's nearly four o'clock and we're going to close the office early today. In fact, I'm closing the office tomorrow, too. You can have a long weekend. I'll call you about coming in on Monday."

"You firin' me?" she asked, concern rising in her voice.

"No, of course not," I rushed to reassure her. "I need to make sure it's safe here before I have you back in the office. Don't need another shooting here."

"I'm so sorry, David. I didn't want to cause you any more trouble," she said.

"Don't worry about it, Mae. I'll call you sometime over the weekend. But you can go now. I'll lock up."

And with that, she gathered up her things and left. I leaned back in my chair and closed my eyes to think. But within minutes, my concentration was disturbed when the front door to the office opened and in walked two window repairmen. They made quick work of their tasks, replacing the glass and repairing the window frame. I made banal chit-chat as they worked and otherwise stayed out of their way. They only took about thirty minutes.

When they left, I straightened up my desk, preparing to lock up and head out when the telephone rang.

Oh, good heavens, who wants me now? I thought to myself. *Whoever it is, I'm not sitting down and I'm getting rid of them fast.*

It was 4:30.

"David Blaise Investigations."

"Oh, my God, David, you won't believe this. I got the job. I. Got. The. Job. THEY HIRED MEEE," Marie shouted so loud into the phone I had to take it from my ear.

Despite tension and stress, I smiled, pleased to hear her joyous voice. "Congratulations, Marie. What can I say? This is terrific news," I said.

"I know, right? Wow!" she said.

Marie's design awards in college had earned her interviews with a couple of important firms in Manhattan, though they mostly interviewed her on campus in Philadelphia. And this was her third interview with someone at Willi Smith, but the first one in New York City.

"I interviewed with them on campus, you know," she said. "They only called me up to New York to introduce me to people and to make the final decision."

I didn't know a lot about fashion designers, but over the past several months Marie had talked endlessly about Willi Smith, an up-and-coming Black designer from Philadelphia, and how much she had wanted to work for him.

"I knew you had it in you," I said, trying to keep any worry out of my voice. "I'm so proud of you. What's the job?"

"Apprentice designer for one of Willi Smith's lesser lines. Not sure which one yet. But you will not believe this," she said, sounding a bit breathless over the phone. "You will never guess who I got to meet. Willi Smith himself. They took me to his office after I finished. They said they were so pleased with my drawings that they wanted him to see them."

Marie continued breathlessly. She apparently couldn't stop talking. "You'll never believe how beautiful this place is. I love it. You've got to come see it."

I didn't want to dampen her enthusiasm but I needed to interrupt.

"Marie, we need to talk about something."

"I know, Boo, I know. But not right now."

"That's not what I was going to say."

"Do you know what he's doing? Willi Smith, I mean. You know what?" she said, moving on again. "He asked me what I thought of some tuxedos he designed. The fabric is exquisite, of course, and the designs looked absolutely fabulous. And I told him that. I think it was a test, because you know what he told me?"

Of course I don't, I was tempted to say. But she knew that. She was just excited. "Tell me," I said.

"They're the tuxedos for Caroline Kennedy's wedding. It's what the groomsmen will wear. *Ha*. Can you believe that? He's designing men's clothes for Caroline Kennedy."

"Marie, I need to talk to you about the necklace," I said.

"Yes, yes, I nearly forgot to tell you about that, too. It's my lucky charm necklace now," she said excitedly, and I could imagine her putting her hand to her neck to touch the necklace. "And I think it's worth more than what I think you must have paid for it."

My heart nearly jumped out of my chest. "What? Why do you say that?"

"Because Mr. Smith took an immediate interest in it as soon as he saw it. He asked me where I got it. I said my boyfriend gave it to me. He seemed to think it was a really expensive piece and he complimented me on it. But I told him it was just a replica of something."

"Marie, about the necklace . . ."

"Oh, David, I gotta go," she said in the same excited voice as before. "Someone's picking me up and their car just arrived."

"Marie, we need to talk about the necklace," I got in just as she cut me off.

"We can talk about it later. I'll call you this evening. Or we can talk about it when I get home. I'm staying for the weekend. Remember? But I gotta go now. Love you, Boo. Talk to you later."

Click and the phone went dead. I held it for a second, just looking at it. My heart was pounding so hard that I could hear it in my inner ears. I hadn't been able to alert her to the potential danger and I had no way of reaching her.

I slowly put the phone down, cursing myself as I did.

At least she wasn't in town and wouldn't be for several more days. That should provide some level of protection. At least, I hoped so.

CHAPTER XI

"You do me wrong, man. You do me wrong."

While not as old or as widely known as the Union League on Broad Street, which is less than two blocks from City Hall, the R. Wharton Social Club has a past just as storied.

Established in the early years of the twentieth century by prominent members of the Democratic Party in a city dominated by Republicans since before the Civil War, the club was named after Robert Wharton, a Federalist and eighteenth century politician who served as Philadelphia mayor more times and for longer periods than any person in the city's 300-year history.

Its current building is a five-story, brick structure with a large front door set in the center and with bay windows on the floors directly above it. Located in Old City, Wharton Social, as it became known, was only a three-block walk east of Independence Hall.

Established in 1862, the Union League was started by Republican patriots in support of the politics of President Abraham Lincoln. But GOP politics grew more conservative over time and so, by the 1950s, Wharton Social, while not as large as the Union League, was the most progressive male-only social club in the city.

Wharton Social admitted its first Black member in 1964, nearly a decade before the Union League, and admitted women as members five years later, more than fifteen years before massive public sentiment coupled with bad press forced the Union League to capitulate and eliminate its restrictive covenant barring female members.

I knew Wharton Social's history, of course, and even understood why Raymond would join. It was undoubtedly a perk of his job. Plus, his personality was all about being seen by, and mingling with, all the right people.

Nevertheless, I thought such present-day social clubs were nothing more than pretentious reflections of a snooty, privileged past — a past I hoped we were moving away from.

I picked up Eli, my fourth for the day's basketball games, from his apartment and drove down to 2nd Street where I found a parking space and walked the remaining distance to Wharton Social. Raymond and another former frat brother from college, Randall Wayne, were waiting. Raymond was dressed in a fancy, expensive running outfit, and carried a bag, probably with a change of clothes for after the game. The bag had a Nike logo. When he saw us approach, his eyes nearly popped out of his head.

"I see what you're trying to do," he said as he greeted us. "Hey, Eli."

"What are you talkin' about?" I asked, innocently, and then quickly introduced Eli to Randall, who had never met my brother before.

Raymond, however, had known Elijah since he was a child.

Randall looked from Raymond to me and back to Raymond. "What's going on?" he asked.

Raymond turned to walk into the club with me beside him. He said over his shoulder to Randall, "It's Snoopy Dog. He brought a ringer. Elijah here played ball in high school . . ."

"Varsity ball," I said, interrupting to clarify.

". . . and in college," Raymond continued.

"Shooting guard. A starter at Clark Atlanta," I interrupted again, with a chuckle. Then, to Raymond, "You said bring a fourth. So here he is. Why are you complaining now?"

"You do me wrong, man. You do me wrong," was all Raymond said in a voice reminiscent of a doomed man headed to the gallows.

Ray escorted us inside, where we were greeted by wood-paneled walls, leaded-glass windows, and ridiculously high, oak-beam ceilings. The place screamed of old money. At the front desk, an older white man, who had a shock of perfectly combed white hair, looked up as we approached. He wore a black suit, a heavily starched white shirt and a black tie, and he greeted us with a smile.

"Mr. Dawson. What pure pleasure it is to see you again, sir," he said without a hint of condescension in a baritone that spoke of decades of refined service work. His manners were impeccable.

"Thank you, Mr. Munson. These are my guests. We'll be using the half court on the south end this afternoon," Raymond said. "I made a reservation."

"Very good, sir. I noted it earlier," Munson said. "And if each of you will just sign in here," he said, indicating the guest registration book. Once we had all signed, he turned his attention back to Raymond. "Enjoy your game, sir. And good luck."

We traveled down a long hallway to the elevators toward the back of the building with nary a turned head, as if we all belonged there. It was an odd feeling, for me, given the surroundings in a fancy-schmancy club.

The locker room was on the second floor, just outside the court. There were plenty of lockers, and we changed into more comfortable t-shirts and shorts and listened to Raymond continuing to complain that, with Eli, the afternoon's play was stacked against him.

The rest of us ignored him.

Just before we headed out to the floor, Eli nudged me and whispered into my ear.

"Is that the Randall that Allen was telling me about?" he asked, looking past me to my former frat brother.

"Huh? What did Allen say?" I inquired.

Eli looked at me and made a quick judgment. "It's nothing. I'll talk to you about it later."

We each grabbed a couple of water bottles and white towels as we headed out onto the empty court with its highly buffed hardwood floor. There were a couple of benches for players and a little space behind them for a few spectators to sit. Since there was not much room beyond the post for the hoop, the walls on either end were heavily padded to protect players who ran or fell outside the court. And there was also a running track on the third floor that circled the basketball court from above. I could see a couple of men up there running.

We agreed to play a best-of-three game set, with a short rest between games. Field goals were for two points, except for those in three-point range, and the first team to reach twenty-one points would win the game. If a player shot and missed but his team got the rebound, they could attempt to shoot and score again. If the opposing team got the rebound, the ball had to be passed out past the free-throw line before a shot could be taken.

I asked Raymond earlier if I needed to bring my own basketball but he assured me it wasn't necessary. There'd be plenty.

There were racks on each side of the court containing basketballs, and we each grabbed a few and started taking practice shots to warm up. Raymond, the only one of us under six-foot, practiced taking long shots just inside of three-point range, undoubtedly knowing he'd be slammed if he tried to dribble in for a lay-up during our game. Randall and I took shots closer to the basket, hitting some, missing some.

With his first ball, Eli dribbled a little outside three-point range and took a jumper. He scored.

Swish . . . all net.

Randall either didn't notice or didn't care. He was there just to play. But Ray looked at me and shook his head as he mumbled, "You're so wrong, man."

After we warmed up for about five minutes, we collected the balls and put them all away, except for one. Then we faced off against each other — Raymond and Randall vs. Eli and me. I won a coin toss and in-bounded the ball to take the first possession.

~*~

Eli and I won the first game, 21-15, though because of Randall, who scored eleven points, the outcome was closer than it looked. But it was a spirited game and all of us, huffing and puffing and drenched in sweat, took a seat on the benches afterwards. I was sitting, hands on my sweaty knees, a towel around my neck, looking out onto the court when Ray sauntered over. He took a long swig of water, wiped beads of perspiration from his forehead with a towel, and sat down beside me.

At first, neither of us spoke. I wondered whether he was gathering up the strength to grumble about Eli. I was surprised when he didn't.

"We fired Stephenson this week," Raymond said, wiping his chest under his shirt. "And Andrew and his cousin, who heads up the store's legal department, plan to bring civil charges against him."

"He was arrested, too, by police, I heard. Charged with theft and possession of stolen merchandise. The cops are going to put the squeeze on him and his accomplice . . . the other guy in the photos I gave you . . . to learn who's behind the fencing operation."

I took some more water.

"Good. We're rechecking our inventory and accounts receivables. We've already found a number of discrepancies," he said, and leaned onto the back of the bench. "We told Stephenson's boss that she was being demoted to assistant manager in shoes at the Plymouth Meeting store, but she decided to quit instead. Her last day was yesterday."

I stood up and stretched my arms. "The FBI are involved, too. You remember the woman in the photos I took? I found out a couple of days ago that she's with the Bureau."

"I didn't know that, but federal agents came in to talk to us on Wednesday."

"Is the fallout going to affect you? Hurt your job?" I asked.

"I doubt it. I didn't hire the guy."

Randall, looking relaxed and refreshed, walked over, followed by Eli, who looked equally composed.

"You guys ready yet?" Randall said. "I know your tricks and moves now, Snoopy Dog. And I'm going to whoop your sorry ass."

I looked at Eli, who was as confident as ever and he shook his head. Ray was about to walk back onto the court but I grabbed his shoulder. "I'm almost ready but I need another word with Mad Dog first."

Ray gave me a quizzical look as the other two returned to the court and started shooting the ball and waiting for us.

"When you said Plymouth Meeting it reminded me of something. I need a favor." His right eyebrow arched and he tilted his head in apparent interest but he said nothing. "There's a woman who works in your store there. I'm not sure which department. But I need to have a word with her. Could you help me?"

Ray backed up, as if leery of the approach of some predatory animal. "Man, I'm not so sure about that. I can't have you interrupting store operations."

"I'm not going to interrupt anything. I just need to know where she works. No one will know I got the information from you." I stopped and exhaled heavily. I looked over my shoulder to make sure the others didn't hear me. "It's for a case I'm looking into. And just like with what I did for you and your stolen merchandise, this is on the down-low."

I watched his Adam's Apple move up and down as he

swallowed — and he came to a decision. At least a partial one.

"What's the case about?"

Now he studied me as I contemplated an answer. "I'm looking into the death . . . the circumstances of the death . . . of Kareem Adams."

"The guy who killed that white chick in Center City?"

I scratched my head and rocked a bit on my feet. "There are a lot of people in the community who don't think it's as simple as that. Or that city officials are hiding something. Not telling everyone the truth. And Sheree Jackson could be the key to unlocking some of it."

I waited to judge his reaction but he just continued to search my eyes for a reason to help me.

"She's his mother. Kareem's mother. And nobody's gotten to her," I said. "Please Ray."

He turned to head onto the court. "Let's play," he said, and my heart sank until he added, "I'll find out which department she works in and her schedule." He stopped and turned back to me. "You cannot reveal how you got that information and you can't talk to her in the store while she's at work. Deal?"

I nodded.

"Good. Now let's play ball. My touch is feelin' hot," he said.

And his touch was.

Rebounding from his mediocre play in the first game, Ray scored a respectable ten points in the second game. But it wasn't quite enough.

On the last play of the game and with the score tied at 19, I in-bound the ball to Eli, who dribbled back to the foul line. I thought Eli would shoot the ball but Randall was too close, ready to attempt a blocked shot or to cover him on a move down the lane. I ran behind Eli and we executed a perfect pick-and-roll. But I was too far out to risk a shot at that distance with a tied game on the line.

Eli rolled to the left and I passed the ball to him but Randall had him covered and Eli quickly bounced the ball back to me. I had both the size and speed over Ray and dribbled once on a drive to the basket.

I scored and the game was over, 21-19.

We heard unexpected applause from a number of guys watching us from above on the running track. We all shook hands and then waved back to the spectators, acknowledging the applause.

On the way to the showers, Raymond complimented me on the game and thanked me for bringing Eli. "I knew you had me on that lay-up," he said and I just smiled. "I'll call you tonight with that information you want."

But just before we reached the locker room, Randall stopped me and pulled me aside. Eli looked back but kept going.

I first met Randall at Temple when he, Ray and I joined Omega. His Que name is Mad Dog. He has a very good upper-management job in an Atlantic City hotel and casino, and is a great physical specimen due to regular exercise and a very healthy diet.

On paper, he's what many women look for in a guy — a strong, caring, sensitive man with soft brown eyes — except he isn't particularly handsome. Plus his hair is cut extremely short, which draws even more attention to his oblong-shaped head and small ears.

While running and workouts in a boxing gym are his forte, he played a good game of basketball today, often overpowering Eli or me under the basket, snagging rebounds, and hitting inside shots.

But basketball wasn't what was on his mind.

"Snoopy," he started and then switched up. "David, I should have mentioned this to you before but I didn't know where things were going and I didn't want to mess things up."

"Okay," I said, now wondering where this was headed.

He was looking down when he spoke again, somewhat timidly, as if reluctant to say the words that needed to be said. "I've started seeing someone," Randall said, and then looked up directly at me. "It's Clara. And I should have told you before."

Clara, my ex.

I was shocked and more than a little surprised, though not at all hurt. Clara and I had had our rocky time together for a couple of years but once we broke up, we moved on. She quickly married nearly two years ago and just as quickly divorced a year later.

Clara and Randall were good friends, having met before I met either of them. And it was an open secret Randall had carried a torch for Clara from the beginning. She firmly but not harshly rejected his first romantic advances, only for him to watch helplessly as she dated other guys, including me, and eventually got married.

He had attended their wedding.

I wasn't invited.

"I briefly dated a woman, you know, from Sicklersville," he said.

"Yeah, Mariah. She moved away."

"Took a job in Arizona. Quite different from here. We called it quits just prior to her move."

"Dude, I'm so sorry," was all I could muster.

Randall waved off the comment.

Then it hit me — Allen's vague comments from earlier this week and even Eli's reaction when first meeting Randall — and it started to make sense. I said nothing, however, and allowed him to continue.

"After Mariah left, and Clara got divorced, she and I were there to support each other and to commiserate. We had dinner together a couple of times in December, around Christmas, and things started to get serious after the first of the year," he said. "We've been very discreet."

Randall hesitated. "I . . . uh . . . didn't know how you'd feel about it but I didn't want you to hear about it through the grapevine. I wanted you to hear it from me. No hard feelings?"

"I've known how you've felt about her for a long time, and how hard that must have been for you when she and I were together," I said. "There's no hard feelings. If you're happy and she's happy, then I'm happy."

I slapped him on the shoulder as we headed into the locker room to change.

Raymond went to the showers but asked me to stay behind for a couple of minutes to talk. Ray and I bid good-bye to Eli and Randall, and I stood outside the shower stall when Ray went in.

I could hear him clearly over the sound of the water splashing.

"I took a bold step this past week," Raymond said. "Audrey and I are going to get married. We set a date. And we'll probably hold the reception here at the club, by the way."

"Oh, my goodness, Ray, that's wonderful news. Really. Wonderful news. What made you come to that decision?"

"You did, after you dropped off the pictures in the office. I was going to do it some time anyway, you know, but you were the catalyst to move me forward."

"I am so happy for you, Ray. You and Audrey. Congratulations. Give her hugs from me."

"Thank you, man. We're looking at the third weekend in August, the sixteenth or the seventeenth," Raymond said. "I'm taking a couple of weeks off in August . . . I'm very tired and need to rest up a bit for the fall. But tomorrow we're driving up to Boston with the baby to tell her family."

"Well, I'll put those August dates on my calendar."

"Yes, you'd better. I want you to be my best man."

CHAPTER XII

Who the hell is Mr. Dennis?

There wasn't much else for me to do for the rest of the day, which was good. I needed to just relax and to contemplate Raymond's big news.

But dinner was another subject altogether. And without outside encouragement, I headed up to North Philly. As I was about to knock, Grammy Taylor opened her door.

How does she do that? Does she sit by the door all day waiting for someone to knock?

"Hey, dear," she said pleasantly, planting a kiss on my cheek. At eighty, she was as spry as ever, despite the scare of the last week's brief hospitalization. And she now seemed as commanding as ever. "What brings you here tonight? I wasn't expecting you until tomorrow."

Even from the front door, I was greeted with the aroma of freshly baked bread. And something else. A roast? And chocolate. I smelled chocolate, too. My mouth automatically watered. I couldn't have stopped it if I tried.

"It's been a rough couple of days and I just wanted to have a nice home-cooked meal and, well, just be around family for a while," I said.

"Come in," she said and then frowned. Her body seemed to tense just a bit. "No Marie?"

"In New York this weekend for a job interview. Should be back early next week."

Relaxing again, she beckoned me into the house. "Dinner's nearly done. Mr. Dennis is already here," she said casually.

Mr. Dennis? The question rushed through my brain. *Who the hell is Mr. Dennis?*

I didn't dare voice the question aloud — Grammy Taylor said the name with authority, as if I obviously must know — but at least a partial answer didn't take long.

We went into the kitchen where Grammy had been icing a chocolate cake on the counter near the stove. Macaroni and cheese was baking in the oven and a beef roast was being kept warm. There were carrots and green beans on the stove, and on the counter were freshly baked dinner rolls.

Sitting at the kitchen table was an elderly man I thought I recognized from somewhere, but I couldn't put my finger on where. He was, more or less, my grandmother's age. (With elderly people, it was sometimes difficult for me to distinguish age.) And he was dressed in the most proper way — dark suit with a neatly pressed white shirt — except that he wasn't wearing a tie. I assumed going without a tie was his way of dressing casually.

He was a large man, though far from obese, and wore his hair short and neat. His skin color was that of a butterscotch sundae, without a cherry on top, of course. A wooden walking cane rested against the table next to where he sat, and his black hat was also nearby.

Most importantly, he hung onto my grandmother's every word and watched with an expression of quiet admiration. Or maybe it was affection?

"Mr. Dennis, you remember my grandson, David," she said, only briefly turning her attention away from the cake.

He rose, using the table to steady himself, and took my hand. "Oh, yes, the private detective," he said in a proper, stately manner that was slowly going out of style. There was genuine honesty and respect in his voice. "We're all so proud of your work. I've heard nothing but good things."

To me, Grammy Taylor said, "Mr. Dennis is with the church."

Well, that explained who he was but it didn't address why he was here. I needed answers but knew I wouldn't get them now. I'd have to talk to Renee, if I could get her alone, or call my sister Valerie when I got home.

"This is a lot of food," I said, looking around the kitchen. "You expectin' an army?"

"No, just Renee and Allen. She's upstairs, just got in from shopping all day. Allen should be here soon," she said. "And I asked Mr. Dennis to stop by because I'm baking a cake. Chocolate is his favorite."

As if on cue, Renee came downstairs. "Can I help with anything?" she asked, entering the kitchen. "Oh, hey, there, Mr. Dennis. Good to see you." She stopped suddenly when she noticed me. "Oh, Davey, I didn't see you. When did you get here? Staying for dinner?"

There was pleading in her eyes. And I could see why.

Feeding people was an act of love for my grandmother and she enjoyed showing her love. When Renee married my brother, she was an average-sized woman. In the few months since she moved in upstairs and started eating my grandmother's cooking on a daily basis, Renee must have gained fifteen pounds. Maybe more.

I often saw her in new outfits — which would explain another round of shopping today — because she was growing out of the old ones. I, therefore, assumed her desire for me to stay meant, in part, that there'd be less food for her to consume tonight or leftovers for the coming days.

There was no way I was going to turn down this meal but there was another reason to stay. I needed to get Renee alone.

"Yeah, sure. I'm staying," I said. Turning to address Renee, I added, "But I could use your help. I'm thinking of getting

Marie a gift . . . for graduation, and all. I don't know what, with so many choices. I have a catalogue. It's in the car outside. If you could help me."

Now my eyes were pleading.

"I don't know, Davey," Renee started.

Mr. Dennis chimed in. "The right present is always a good idea for a lady. It says something special to her."

Oh, my goodness, if I didn't know any better, I'd say my grandmother just blushed as she stood over the cake.

"It's okay. You two go ahead. You have a few minutes before I have everything ready to eat," said Grammy Taylor.

Once Renee and I were outside and away from the house, she said to me, "David, what's this about? Do you really want my opinion on a gift for Marie?"

"No. I've already given her a graduation gift. It was a portfolio. This is about . . .", I said, looking back at the house. "It's about Mr. Dennis. Who the hell is he and why's he here?"

Renee gave a hearty laugh, her hands at her stomach as if to stop herself from busting out of her pants. She still held a broad smile when she settled down. "They know each other from church. He has a car and still drives. That's his car right there," she said, pointing to a late model dark gray Buick Park Avenue.

Very nice and very clean, as if it got washed several times a week.

"For the last several months, he's come by to give her a ride to church on Sundays. They usually have lunch together afterwards," Renee said. "And during the week, he comes by sometimes to take her on errands, grocery shopping and whatnot. Or he might stop by for lunch. At their age, it's real sweet. And all very, very proper."

"Proper? How is any of this proper?"

"Oh, please, Davey, get over yourself," Renee said with slight reproach. "They're relentlessly proper. Grammy Taylor only calls him or refers to him as Mr. Dennis. I don't know his first name. Hell, I don't know if he even *has* a first name, though I assume he does. He's just Mr. Dennis," she said with a chuckle. "And he only calls her Mrs. Taylor."

"Why don't I know any of this?" I said, leaning against my car.

She looked at me with her hands on her hips. "Oh, please, David. Your grandmother has what old folks call a 'gentleman caller.' And the companionship suits them both."

"Why am I just finding out?" I pressed again.

"Because they're private and you don't ever go to church with any of us. And you aren't around when they go grocery shopping together or to lunch. They like going to Arthur Treacher's for seafood. I think she dresses up a little when he's around," Renee said.

"I'm over here every Sunday night for dinner and I've never seen him," I said.

"He probably eats Sunday dinners with his own family. I'm sure he must have one."

"And what about when she was in the hospital? I didn't see him then."

"Grammy Taylor called and talked to him before you got there. He wanted to come by but she said no. She didn't want to worry him," Renee said. "But he was there when we arrived to take her home. They were holding hands when Allen and I walked in but then stopped. It was sweet."

An insane thought rushed into my head and I stood up from the car. "Good Lord, you don't think he's mar. . . ."

Renee cut me off before I finished. "David. No. He's widowed, just like Grammy Taylor."

"And you and Allen are okay with this . . . Mr. Dennis?"

"Yes, we are. Well, Allen not at first. But he didn't react

like you . . . like he's nuts . . . and he quickly accepted it," she said. "It's sweet. Really sweet. Two elderly people finding companionship together. That's all it is." Renee looked back toward the house. "Let's get back inside before dinner gets cold."

Grammy Taylor was standing in the kitchen doorway when we entered the house. "Good, you're back. And just in time. David, go set the table in the dining room. We'll be eating in there this evening," she said.

Mr. Dennis, using his cane this time, rose from his seat. "Can I assist you, young man?" he said to me. But it was my grandmother who replied.

"We're using the dishes and silverware from the cabinet in there. The napkins are in the drawer. David knows where," she said, indicating the dining room. "And he can show you where I have the serving platters, too."

Mr. Dennis and I went about setting the table for five. I hoped that was all who were coming. But who knows? There could be a whole host of others that Grammy Taylor failed to mention to me.

Allen, who is two inches taller than my five-foot-eleven but who seemed to have lost some of the weight his wife gained, got home just as we finished setting the table and dinner was about to be served. Grammy Taylor undoubtedly timed that, too.

"Go upstairs and wash your hands so we can eat," she told him. When he returned, we all took our seats at the table, with Grammy Taylor at the head and closest to the kitchen, and Mr. Dennis and me to her right. Renee and Allen were to her left.

I wondered which of us — Allen or me — would get the nod to bless the table. Allen was living in the house but I was the oldest male family member present.

However, I was surprised when my grandmother nodded at Mr. Dennis. The guest at the table. He gave a stirring supplication to the Lord that made it clear to me that, at the very least, he was a trustee, but more likely a deacon, in the church, a position to which neither Allen nor I would ever aspire.

But once the grace was said and a Bible verse was recited by each person, we started serving the food. There was little conversation other than requests that a plate, food platter, or some condiment be passed along. With a visitor at the table, I assumed any conversation would be banal and inconsequential.

However, I totally failed to consider my brother.

"Davey, I heard you shot someone this week," Allen said as he shoveled a forkful of beef roast into his mouth. Even while chewing, he managed a playful smile.

All eyes went to Allen, and then to me. And then the questions started to fly.

"King-David Anderson Blaise. Is this true?" my grandmother asked with a mixture of fear and horror. "Did you kill someone? With that cockamamie job of yours, I knew you'd kill someone sooner or later."

"I didn't kill anyone," I protested. I looked at my brother and said, "And thank you very much for bringing up the subject, Allen."

"It's no pro-blamo. It's what I do," he said, clearly amused and barely getting the words out with his mouth full of food.

Now I was regretting the decision to come over. I hadn't worked out yet how I was going to tell my grandmother about the incident, or when. And I had forgotten that Allen, as a SEPTA transit police officer, could have heard of the shooting, since city police would have filed a report that would be available to other law enforcement departments in the city.

"Who did you shoot?" my grandmother said as she over-salted her food and took a bite of green beans.

I explained about the guy, the confrontation with Mae, and the shooting. I left off anything about the necklace and Marie.

Fortunately for me, that wouldn't have been in the police report.

"I'm sure the detectives will figure it all out, based on what you've told us," Mr. Dennis said. "I was in the department for more than thirty years and there's some good officers over there. They'll sort it out."

Allen and I exchanged glances while passing a bowl of cooked carrots. "You were in the Philadelphia Police Department?" Allen said. "I didn't know that."

"I was a patrolman for many years and then rose to detective. Assigned mostly to the Nineteenth District in West Philly. Frank Rizzo was my captain for a while. I know him personally."

That admission shocked the table.

"Mr. Dennis doesn't like to brag," Grammy Taylor said, reaching over to touch his hand.

"Frank is boisterous and loud and all, but he's serious about fighting crime," Mr. Dennis said. "And to that end, he's willing to bend the rules. But in the district, all of us officers, white and Colored alike, worked hard to improve communications and relations between the Negro community and the PPD."

"How long have you been off the force?" I asked.

"Retired in '68. Right after Frank was named commissioner," he said. "I had had enough. It was time to get out. But I keep in touch with some guys in the department."

"I'm investigating a case involving stolen merchandise," I said. "You think you could give me some pointers . . . on what to look for and where to look?"

"They took your gun, right?" he said. "After the shooting in your office?"

"Yes."

"They'll give it back. Don't worry. You were protecting your office and employee."

True, I thought. But Gregory will keep the gun for as long as he can.

"Does your case of stolen merchandise involve the guy who came to your office? That sounds dangerous," said Mr. Dennis.

"I doubt it," I replied.

"Good. But be careful."

"David, that's enough, now. Crime and shootings are not good dinner talk," my grandmother said sternly.

"I'm sorry, Georgie," Mr. Dennis said in a gentle, almost intimate voice. "I didn't mean to be rude."

Renee, Allen, and I were shocked into silence, as we might have been when we were little children listening to grown-ups' conversations. We knew our place.

"That's okay, Homer," she said softly, revealing, for the first time, that Mr. Dennis did, indeed, have a first name. "David got you into it. You both can exchange information after we have dessert."

He looked up at her and they locked eyes. Grammy Taylor smiled in a way I had never seen before, and then went back to eating.

After dinner was over and dishes and plates returned to the kitchen, we each enjoyed a slice of chocolate cake, served with ice cream. It was, indeed, delicious. And when Mr. Homer Dennis left the house, he carried a couple of large pieces of chocolate cake wrapped up in waxed paper.

Over the course of dinner and dessert, followed by clean-up, I had grown comfortable with the delightfully disarming Mr. Dennis, though I was no more likely to address him by his first name than I was to address my grandmother as Georgie Mae.

Before I left the house, Mr. Dennis gave me the names of a couple of contacts in the police force, and promised to help me with my cases in any way he could.

As I walked out, I had enough leftovers for two full meals, and the gratitude of my sister-in-law Renee that there would be a lot fewer leftovers for her as evidence of Grammy Taylor's love.

CHAPTER XIII

"What the heck happened in here?"

With all the new business I've had in the last year, I was able to rent a nice brownstone on Delancey just below 22nd Street. It was a very pricey neighborhood that, even with my new financial success, was out of my financial reach. But the owner, recently widowed Dinah Merriweather, who had lived in the house since she got married four decades ago, couldn't — or didn't want to — manage the house any more. However, she also refused to sell it because of all the memories it held. And while they tried mightily, her adult children couldn't force her to get rid of it.

Several years ago, the Merriweathers had hired me to do a pre-marital investigation into the guy their youngest daughter planned to marry.

Because of my detective work, Mrs. Merriweather took an instant liking to me, and treated me with considerable affection even after my work for them was done. And when I started to seriously consider returning to law school last year, I called Mr. Merriweather, a Penn law professor and the third-generation scion of another wealthy Quaker family. He put in a good word on my behalf with the law school dean.

I had Mr. Merriweather in my first law class on contracts but he cut the course short after only a couple of weeks once he and his wife realized he had Stage 4 prostate cancer, and it would cut short his life.

Dinah offered me extremely reasonable rent, which was great, considering the place was more than 4500 square feet over three floors, and with an option to purchase the house later when she decided to sell.

One of my favorite things about the property was that it had a small two-car detached garage in the back that was accessible down a very narrow alley. It took some skillful maneuvering to get the car in the garage, though it was much better than constantly having to search for what limited street parking was available.

I decided to rent the house in the first place because of its nice neighborhood, the promise to buy it later, and because of its roominess. I didn't really need anywhere near that much space, but I had always felt cramped as a kid in North Philly. Growing up, I lived in a two-story, three-bedroom house with my parents and three siblings. I lived there all the way through college and until I enlisted in the Navy.

When I got my first apartment in West Philadelphia after the military, I vowed that if I ever had the money, I was going to have a lot more space.

From the garage, I walked up a short path to the backdoor of the house. Once inside, I continued through the spartan kitchen and down a hallway to the front of the house. On the floor inside the front vestibule was my mail, which had been left through a slot in the front door. There was all the standard stuff — utility bills and grocery flyers — and a small white envelope that was addressed to me by hand. But there was no postage on it and no return address. That meant it was hand-delivered.

I didn't recognize the writing.

Going to a newly acquired wooden desk from an antique dealer on Fairmount Avenue near Marie's apartment, I picked up a fancy letter opener that was a house-warming gift from Mae. Slicing open the envelope, I took out a single sheet of stationery with the name Angelo De Luca embossed at the top.

A business card fell out and onto the floor.

The note was hand-written in a commanding script that tilted forcefully to the right.

I knew De Luca, had met him once, in my office, near the conclusion of a murder case last year. He was the head of The Henderson Group, the largest and best-known private investigative and security agency headquartered in the city. He had satellite offices across the country.

What I didn't know was why De Luca was contacting me.

Dear David,

It was such a pleasure meeting you last year. I see you are doing quite well for yourself now.

That case last year was a complicated one and I liked how you later resolved it. At the time, I made a sincere offer to discuss ways we could work together in the future. Unfortunately, our paths have not crossed again until now.

I hear you are involved in a matter that may concern a client of Henderson, and I would like to discuss matters with you. Financial incentives would be in order for your assistance.

Please contact me at your earliest convenience at the number on my card.

Angelo

I had no idea which case he meant but, given the timing, there were a couple that came to mind. But it didn't matter. Without Marie or my family around, I planned to spend the rest of my weekend in quiet solitude, reading the paper and jogging along the river.

I contemplated my cases as I jogged along Kelly Drive on Sunday morning. The weather was nice, just cool enough for a good run. I was joined on the path with other runners, casual walkers, and a few people on bikes. The Schuylkill River was full of rowers, which I love to see as I run.

I showered as soon as I got home, and then called Mae. I told her to come into the office at her regular time on Monday and informed her of what I needed to have done. After I relaxed quietly for a while, I went to a restaurant bar and ate a burger and fries as I watched a Phillies game on television.

I had already decided that whatever Angelo De Luca wanted, it would wait until Monday.

Monday came soon enough and I arose early, showered and had a small breakfast of toast with jam and coffee. I picked up a copy of the Daily News on the way into the office. I have a subscription to the Inquirer and a copy is delivered to the door of my office each weekday morning before anyone arrives. As I got to my floor and turned toward my office, I saw that the paper was there as usual, but the light was on in the office.

That was odd, because I knew I had turned it off before I left on Friday.

After I picked up the newspaper, I checked that the security alarm was still on. However, the door was unlocked. I entered and saw a mess.

Someone had come in during the weekend and rifled through all my files, leaving the cabinet doors open and most of their contents scattered around the floor. I walked into my office and it was much the same: files everywhere, desk and cabinet drawers open.

"What the heck happened in here?" Mae said. I hadn't heard her enter. I walked back out to the outer office to see her standing there with her hands on her hips.

"Someone must have broken in. And from the looks of things, they were looking for something. Something specific," I said.

"How'd they get in?"

"No idea. I locked the door and set the alarm. But it didn't go off. They somehow disarmed it first, got in, looked around and left," I said, scratching the back of my head. I had already absentmindedly checked for my gun.

"What did they want?" Mae said as she rounded her desk, inspecting the top to see if any of her personal belongings were missing.

"I can't tell. That's gonna be for you to find out."

"Me? Why me? How would I know? I didn't do it."

"I know that, Mae. I didn't say that you did. It's just that I can only determine what they were looking for after you clean everything up and reorganize the files. Then we can look for what's missing."

She stood up, taking a random file and seeing if it belonged in the closest folder to her left. It didn't.

"I have to do all this by myself?" The pitch in her voice went up.

"No, I'll help, but first I have to handle a couple of things. I'm going to make a couple of calls and go downtown after that. When I get back, I'll help. But first, I gotta make those calls."

I returned to my office as she mumbled and I ignored her. Back at my desk, I called John Thompson.

"Good morning, detective. How are you today?" I asked.

"I'm good, Blaise. What do you want?" he said bluntly.

"No 'How do you do?'" I said and waited. Once it was obvious there'd be no answer, I continued. "I just got to the office and there was a break-in."

"When did it happen?"

"Not sure. Sometime over the weekend."

"Anyone hurt?" Thompson said.

"Why detective, I'm touched by your concern."

"It wasn't so much out of concern, Blaise. It's a standard question and it's my job."

"No. No one was here at the time."

"Anything taken?"

"We're assessing that now."

"Did you get your gun back from us?"

"Yeah, on Friday."

"Then why are you calling? To report the break-in? I'm not the person you report that to," he said. "Uniforms get it first."

I inhaled deeply and blew it out. I wasn't sure if Thompson heard it. "No, I didn't report it. Yet. But I will. It's not the real reason I called you. I need a favor from you." He didn't respond, apparently wanting to drag it out of me. "I need you to make an introduction for me. To someone at the Bureau."

"And why would I do that?"

I couldn't say friendship, and professional courtesy was too flimsy. "I need it for the case I showed you last week and I thought it would be easier getting it if I had an introduction first . . . from you."

"David, these are the Feds. They won't tolerate your crap like we do," he said seriously. "They'll hold you and question you for hours, even slap you in jail, if they think you're holding out on them. It's called accessory after the fact."

"Please. Just make the introduction. Vouch for me a little. I'll take care of it after that. It won't be on you."

"The hell it won't," he protested.

"Please, detective. I need this," I said, inhaling and exhaling heavily again. I'm sure he heard it that time.

He paused, then said, "Who do you want me to call?"

"Darcy Hayes."

"The agent in the picture you took," he said.

"She's the one. Will you do it?"

"I'll do it, for all the good it'll do you."

"Thanks, John. I appreciate it."

"You'd better. And you'd better fill me in right away if this has anything I need to know about. I don't want to hear it first from the Feds. Or from my captain."

I hung up and walked into the outer office to help Mae until the phone rang. Then I went back into my office and called the federal building at 6th and Arch, where the FBI has its offices. I made arrangements to meet Hayes at noon on Independence Mall, across from the glass pavilion that holds the Liberty Bell.

~*~

I got there early.

I picked an open park bench near a street vendor where I got a meatball sandwich and a Coke. I knew it could be messy so I planned to eat most of it before Hayes arrived. I was on one of my last bites as I saw her cross crowded Market Street and head in my general direction.

I wondered whether she'd have agents around to observe us. Or would she come alone to a hastily requested meeting with some random person she had never met before? I think it would depend on Thompson's introduction. I looked around and didn't notice anyone who might fit that bill but I could be wrong. In the end, it didn't matter. I needed the meeting and this was a way to get it.

I got up as she approached and I stuck out my hand. "Hi, I'm David Blaise."

"FBI Special Agent Darcy Hayes. Nice to meet you," she said casually, and took my hand.

I indicated for us to sit.

She visited me with an appraising look. I had done the same as she walked across the street. Then again, I also had pictures of her. But this Darcy Hayes up close looked somewhat different from the version of her that I had photographed from dozens of yards away.

"I've heard about you," she started.

It caught me off guard, although it shouldn't have. "Really?"

"Yes. You were involved in that mob case . . . when, uh . . . two years ago? It was just before I got to the Philadelphia field office but you were all the talk in the bureau back then. And then you handled that case last year of the man who was laundering money in the Cayman Islands and hiding it from his wife.

"That's right. I'm surprised you knew."

"Because of the money going overseas, we looked into it after you closed the case," she said. "I was reminded of those cases by Detective John Thompson of the Philly police force when he called. In addition to his recommendation, those cases are a large part of the reason why I agreed to meet with you today."

"I see," I said. "Thank you." Then I remembered my manners. "You want something to eat? Hot dog, maybe? My treat."

"I have a salad on my desk for when I get back," Hayes said. "What's going on?"

The folder with the pictures were on the bench under my right leg. I got it and pulled out a picture. Her surprise was quick but she covered it just as quickly.

"Where'd you get this?"

It was an obvious question that surprised me that she asked. "The parking lot."

"Why were you following me?" she asked, the first hint of concern in her voice. She made a quick glance around the park. There wasn't anyone close enough to hear our conversation.

"I wasn't. I was following him."

"Why? What's this got to do with you?" she said, handing back the picture.

"That's the question."

I took a swig of the Coke.

"What are you saying? Who was it who hired you? Who's your client?"

"My client wanted evidence that their merchandise was being stolen and given to someone. That's what I recorded in these pictures. I just want some answers."

"They're evidence of a crime. Can I have the pictures?" she said.

"Certainly," I said, handing them over. "But I doubt you need them as evidence."

"No, not really, but I'll take them anyway," Hayes said.

"Doesn't matter. I have additional copies."

"I won't go into details of our investigation, other than to say it's focused on stolen merchandise fencing in and around the Philadelphia area," she said.

"And the guy you got the stolen merch from is a figure in that operation?"

Hayes gave me a hard stare, one of the hardest I've ever felt. It was like she was burrowing into my soul. She had come across congenial enough, until that moment, but it was clear there was a steel edge under the exterior.

She cleared her throat and rose. I remained seated.

"We're done here. However, I'm sure I'll be talking to you again. Soon."

And with that, she headed back to the FBI building, leaving me as confused as ever. However, it wasn't going to be the only confusing conversation I'd have that afternoon.

I threw the paper my sandwich was wrapped in and the Coke can into the nearest trash bin and walked to my left in the direction of Independence Hall. I crossed Chestnut Street, headed through the archway at Independence Hall and over to Walnut Street. Then I headed up toward Seventh.

CHAPTER XIV

Jeweler's Row

Jeweler's Row in Philadelphia is the place to shop if you want really good jewelry, especially diamonds, at truly reasonable prices. There are scores of small jewelry stores on Samson Street, stretching from 6th to nearly 9th. There's jewelry at every price point to satisfy the pocketbook of any buyer. There are necklaces, bracelets, pins, watches, rings for the fingers and rings for the ears. You could even get a single diamond placed in your beard like the guy who did the television and radio ads for his store, Robbins 8th and Walnut.

And surprisingly, there was little crime on Jeweler's Row.

I walked into M. Rubinstein's Jewelry, a store recommended to me and whose long-time owner was a man named Malachi Rubinstein, but was operated by a generally nervous little guy named Joseph. I took it that he was old Malachi's son.

He was standing behind a case full of more sparkly things than existed in many entire cities.

"What can I do for you?" he said, eyeing me closely.

"You remember me?" I said. "You sold me a silver necklace with a jade pendant last year for my girlfriend."

He said no, but I could tell he was lying. His nervous, jerky movements became more pronounced.

"Let me see if I can't jog your memory," I said. I took a picture of the necklace out of my pocket and showed him.

"Yes, I think I remember that now," he said, moving along the wall toward the back of the store.

“I thought you would.”

“It’s a nice-looking piece. Hard to forget,” he said.

“Where did you get it?”

He was so nervous now that I thought he’d have a seizure. “I don’t remember off the top of my head. I’d have to go check our records. We use many different wholesalers and middlemen. And we also get many items in estate sales. Families unloading old heirlooms.”

I raised my voice. “Where . . . did . . . you . . . get . . . it?”

“Hush,” he said, moving from behind the counter and ushering me over to the side as he looked toward the door in the back of the shop. He held a tight grip on my forearm. “Keep your voice down.”

“Are you fencing stolen merchandise? Is that why the price of that necklace was so low?”

“We do not sell stolen merchandise. My dad would kill me,” he said in a voice barely above a whisper.

“Is something wrong, Joseph?” asked an old man who walked out from a door in the back of the store. But also at that moment, two men walked in from outside and pulled out guns.

“Move to the back, move to the back,” hurriedly said the first man, a short, stocky guy with a bald head. He looked a lot like a Buddha. His partner, taller but also thick through the middle, stood near the front window to keep watch. They looked mean. The Buddha, who did all the speaking, also sounded mean. And serious. He wasn’t a man to fool with.

The Buddha looked around through the cases, stopping at the one that contained necklaces. “Where is it? I want the necklace.”

“I know nothing about what you’re talking about. And I want you to get out of my store,” said Rubinstein, the elder. The Buddha struck him across the face with his hand, knocking the old man to the floor. Blood spilled out of his mouth. The Buddha looked to Nervous Rubinstein, the younger. "Tell me now where it is or I kill all of you . . . right now."

From out of nowhere, shots rang out. Buddha stumbled back onto a jewelry case, slamming the glass as his body slumped forward and fell to the floor. Blood was coming from wherever he had been hit.

More shots followed, and the taller man, who had turned to rush out, was hit in the right shoulder blade and he fell into the doorframe. He was hit again in the left leg as he got the door open and stumbled out onto Samson. Through the window, I saw the door to a maroon-colored car open and he fell inside before the car sped away.

Another man came from the back. He was older and more stable looking than Joseph and carried a .357 Magnum.

"Pop, you all right?" he said to the man on the floor. To his brother, he said, "Joseph, call the police."

To me, he said, "You might want to get out of here."

I took his advice.

~*~

It didn't take long for the police to arrive as I watched from the steps of the Curtis Center at the corner of 6th and Walnut. I pondered what to do. Clearly, someone wanted that necklace and had traced it back to Rubinstein's, although I wasn't sure the old man knew anything about it. The son, Nervous Rubinstein, the younger, however, was a totally different matter.

But I doubt the men who rushed into the store had anything to do with the guy who came to my office. They seemed totally different, both in look and approach.

While both my most recent and active cases were important — looking into the death of Kareem Adams for Eli, and the shooting in my office by a guy looking to recover a piece of stolen jewelry — coming to understand what was going on regarding the necklace was now my top priority. The shooting just proved that. I needed to collect my nerves and do my job, for everyone's safety.

CHAPTER XV

Rampant, raw, and unfiltered

The Rev. Dr. Martin Luther King, Jr., the iconic Civil Rights leader whose life and struggles had recently been immortalized with a national holiday celebrated in January, once famously said the most segregated time in America is at 11 o'clock on Sunday mornings. Despite advancements in equality in education, housing, and employment in reshaping America into a more inclusive society, most Black folks attend Sunday services in predominately Black churches, though some congregations might have a sprinkling of white folks here and there. Whites tend to attend churches where it's unlikely that they'll be sitting next to a Black person, except on the rare occasions when two churches hold a joint service.

And it's often that way even when Black folks move away from the community.

Take Stuart and Valerie, for example.

They have a large house in a predominantly white neighborhood in Elkins Park in Montgomery County, just north of the city, and live within walking or easy driving distance of several Protestant and Catholic churches. And yet, Valerie, the twins, and Stuart, when he can tear himself away from the golf course on Sunday mornings, drive back down into North Philadelphia to attend services with Grammy Taylor at Beulah Baptist, the church where we grew up.

But there's another major institution in American culture that remains mostly segregated along racial lines — beauty and barber shops. Virtually everyone in the Black community, regardless of gender or age, goes to a beauty parlor or barber shop on the regular. And while there are salons — and a growing number of them — that have a diverse clientele, it's generally not the case in Black America.

If someone wants to gauge the pulse of the Black community, a good place to start would be at a barber shop or beauty parlor. Gossip as social currency is the coin of the realm. It is rampant, raw, and unfiltered.

You can learn all sorts of information about people, places, and things in a barber shop, and some of the information is even true. There are many things listed on the menu in a barber shop — haircuts, with or without razor edging, trims, shaves, and many more selections. But the conversation is plentiful, free, and well worth the cost.

At the moment, information was what I needed. And, crossing my fingers, I knew a place where I'd start looking.

~*~

It'd been a year since I first set foot in Charlie's Barber Shop up in Germantown, close to Chelton Avenue. It had been within a day or two of the police bombing of the MOVE house in West Philly. Since then, I've visited the shop every couple of weeks to get a trim and to listen to the same old, sorry-ass men talking shit.

Situated in the middle of the block and without a white, red, and blue barber pole outside, it was easy to miss Charlie's.

On its right was a small, women's clothing store that was struggling to stay afloat, and on the left was an empty storefront, which had been a coffee shop a year ago. There was a handwritten sign on the door that said they were temporarily closed. But since the sign went up nine months ago, I was sure they were gone for good.

I had been thinking about this visit since Mae mentioned

that a man she called Mr. Charlie had threatened her and, by extension, me. She said he was a small, older man, who was a fancy dresser and fast talker. And he liked to flash his cash around.

My barber Charlie didn't come close to fitting that description. He was a big, powerfully built man whose stomach showed he rarely, if ever, missed a meal. And he had short, wavy hair that was an unnaturally dark black for a man of his advanced age.

However, aside from being older men who shared a name, the two men shared another characteristic I hoped would help in my investigation.

They both wore a Process, a once-prominent Black male hair style that mostly died out with the ascent of the Afro in the late 1960s. A Process, also known as a Conk in many Black neighborhoods, required the use of corrosive chemicals containing lye to straighten naturally curly hair. If not done properly or carefully, the client's head or neck could easily suffer first- or second-degree burns. The style left the hair oily and slick in appearance, and required nightly upkeep, generally in the form of a stocking cap made of women's hosiery.

In terms of maintenance, the most important thing was to avoid, at all costs, any kind of wetness or moisture — be it in the form of perspiration, rain, high humidity, or, most especially, from being in a swimming pool. Otherwise, the hair would quickly return to its naturally curly, kinky state.

It wasn't just that Charlie, my barber, wore a Process that seemed to perpetually need a touch-up — or as people would say, "His Process is taking a recess." What was important is that Mae said her Mr. Charlie's hair was always neat and well-kept. No nappiness at all, which meant he got it touched up regularly. And since the style was no longer *en vogue*, there were only a few places in the city to get it professionally done.

Charlie's Barber Shop in Germantown was one such place.

~*~

"What you gonna say at the barber shop when you go there today?" Mae asked this morning as I helped clean up some of the mess in our burglarized office. But then she also decided to make a point, "It's a good thing you goin', though. You need a haircut."

"Um," I said haltingly, "I've been thinking about it but I don't know yet what I'll say."

I handed Mae a file and she gave me a look of haughty derision, then turned away to add the file to a stack of files on her desk, which was next to other stacks of files. The look told me more of what she thought than if she had actually spoken. We continued working for a while in silence before she said, "You should have me go. To see the barber."

"No," I said quickly. "For your safety, I can't do that. I won't put you at risk."

"I can take care of myself," she snapped vehemently. "And I can get information out of men easier than you."

It was a fair point and she was probably right.

"I don't doubt it, Mae," I said, not wanting to bring up or acknowledge her past as a working girl. "But being in harm's way is not part of your job description." I was lucky she didn't bring up the stakeout in Fairmount Park I took her on recently. "What if he recognized you there?"

"The same as if he recognizes you," she countered. "But you don't know if your barber even knows my Mr. Charlie."

I picked up a stack of papers from the floor and stood up. I put the papers on her desk. "Mae, you are an integral part of my operation. We're partners. I won't risk your safety."

Mae was speechless. She didn't have an argument for that.

~*~

Many times, I've imagined what Charlie's Barber Shop must have looked like when he opened it in the late 1940s or early 50s. He had used the GI Bill to go to barber school. Savings from his wife helped to buy and open the shop.

Back then, the front window would have been new and clean; the paint on the interior walls would have been fresh and bright; the equipment, including the bright red leather barber chairs, would have been new; and there'd have been the latest weekly copies of Jet magazine on the tables for customers to read.

But times had changed. The window looked like it hadn't been cleaned in a while, many of the interior surfaces needed a dusting, the paint was dull, and the barber chairs were well worn and the red leather cracked. What Jet magazines that were lying around were old — some by mere weeks, but most by months and others by years.

The jingle of a bell on the door announced my arrival in the shop. There were five people inside — Charlie; a second barber, Clifton, who had a customer in his chair; a youngster sitting near the front; and a tall, heavy-set man in a brown suit and wearing a hat who occupied a chair along the wall as if on a perch. Most of the men welcomed me with a smile or a pleasant nod, though the boy never looked up from his comic book and the man along the wall merely grunted.

"Dave, good to see you," Charlie said, rising from his barber chair and dusting it off with a dingy old towel. "Come on over. I'm ready for you."

"Hey, Charlie," I said as I wandered over. Once I was in the chair, Charlie placed a smock around me, fastening it at the neck. Then he swung me back around to face the mirror and used a hand-crank on the side to raise the chair up to a comfortable height for him to do his work. Looking at me in the mirror, Charlie ran his hand over my head as if to re-acquaint himself with my hair, though it had only been three weeks since I last saw him. Except for its length, how much of a change could it have had?

"You got good hair. Soft, not too nappy," which is what he always said to me just before he started to cut it. "You want the usual?"

"You know he do. Muthafucker always have you do the same cut," said the man along the wall.

"The boy, Harlan! The boy. Watch yo language," snapped Charlie, as he turned quickly to address the tall, fat man.

But the man continued talking. "How long it been he been coming in here? Gotta be a year and he ain't changed up once in that time. He don't know no bettah."

"This ain't none of your concern, Harlan. You just sit there, quiet-like. Okay?" Charlie said.

Harlan grunted again but said nothing more.

When Charlie returned his attention to my reflection in the mirror, I answered Charlie's question. "The same. Even all over, just a little taper in the back."

"No razor edge?"

"Nope."

And with that, we got started. He reached for his clippers, selected a No. 2 guard and attached it. Large chunks of black hair fell to the floor as he mowed it down from front to back. Charlie's body partially obscured my view in the mirror as he worked in front of me, so it was difficult for me to see his expressions when we talked. Nonetheless, I needed to move things along.

"You know, Charlie, I admire your choice of hair style . . . and your dedication to it," I said.

"He's been wearing a Conk since before I started workin' here," Clifton said as he finished his customer's hair. To Charlie, he added, "You need to come over here tonight before we lock up so I can fix you up."

"It's all he know," Harlan said from along the wall.

"Takes a lot of confidence," I said. "Not a popular style now but you wear it proudly. Not easy to get it done, nowadays, I'd guess."

"We have a few customers who ask for it," Charlie said, having switched to a closer guard on his clippers.

Clifton's customer paid him ten dollars for the cut and Clifton motioned for the youngster, his grandson, to come over. The boy at first was so engrossed in the exploits of Superman in the comic book that he didn't hear that he was summoned.

"Boy, get up and come on over here," Clifton said. "Don't make me say it again."

The youngster got up without comment, walked over, and got in the chair.

"Charlie, you got that one skinny old dude who has it done. Ain't it 'bout time he be showin' up? What's his name?" Harlan asked, snapping his fingers as he tried to recall the man's name.

"Charles Pennypacker," Charlie said.

"Yeah, that's it. People call him Charlie like you, boss," Clifton said as he prepared to cut the boy's hair.

I just listened to this and mentally took notes, hoping they'd keep talking and say more. *Charlie Pennypacker*. Must be him.

"I think he oughta be in tomorrow or the next day, I think. Should be about time," Charlie said.

"Doesn't he make an appointment?" I asked.

"No, he just come in, usually shortly after the weekend," Charlie said.

"He's a sharp dresser, though. Where he work, Charlie? You know?" Clifton asked.

"Down on the railroad, though he should be retired by now. He told me he was the chief porter on the trains going out West," Charlie said. "He supervised the other porters."

"You don't say," was my only comment.

"But I know he still be hustlin' 'round here. He can get his hands on all sorta stuff," Charlie said as he used some scissors on the top of my head. "He got me some new designer clothes for my wife Tootie. Told me last time he can get me some new barber chairs real cheap."

"The little pecker nearly got his little pecker in a pickle, I heard," Harlan said without prompting. I inwardly smiled at the alliteration.

Though I couldn't see it, I imagined Charlie giving Harlan a hard look, though he didn't take the hint, for Harlan continued. "I hear he was with some floozy who wasn't his wife and they was just taking off their. . . ."

"Harlan! The boy. I told you," shouted Charlie as he stopped cutting my hair and pointed the scissors at the fat man. "This ain't no time and place for that talk."

Harlan smirked. "I was just sayin', they was taking off their . . . *shoes* . . . when someone saw them."

"Harlan's right," Clifton chimed in. "He told me that one day when you weren't here, boss. He tried to laugh it off but he be scared of his wife. From how he talk 'bout her, I be scared, too."

The youngster, who was once again looking at his comic book, didn't seem to notice any of this conversation. I wanted to laugh but held it in. After all, it appeared I had found my man. I let them talk as I worked out in my head what my next move would be.

But for sure, I'd ask Mae to talk to Rita. She might have some leverage I could use when, eventually, I'd have to meet Charlie Pennypacker. And I started making plans on how to bring that about.

I couldn't linger in the shop after the cut. Too much to get done today.

Handing me a mirror to view the cut from the front, Charlie swung the chair around so I could see the back of my head reflected in the mirror on the wall.

"Looks good, Charlie. Thanks," I said as he swung me back around again and lowered the chair. He unfastened the smock and pulled it away from me, allowing any clippings to drop to the floor.

I paid him ten dollars, plus a generous tip, all of which he just shoved into a drawer that contained loads of loose cash.

Walking to the door, I said good-bye to everyone and the two barbers returned the sentiment. The boy, who never really noticed me to begin with, said nothing.

And Harlan, as usual, just grunted from his perch along the wall.

CHAPTER XVI

"Angelo, please. And my friends call me Angie."

After my trip up to Charlie's Barber Shop, I intended to head back to the office until it was time to get Marie. Calling Angelo De Luca wasn't part of the plan but after looking at my watch and checking the time, I decided that, on the off chance he had something informative to say and I had the time, I was in the mood to listen. I wasn't happy that he had had some lackey drop a note into my mail slot at home. I'm sure he'd never do such a menial task himself. It was a power play. He could have called and left a message at the office, but he didn't. He could have even called my house. But no, he wanted to let me know that he knew how to find me.

What an ass.

I called and got an immediate appointment.

The Henderson Group was located just to the northwest of City Hall, on the top two floors of the PennWalt Building at 16th and Cherry. The detective and security firm had placed nearly as many antenna and listening devices on PennWalt's roof as the Philadelphia Police Department had at its headquarters a mile to the east. Given its location, the firm was probably listening in on every telephone conversation taking place in City Hall.

I took a private elevator to the 19th floor and was surprised that the offices were so conspicuously opulent. I expected more reserve. What didn't surprise me was the thick, plush carpeting. What better way to muffle footsteps so that the myriad of microphones in the entry could pick up every sound, from conversations to heartbeats?

"Hi, I'm David Blaise and I have an appointment to see Angelo De Luca," I told the receptionist, who, also a surprise, was a man. He wore a black suit and a white shirt — and probably a gun.

"I'll let him know you're here. If you'd like, you may have a seat over there while you wait," he said, pointing to two dark leather chairs to his left.

I had barely rested my feet when a hidden door in the wood-paneled wall behind the receptionist opened and out came De Luca himself. "David, how nice of you to come by. Come on in." He waved me toward him.

De Luca wasn't a big man and generally carried a stern expression. While he wore casual yet conservative civilian attire — a tan jacket and gray slacks, and a blue, Oxford-cloth buttoned down shirt — he moved like a military man. Shoulders back, chest out, back straight. He barely moved his arms as he walked to maximize movement with the minimum of effort.

We disappeared behind the wall and down a dark-paneled hallway that opened at the end into a brightly lit conference room. There was a nice view of City Hall through its tinted windows, which provided visual security from the outside. The floor to ceiling drapes, when closed, undoubtedly would keep any eavesdropping at bay.

"Have a seat," he said, and I took the seat at the head of the table, the most dominant position, forcing him to take one to the side. While I knew he was a master at the power-playing sport, two could play the game. I wasn't prepared to lose it before we started. "I see you got my note. So nice of you to drop in."

"It was no problem. I was handling something for a client downtown and was nearby," I lied.

"I'm sure you were," he also lied. "I see you've been doing quite well for yourself since we last met."

"It's been a good year."

"I'm so glad to hear it. Being a one-man shop can be such a monumental task."

"I manage. And I do have an assistant," I corrected.

"Yes, Miss Mabelene Washington. She must be quite a help," he said with the slightest hint of sarcasm.

I was getting tired of his power games so, playing a mind game of my own, I casually looked at my watch without saying anything. He took the hint.

"Let me come to the point," De Luca said, leaning forward onto the highly polished conference room table. "David . . . oh, excuse me. May I call you David?"

I waved my hand, dismissing the question as being trivial, just as there was a knock at the door and the smartly attired assistant entered the room. The man stayed near the door, perhaps out of a false sense of safety from De Luca's anger at the intrusion.

"Uh, sir," the young man said.

"Yes, Jason," De Luca barked. "What is it? I thought I said I was not to be disturbed."

The young man coughed to clear his throat before replying. "Yes, sir, but it's a call from City Hall . . . the Council President's Office. They said it's quite urgent that he speak with you immediately."

I could see that De Luca still was angry with the interruption but I wasn't sure who would absorb the brunt of his wrath — Jason or Crocker Smithson III, the president of the Philadelphia City Council.

"David, excuse me for a moment, will you, please? I won't be long but I have to take this," he said as he rose and headed for the door, which Jason held open.

I sat quietly for a while, then stood and walked over to the window to gaze out onto the lower section of the Ben Franklin Parkway. I was there, at the window, thinking, when the door behind me opened again and De Luca re-entered.

I returned to my seat at the table.

"Now, where was I?" he started as he was mentally shifting gears. "Yes, I recall." He took another breath to center himself before continuing. "David, I have a client who had some property stolen some time ago. And it appears you have come into possession of that property. My client is willing to pay a considerable reward for the return of the property."

De Luca's interest was now clear, but I frowned as if I didn't comprehend.

"Property? What kind of property? I don't have any stolen property."

"Oh, come now, David. I know you aren't that naïve," he said, sounding genuinely surprised at my reaction.

"Mr. De Luca," I started, also leaning forward.

"Angelo, please. And my friends call me Angie," he said.

"Yes, I'm sure they do," I said, leaning back again, trying to appear more relaxed. "What is it you're looking for?"

"A silver necklace with a jade pendant. It's called The Jade Empress. It was designed in the 1930s by one of the most famous European jewelers of the time. It was to be a present to a famous actress."

I was sure his monitors and listening devices in the conference room could hear my heartbeat and detect the increase in my respiratory rate. "What happened to it?" I asked.

His pointer finger tapped the table twice, almost as a reflex. If I hadn't been paying attention, I might have missed it. But it was clear he was formulating an answer that might or might not be truthful.

"I'm not altogether sure. But my client says it was stolen," he said. "However, that's not the point of this discussion. The point is, do you have the necklace?"

I had already contemplated lying but there was no point. Besides, the truth might work to my advantage in this situation, as long as he didn't probe.

"No, I don't have a necklace such as you've described," I said as calmly as possible.

"Damn," was his reaction as his shoulders relaxed somewhat, as if we had been in a battle up until that moment. Then, he studied me closely, undoubtedly looking for the lie, which he wouldn't see. His next statement sounded sincere. And I took it as such.

"David, there are several very serious people looking for that necklace, people you don't want to mess with," he said. "They hire people like the man you put into the hospital last week. Dangerous men."

I wasn't surprised that he knew about Benjamin Floyd. Since he didn't mention the two guys in the jewelry store, he must not know about that incident yet.

"Even if I had the necklace, which I don't, how would giving it to you keep dangerous men from looking for me?"

"They would know to look somewhere else. And even if they didn't, I would use the resources of my agency to protect you," he said. "And don't forget, there'd be the reward for you, or whoever returned the necklace to its rightful owner."

"And you can prove your client is the rightful owner?" I said. "You have a provenance?" Again, De Luca paused. "I guess I'll take that as a no."

De Luca pushed back in his chair. The meeting was over. "All this is academic, since you don't have it," he said, shaking his head. "My source was positive. And he's usually reliable. One of my best."

Not like one of your men who tried to kill me last year, I thought to myself.

I shook his hand, and he walked me back to the front and through the hidden door in the lobby.

"I'm sorry to have wasted your time," I said.

"Don't worry about it. I had to ask," he said and smiled. It was the smile of someone who didn't smile often. "And do contact my office sometime. I'm sure we can work together on some future project."

"I'll do that. I'm sure we can." I lied.

Twice.

CHAPTER XVII

The Jade Empress

I was glad De Luca ended our meeting when he did because I had been about to, anyway. Marie's train was due at Penn Station in less than twenty minutes.

It was a short hop from De Luca's office to the Amtrak station. I drove two blocks to JFK Boulevard and then a mile west. I went around to the back of the station and parked on the west side, which is across the street from a regional banking office of the Philadelphia Savings Fund Society. My sister Valerie was a vice president at PSFS, responsible for overseeing a large group of regional bank branches, and her office was in the building across from the train station. If all went as I was planning, Marie and I were going to visit Val as soon as Marie got off the train.

Marie's train was scheduled to arrive at the moment I entered the station. I looked up at the display to see which track she was to arrive on and saw that her Metroliner service was running fifteen minutes late. I had time to spare.

I had been in 30th Street Station, as it was commonly called, more times than I could remember or would bother to count. But seldom did I linger and look around. It was all rush, rush, rush, as it is every day in major train stations worldwide. But Penn Station has its charms.

The east and west exteriors of the stone structure have porticos with Corinthian columns. Inside, the main concourse has an Art Deco design with six-story columns on the east end. And it's there that the most striking feature of the station stands: a thirty-nine-foot tall bronze memorial to the more than 1,300 employees of the Pennsylvania Railroad who died during the Second World War. The *Angel of the Resurrection*, which stands on a black granite base, depicts the archangel Michael, his wings pointed skyward, as he lifts a soldier fallen in war.

As I stood there staring upward, I considered for perhaps the first time that it was one of the most moving tributes in the city, on a par, though not near in size, as the Lincoln Memorial in Washington. As a veteran, I truly appreciated the sacrifice those men and women made.

I was lost in thought when the public address system announced that "Train Number 93, Metroliner service from New York to Washington, via Philadelphia's 30th Street Penn Station, is now arriving on Track Seven."

The floor rumbled ever so slightly as the train rolled in on tracks on the lower level. And I went over to the stairs leading down and waited for Marie to come up.

In low-heel ankle boots, a tight pair of jeans and a crisp light-green shirt, Marie was a wonder to behold. It certainly was not her first trip to Manhattan, but this trip to the Fashion Capitol of the World had taught her how to accentuate her beauty, which the jade necklace around her neck only enhanced more.

And seeing it nearly caused my heart to stop.

She rushed over and, dropping her things on the marble floor, threw her arms around me as if it had been years instead of a mere four days.

"This was the best time of my life," she exhaled into my ear. She kissed me and I nearly cried. "And this necklace you gave me is my lucky charm."

I didn't have the heart to tell her that I couldn't see any

scenario other than, one day, having to give it back to someone. Such thoughts would have to wait at least until we reached the car.

"It's so good to have you back home," I said and I felt her emotions shift throughout her body. And I knew in that moment she no longer thought of Philadelphia as home.

Letting her go, I picked up her bag and she grabbed her portfolio and, with our free arms around each other's waist, we headed for the door.

With Marie's belongings in the trunk and her situated in the car, I started the conversation I had been dreading for some time. The only chance I would have to keep her safe required that, as a first step, I tell her the truth.

"I have something to tell you, Marie, about the necklace," I said, turning in my seat to face her. "It's not as I thought it was . . . as either of us thought it was. It's a real piece."

"I know."

Surprised.

"You know? How?"

"Willi Smith told me. Once he saw it, he could tell it was real," she said. "And he had one of his jewelry experts look at it. All of it . . . the jade, the diamonds, the silver . . . all of it's real."

"If you knew that, why are you just cavalierly walking around with it on? It's real and it's genuinely expensive. Aren't you afraid someone might just walk up and yank it off from around your neck?"

"Once I knew, I stopped wearing it. And I didn't tell anybody about it, either. I only put it on just before I got off the train. I wanted you to see me wearing it," she said, anger rising in her voice. "What's your problem, David?"

I gripped the steering wheel and looked out the front of the car. Then I turned on the engine and started to back up.

"When I got it, I thought it was just a nice pretty piece and I wanted you to have it. It still is pretty but. . . ."

"But what?" she said.

"You remember that guy who came to the office last week, demanding something from Mae?" I said.

"Yeah, that guy you shot in the leg."

I turned out of the train parking lot onto 30th Street, then turned into PSFS's lot. I parked the car again.

"Why are we stopping here?" she said.

"The thing that guy was looking for was the necklace. Apparently, a number of people . . . dangerous people . . . are looking for the necklace. I didn't know it, but it was stolen and probably fenced at the jewelry store where I bought it. And it has a name. It's called The Jade Empress."

~*~

"You're a jerk," Valerie said, hitting me in the shoulder with her fist, "you know that?"

Hurt a little, both the comment and the punch, and I said so.

"How am I the Bad Guy here? I'm only trying to protect her."

We were alone outside Valerie's office as Marie, who, after a lengthy discussion in the car, only reluctantly agreed to my suggestion that we get a safety deposit box in the bank and put the necklace inside. She cried as Valerie handed her the paperwork to sign. Once it was done, Marie alone took The Jade Empress back to the deposit vault.

"You gave her this beautiful piece of jewelry and now you say it's stolen and too dangerous to keep. You should have known that before. That's why you're a jerk," Valerie said. "And you need to make it up to her. You owe her."

That was something I understood and was resigned to accept.

"I know."

"And you owe me, too," she said.

"You? How's that?" I said.

"For dragging me into your problems with Marie. And you owe Stuart, too."

"Stuart?" I asked, not adding that I saved his ass two years ago when he was having an affair. As I had promised Stuart, I never mentioned his affair to Valerie, though I kept the promise more to save her from mental anguish and hurt than in any way to help Stuart.

"For shooting up the windows in your office, which you're leasing from him."

"It's covered by insurance, Valerie. And I didn't invite the guy to come in and shoot up the place."

"You just don't get it, do you?" she said.

And with that, she turned and walked back into her office, leaving me to wait for Marie in silence.

The cold shoulder I was getting continued between Marie and me in the car, and was only broken by a request.

"Can I stop by the office real quick before I take you home? Please."

"Sure," she said, dejected, just staring out the passenger side window and away from me. "Doesn't matter."

I didn't believe her but I let it go. Marie merely sat with her arms folded tightly across her chest and watched the buildings of West Philadelphia go by.

By the time we arrived, Mae had gotten all the files off the floor and mostly arranged on her desk. A broad smile appeared on her face when she saw Marie.

"Girl, look at you," Mae said. "Don't you look fabulous?"

"Thank you, Mae. What happened here?"

Mae looked at me, almost as if saying, "You haven't told her yet?" But I said nothing and she spoke up. "Somebody broke in over the weekend and trashed the place lookin' for somethin'."

"Was probably related to that guy who came into the office looking for something about the necklace," I said.

"No it wasn't," Mae said, passing her hand over the files in stacks on the desk. "That wasn't it at all."

I caught my breath. Marie looked puzzled. What else could it possibly be? I didn't have any other controversial cases, certainly none that would warrant a professional breaking into my office and searching it.

~*~

I walked into my office and just sat behind my desk and thought.

Who would want those files? It was a run-of-the-mill, non-violent, white-collar case regarding allegations of bank fraud. And I was nearly finished. Mae should have been in the process of typing up the report for me to give the client, a suburban wife whose husband was implicated in some bank scheme. I had followed him around for a couple of weeks and once saw him meeting up with a woman in a hotel near his office.

Unfortunately, I didn't get a good picture of her and him together.

Since banking issues would involve federal law, I'm sure the FBI was looking into the broader issues in the case but at the time of the break-in in my office, the Feds didn't know of my involvement. And besides, if they thought I was hiding evidence related to a federal crime, they wouldn't have broken in. They would have gotten a subpoena, served it on me in the daylight hours, and carted away everything they wanted.

Mae appeared at my door, with Marie directly behind her.

"You have another problem, boss."

"Oh, good grief, what is it now?" I said.

"The police are looking for you," she said.

"They're looking for David?" Marie said, coming to stand inside my office and looking back and forth between me and Mae. "Why?"

"They didn't say why," Mae said to Marie before looking back to me. "I don't think they want to arrest you, but they were intense when they came in this afternoon looking for you."

"Who was it, do you know?" I said.

"That guy Thompson and his partner."

Holy crap. That's not good, I thought. I didn't say it aloud.

"After I drop Marie off, I'm giving you a ride home from work today," I said to Mae. "Just to be safe." She started to interrupt but I sternly cut her off. "Mabelene. . . ."

Marie held up her hand to stop me, and stepped closer to my secretary. "Mae, David is right. It's for your safety," she said softly. "For all our peace of mind, please, Mae. Let him drive you home."

It didn't take me long to get Marie home and to rush back to the office for Mae. I wanted to talk to Mae alone on the drive to her apartment.

"I haven't had a chance to check yet, of course, but on the off-chance that whoever broke into the office over the weekend . . . and we know they're professional because they got in without setting off the alarm . . . on the off-chance that they also bugged the office, let's not have any sensitive conversations in the office, and especially over the phone."

She looked at me in shock. "Do you think someone would do that?"

"I'm not sure, but until I can check the office and the phones, it's a precaution," I said, hoping to reassure her as I pulled into a parking space up the block from her apartment. "And also as a precaution, I contacted someone to look after the office when you're there alone."

"Who?"

"I don't want to say for now. But trust me, it's fine."

"If you discover we're being bugged, what ya gonna do 'bout it?" she asked.

I had thought about that very issue several times during the day and I hoped the response wouldn't worry her too much.

"For the moment, nothing."

"Why not?"

"Because the person doing the eavesdropping has the advantage if the target . . . in this case, that's me . . . is unaware of the bugging. But I have the advantage since I *am* aware of the eavesdropping without the bugger knowing I'm aware," I said. "Leaving it in place would give me some time to learn who the bugger is and perhaps what they're looking for."

~*~

Seeing my office in disarray — and hearing that police wanted to see me — had helped Marie understand the difficulties and the dangers of the cases I had. And by the time I reached her apartment, her attitude had softened, but not enough that she agreed to have dinner together after I dropped off Mae. The excuse was that it had been a long, busy weekend and she was tired.

I had promised her I'd contact the police as soon as I got home, which was true, but I didn't plan to go directly home. I had work to do first.

I went through a drive-through and picked up a sandwich of undetermined nature and ate it absentmindedly as I drove back downtown. I got some ketchup on my pants but didn't notice that until later.

Grateful to find a parking spot near 20th and Ben Franklin Parkway, I was equally grateful the Central Library was open late.

~*~

I left the library when it closed and went directly home, planning to call and leave a message for the police detectives to call me in the morning when they arrived in the office. It had started raining and I was glad there was only a short distance between the house and the detached garage which I accessed through an alley. I went in through the back door, of course, and walked through the house. As I was in the foyer picking up my mail, I looked out the window in the upper half of the door and saw a familiar car parked on the street.

When I turned on the exterior light, I knew they'd immediately notice someone was home. And less than ninety seconds later, the buzzer sounded AND there was a knock on the door.

Guess they wanted to make sure I heard. Since I was still in the foyer, it wasn't a problem.

"Detective, how nice of you to stop by," I said as I opened the door for John Thompson, happy that he was alone. "I just got in and was about to call and leave you a message."

"Cut the shit, Blaise."

He seemed more irritated than hostile or belligerent. Couldn't have been because of the rain. He had been sitting in the car. And now, only a few droplets of rain appeared on the shoulders of his all-weather raincoat.

I welcomed him in and we walked into the kitchen. I was still hungry. It wasn't much of a sandwich that I ate in the car and that was hours ago.

"How long were you out there? You hungry? I'm about to make something. You're welcome to have some."

"This isn't a social call, Blaise."

That wasn't a surprising statement given that Thompson had never before visited my residence on a social call. But I didn't point that out. I just went to the refrigerator and looked to see what my limited options were. Looked like it would be a grilled cheese sandwich.

"There was a botched jewelry store robbery early this afternoon on Sansom. You hear about that? It was at M. Rubinstein's."

"Yeah, I heard something about it on KYW this evening. Some guy got shot and another guy got away," I said as I got out a skillet and started heating it. Everything I needed was already out except one crucial ingredient. "Could you hand me the butter from the refrigerator?"

He was leaning against it and just looked at me for a moment in disbelief before opening it and getting out the butter.

"Thanks."

"They said a Black man who greatly matched your description was seen leaving the store just after the shooting and running up the street. You know anything about that?" I continued prepping the sandwich in silence, so he went on. "Then I read an internal report on the shooting and you know what?" he said, but again I didn't answer. "You came to mind. I looked at the report of the shooting in your office last week and it appears that the guy you shot, Benjamin Floyd, was somehow connected to some suspected illegal activities in that jewelry store . . . M. Rubinstein's."

I had buttered the bread, sandwiched the cheese and was heating it in the pan by that point, shaking the skillet to make sure the heat was distributed evenly. I finished and put the grilled cheese on a plate and walked over to the table and sat. Thompson continued standing over me.

"Okay, so I was there. But I didn't shoot anybody."

"They have one dead body and the shooter and his gun," he said. "But the questions remain, why you were there and why you left? That's leaving the scene of a crime, David, which is a felony."

"Aren't you going to sit down? Standing over me as I eat makes me nervous," I said.

"And me saying you could have committed a felony doesn't?" He pulled up a chair. "That's the least of your problems, if the Feds figure out that it was you in the store."

I stopped eating. "The Feds?"

"They're taking the lead. Why were you in the store, David?"

"It's where I got the necklace that that guy in my office apparently wanted. I went there to find out how they got it. I wanted to talk to the guy who sold it to me. That's all."

"For some reason, I believe you. What did you learn?" he said.

"Nothing," I said as I took another bite and chewed. "I had just started talking to the nervous younger guy I bought it from when two guys with guns burst in, demanding to know where it is."

"Where *what* is?"

"Never had a chance to find out, but for some reason I'm assuming it's the necklace. That's when someone from in back started shooting. Once it was over, he said I should get out quick, so I did. What's so important about that necklace?"

"Not sure, but the Feds are hot about it," he said, getting up again. "Sooner or later, they're going to figure out it was you in that jewelry store. And when they do, you won't just get to offer them a sandwich."

I was nearly done. I put the last piece into my mouth before I said, "Are you going to tell them?"

He smiled and stuck his hands in his raincoat pockets. "Against my better judgment, no."

Thanks for small favors. "If they don't know about me, should I call them in the morning?"

"No. I'll handle this for now." He headed back toward the front of the house. "Just be on your toes, David. And stay out of trouble. This is important law enforcement work. Stay out of it."

I unlocked the door and opened it for him. It was still wet outside.

"I would but, if you noticed, trouble came looking for me. I told you, I didn't know the guy who came to my office. I had never seen the guy before. And at the jewelry store, I was there to talk to the guy who sold me the necklace. I wasn't looking for trouble. But then two guys with guns walked in and threatened to kill people. I was a bystander."

"Just try. Someone from the bureau will likely call you soon, maybe tomorrow," Thompson said. "I think your name has already come up."

Thompson pulled up the collar of his coat and started to walk out into the rainy night. But he turned and came back to me, his hands still stuffed deep into his coat pockets.

"After I saw you in the office this morning, I got a call totally out of the blue from an old colleague. A mentor, actually. I was new on the force and green as can be. But he took a liking to me. Taught me everything I know, and then some," Thompson said as he reached up to scratch the back of his head as if doing so helped retrieve his memories. "He retired some years ago. I hadn't seen him in years. Probably not since I went to his wife's funeral five or six years back."

Thompson stopped again and looked me seriously in the eyes. "His name's Homer Dennis. And if he ever gives you advice, you should listen. He's a good man."

With that, he turned back into the night and left.

~*~

I was up early the next day, determined to talk to Kareem Adams's mother. I called Eli to check on his availability for a trip up to Plymouth Meeting. Once that was done, I considered how to get a handle on The Jade Empress case.

If The Jade Empress is such a big deal, who do I go to for information who doesn't have a dog in this fight? What hoity-toity person do I know? I asked myself.

A name came to mind of someone who could potentially help me — if they were only willing. But it likely would be tricky. I could virtually see Mae holding up her nose if I mentioned the contact to her. And Mae would be right. The source was pretentious, always putting on airs. It's why I decided to look sharp.

I put on a white shirt and a dark blue print tie. The jacket was blue, the pants gray. While I prefer sneakers or at least rubber-soled shoes, a pair of polished black loafers was more in order.

I examined myself in the downstairs mirror as I headed out and pronounced myself "okay." And I made the quick decision to take off the tie and change into jeans after my surprise visit to my hoity-toity source.

I wouldn't go there immediately. I picked up Mae and drove her to the office first.

"My, my, my, don't you look handsome?" flirted Mae. "You dress like you're going to see. . . ." She stopped, but eyed me closely. "You're not going to see that crazy ho, are you? Why?"

"Yes, and let's just leave it at that."

I gave her instructions on what I needed done while I was out and took some supplies from a cabinet in my office. "I'll give her your regards," I said with a laugh. Mae, who had been in the doorway to my office writing down my instructions for the day, gave a huff and turned to walk back to her desk.

My next two interviews would be interesting and, hopefully, enlightening.

CHAPTER XVIII

"Come to falsely arrest me again?"

My mind wandered as I drove up Lincoln Drive toward Mt. Airy, though I should have kept my mind on the difficult task ahead.

West Sedgwick Street looked much the same as it did a year ago during my last trip, as did the comfortably large lot where sat a big, white, two-story house with a porch. As I parked and sat for a while, I considered that the year-old Mercedes coupe was likely in the detached garage in the back.

Come on. Let's get going. It's not going to get any easier the longer you sit here, I said to myself.

Elise Carmichael opened the front door, and surprise and disappointment showed in her eyes. But she was stunning in tight black slacks and a black t-shirt with a red Delta symbol for her college sorority stitched just over her heart.

I was definitely overdressed.

"Come to falsely arrest me again?" she said. "You have heard of double jeopardy, haven't you? And harassment?"

I wanted to sink into the ground. "I didn't arrest you, Elise. That was the police."

"On your advice and recommendation," she countered.

Off and on over the past eighteen hours or so, I had pondered what I would say at this moment. The conversation wasn't going as I planned so I stood, not saying another word, waiting for the door to be slammed in my face.

I hoped it wouldn't happen but I had expected it.

Last year, Elise had hired me to follow her philandering husband, Reuben. But in the course of the investigation, I found evidence, although circumstantial in nature, that Elise was being blackmailed by a former lover of hers and that she likely killed him. And it was based on that evidence that I had helped arrange for her arrest.

Although Elise had quickly been released from jail, we had never had a chance to speak. We moved in different social circles and I never got around to apologizing to her.

I finally found a voice again. “I’m really sorry about last year. As soon as I realized the error, I informed the police and told them to let you go.”

“When I hired you to follow my cheating husband, it’s a good thing I didn’t pay you more. You could have gotten me convicted and executed before you realized how wrong you were.”

There was nothing more for me to say on the matter. Therefore, I got to the point. “I need your help, Elise. Please.”

Elise studied me quietly, undoubtedly calculating. After an eternity, she backed up two steps and moved out of the doorway and I walked in.

Though the house looked the same — it opened into a sizable foyer and in the middle was a round mahogany table with a large vase with fresh cut flowers and a massive chandelier hung overhead — the atmosphere felt different. I had an idea why but I still couldn’t put my finger on it.

We went into the library, which was to the left. There, the differences from my previous visits were more apparent. Pictures and various knick-knacks now filled the floor-to-ceiling walnut shelves that were once filled with dusty old books. The few volumes present all suggested female tastes. Most were by female authors or focused on women’s issues.

With all the old books gone, the room smelled fresher.

Gone was the desk with the electric word processor, replaced by the piano that once graced the living room. The sofa, chairs and rug had all been replaced. A new textured wallpaper was on the walls. The room was brighter and felt more like someone actually used it as a living space, instead of it being mostly for hosting guests who were not close enough or intimate enough to be allowed further into the house.

We sat on the sofa, one at each end, as if hesitant to sit closer.

"If I help you, are you going to have another innocent person locked up?" she said. Elise didn't smile so I wasn't sure if she was joking. I took her as being serious.

"No, I'm not."

"Then why are you here?"

"Because I thought you might have the answers to some questions I have in a case I'm currently working. In fact, it was my secretary, Mae, who suggested I contact you," I said.

At the mention of Mae's name, Elise's upper lip turned upward, giving her a snide expression.

"I'm surprised you still have her working for you. But then, I haven't seen her name in the newspapers lately," Elise said, turning back toward me. "You want something to drink?"

I said no as she poured herself some water and came back to the sofa, placing a coaster under her water glass.

The comment about the newspaper, of course, was a reference to Mae being arrested once last year for engaging in the world's oldest profession. I understood why the two women didn't care for each other. Mae thought Elise was an uppity, pretentious skank who needed to be put in her place, while Elise thought Mae was a common street ho who rented out her pussy in fifteen- to thirty-minute increments to any man willing to inhabit it.

I found Elise's comment regarding Mae ironic given that

I knew that Elise financed her own college education through prostitution.

"What can I help you with?"

"When we were talking last year, you once said you worked for some time in the jewelry business when you first married and moved here from Atlanta after you graduated from college," I said.

"Yes, Reuben was in law school and we had to pay bills. So?"

"Given your background and obvious expensive tastes, I thought you'd know about something going on in the jewelry business."

She moved forward on the couch. Her interest was obviously piqued. "Go on."

"Have you ever heard of a silver necklace with a jade pendant and diamonds called The Jade Empress?"

Elise had masked her emotions well up until that moment, but the mention of the necklace brought a quick smile. "Ah, yes. The Jade Empress," she said, taking a sip of water and sitting back on the sofa. Her head back, she closed her eyes and savored the moment, as if enjoying some exquisite memory. Elise finally returned to the here and now but the delight was still obvious on her face. "It's currently the most sought after piece of jewelry in the Western world."

Damn, I thought. "Tell me about it."

~*~

"The Roaring Twenties were over. The stock market crash and the Depression took care of the rest for most people. But there were places in the thirties where glamour still ruled. Hollywood was one of those places; not as much as before, but close enough.

"One of the biggest stars of the thirties was actor William Powell. He was tall, handsome, witty and sophisticated, with a charming sense of humor and great film presence. Powell made a name for himself in the movies and romanced some of the top blonde bombshells of the time — on-screen and off. Though fifteen years her senior, Powell married Carole Lombard for a brief second, as her star was on the rise. But three years after their divorce, they paired together in *My Man Godfrey*, a highly successful romantic comedy," she said.

"What does that have to do with anything?" I asked, impatient for where she was going and wishing I had taken up her offer for a drink.

"I'm getting to it. You want my help or not?" she retorted, scolding me as if I were a mischievous child.

"Go on."

"The love of his life at the time was the legendary Jean Harlow. By all accounts, he doted on her. He asked her to marry him and they got engaged," Elise said. "It was during that time that he reportedly commissioned noted European jeweler Albert Leopold of Belgium to design the jade and diamond pendant necklace that later became known as The Jade Empress. The design was in honor of some Hapsburg empress or another. And jade was one of Harlow's favorites. It's rumored that somewhere inside the piece Powell had it inscribed, 'My dearest darling.'

"But apparently Harlow never saw it. It was going to be a present, maybe for when they got married, but before they did, she got sick and died," Elise said. "That was in 1937."

Now I was fascinated. This stuff was edge-of-the-chair captivating. "What happened to it? Did he sell it or give it away?"

"He did neither. Powell was so devastated by Harlow's death, he couldn't bear to part with it. Plus, he also got sick around that time. He kept the piece. He must have just put it away somewhere, because he kept it even after he married another woman several years later. He stayed married to that wife for the rest of his life."

"This is just too Hollywood to believe," I said.

"It's what legends are made of," she said. "Powell's only been dead for a couple of years and the necklace was in his will, I've heard. It was to be donated to some Hollywood film charity in honor of Jean Harlow. But before that happened, it was stolen and disappeared. And no one knows where it is."

I do. It's in a bank safety deposit box less than twelve miles away, I thought but didn't say.

"What's it worth in today's market?" I asked.

She looked at me strangely, as if I were from another planet and she were seeing me for the first time. "You can't put a price on that. It's priceless."

"Oh, come on, Elise. You know it has some value, if only for insurance purposes," I said.

"Powell's widow has offered a huge reward for its return. But to be sold, I don't know. A couple million, I'd guess, at an auction. But to a collector of film memorabilia or of exquisite or rare jewelry, it would be invaluable," Elise said, straightening again. She studied me seriously, showing a modicum of both concern and worry. "I've heard rumors that it's surfaced. Some say in California, others say on the East Coast. You aren't planning on searching for the Empress, are you?"

At that, I smiled. "I can assure you, absolutely not. I'm curious about it but I'm not going looking for it."

"Good, because in addition to law enforcement, there are some truly nasty people looking for that necklace. And they will kill anyone who gets in their way. Or so I've heard," she added quickly. "And I've heard that snake Angie De Luca is on the scent of it for some client. You remember him. Reuben invited him to your office on the day you had me arrested."

"He's the head of the largest detective agency in the city," I said. "In my business, he's hard not to know."

"He's into other things, too, I hear. Illegal stuff," Elise said. She rose from the couch. Our meeting was over. "Is that all?"

"That should do it," I said, getting up. "Thank you for your time."

We walked toward the front door but just before she opened it, I stopped and turned to her.

"There is one more thing, Elise," I said. She cocked her head to the side but didn't say anything. "Professionally, I've had an incredible year since I had your case. I'm taking classes at night to get my law degree. Had this semester's final only a few days ago."

"Good for you," she said in a perfunctory way, as if it was a trifling matter. "How did it go?"

"Much easier than I thought. But that's not what's on my mind right now," I said, adding, "I've gotten a lot more work . . . cases steered my way, people I wouldn't normally have had access to . . . I think, because . . . of you. We haven't spoken, you and I, for obvious reasons since last year. But I wanted to say thank you, and that I appreciate the support."

She didn't respond at first but opened the door. I thought she was going to deny it and that would be it.

"I wanted to repay you for finding Wilbur's killer. He was a bit of a heel . . . at the end. But he deserved better than he got. He didn't deserve to die," Elise said. "And despite all the sadness and tragedy and death, I got my life back. And it's a happy life." She stopped again, as if what came next was difficult to voice to my face. "I have you to thank for a lot of that.

"Good bye, Mr. Blaise."

"Good bye, Mrs. Carmichael."

CHAPTER XIX

Only time would tell.

On the drive from Mt. Airy back toward my office, I found a pay phone outside a Sunoco gas station and called Eli to arrange for where to meet for the drive to Plymouth Meeting, and called Allen to ask a favor. I needed some brains and some muscle, and my brothers fit the bill.

"Did you see that snooty, pretentious bitch?" Mae asked as soon as I returned to the office.

"I did. And she asked me to tell you hi," I replied.

"Right. Sure she did."

I went into my office and changed out of gray slacks and into blue jeans. Sneakers were also handy. From inside my office, I called out to Mabelene.

"Get Marie on the phone for me, please. Thanks," I said, then added, "Did you talk to Rita as I asked?"

Mae paused, as I'm sure Rita must have if Mae had called her with my request.

More than a year ago, at some point after Mae had been working for me for several months and her level of trust in me had sufficiently risen, she had shared a deep secret with me. Some of the rooms in the gentleman's club where she worked as a hooker had recording devices installed. Additionally, clients were not generally aware of that.

The equipment wasn't in all rooms, apparently, but Rita kept the recordings as a layer of insurance and protection. She always steered cops and politicians into one of those rooms, though not exclusively just them, Mae informed me.

"When I met you, I wasn't in one of those rooms, was I?" I had asked, suddenly anxious, though, by then, some time had passed since we had shared our only sexual encounter.

"Oh, no, David. We weren't in one of those rooms," she had assured me at the time.

It didn't initially calm my anxious nerves but, by then, my trust in her had also risen to the point where I trusted her not to lie to me. And, given my signal intelligence training in the Navy, I thought I would have noticed even the most discreetly placed camera.

Now, standing in the office, I asked Mae, "Is Rita willing to help me protect you and me?"

"She keeps and catalogues all the recordin's but she don't store them at the club. They someplace else," Mae said.

"And?"

"She thinks she got some pictures of Mr. Charlie, and, of course, of me. And some of the other fella you asked about," Mae said. "And she say she willin' if it can keep us safe. She takes my word that youz ah good guy. And I think she's kinda sweet on you 'cause you hired me."

After dropping that gossipy nugget, she went back to her desk to call Marie. I wasn't altogether sure how Marie was going to take what I had to say, but I was more determined than ever to protect her.

"I wanted to confirm we're having dinner tonight and one more thing," I said once I had her on the phone.

"Where we goin'? she asked brightly.

"Friday Saturday Sunday, that restaurant you like near my place," I said.

"Fancy tonight, are we?" she said lightly.

"I guess. But that's not what I'm thinking," I said, bracing for what I had to say next and her reaction to it. "Marie, given what's happened the last few days, I'd feel better if you stayed somewhere other than at your apartment. Just for a night or two. As a precaution."

At first there was silence on the phone. And then shock, and perhaps anger.

"What are you saying? I can't take care of myself without *your* help? Because I was doing just that long before I met you, David Blaise," she said defiantly.

"Yes, I know that, Marie. But like I said, I'd feel better if you weren't alone." I know I sounded desperate but I didn't care. "Marie, please. Can we at least talk about it at dinner?"

~*~

I picked up Eli at his office, then proceeded through the city over to Germantown Avenue, which, once we left the wealthy Chestnut Hill section and entered Montgomery County, becomes Germantown Pike, the road on which the Plymouth Meeting Mall is located. It's a fairly standard, two-story indoor mall, with two anchor stores on either end — Strawbridge's being one of them. But what is increasingly drawing people to that area is a brand new European-based store located across the parking lot. It had opened last year to great fanfare.

IKEA.

I had visited the Swedish retailer several times in the last year with my sister and her kids, and had even decorated some of the rooms in my new digs with IKEA furniture. I liked the store and enjoyed its merchandise but, with only one location in the United States, I thought its chance for survival here was pretty slim.

Only time would tell.

We parked and entered the mall on the north end, which was closest to Strawbridge's. Sheree Jackson worked in the home goods department. So as not to barge in on her and surprise her unannounced, I had prevailed upon my Tribune friend, Randolph Williams, to call and make an introduction and vouch for Eli and me.

By agreement before we arrived at the store, Eli and I decided that he would approach her first. It might be less intimidating than a private eye making first contact.

Jackson, an attractive woman who appeared to be in her late forties, was in the kitchenware section next to a display of fashion cutlery. She wore a long blouse in a bright floral color and was standing behind a customer counter apparently doing some paperwork. She looked up as we approached.

"May I help you?" asked Jackson, who took off her reading glasses, leaving them hanging around her neck.

"Hello, Ms. Jackson. I'm with the Justice Consortium downtown. You've heard of us, haven't you?" Eli said. She nodded but otherwise remained silent. "We seek justice for those who are so often deprived of it. Can we talk?"

She nodded again. Her face was a mask of infinite sadness, as if the concept of joy did not exist. "I got a call from the Tribune reporter, who said you might be stopping by."

"This is my brother, David. He's a private detective and he's working with me on finding the truth about what happened to Kareem."

"I'll be on my break in a few minutes. Can we go to the food court in the mall to talk?"

"Certainly," I said. "It's what I wanted to suggest. We'll shop around for, say, fifteen minutes and meet you, where? I'll pick up the tab."

She almost seemed startled at the suggestion. "I can pay."

"We insist," said Eli and she relented.

"There's a restaurant and ice cream parlor down at the other end of the mall near the carousel. I'll meet you there. I'll see if I can take a longer break," she said.

With a little time on our hands, Eli and I walked through the mall, stopping occasionally to look in a store window before commenting on something and moving on. Neither of us was much for aimlessly window shopping. Plymouth Meeting wasn't an upscale mall, and all the offerings were Middle American and not too edgy, thus easily allowing clients from nearby Philadelphia suburbia to feel comfortable and sheltered and safe.

We finally made it down to the ice cream restaurant, where we requested a booth. We sat facing each other until Jackson arrived. I rose, allowing her to take my seat, and I moved next to Eli. It had been twenty minutes since we first met her.

"I normally don't take a lot of time for a break but my boss understands and said I don't have to rush back," she said. But still, when the server came, she ordered the simplest and quickest meal on the menu — a grilled cheese sandwich with a cup of chicken noodle soup, and a diet soft drink. I had already ordered a single serving of butter pecan ice cream in a cup and Eli ordered a cup of strawberry.

The meal wouldn't be a strain on my budget.

"First of all, I want to express to you our sorrow over the loss of your son," I said, indicating Eli and me. "We're just searching for the truth and want to see that justice prevails."

She managed a "thank you", but just barely.

"Mind if I take notes?" I asked and took out a notebook and pen.

My dessert arrived and initially I left it untouched as Eli started the conversation.

"What was Kareem like as a child?" he asked.

As Eli and I had talked about it in advance, the question allowed Jackson to hopefully focus on happier memories of her son — and it worked. She talked about his growing up in poverty in North Philadelphia, being raised by a single mother without much family support, and his going to a poor, broken-down school, where he sometimes struggled with his grades. Because she was always looking for work or working long hours in order to survive, she had limited time to help him with his schoolwork. She said there were times when she didn't eat so that Kareem had a meal at home.

Yet, he somehow seemed like a happy child.

"He made friends fast . . . at school and in the neighborhood and at church . . . and that helped him socially," she said as her food arrived and she started eating.

"You mean at the community church on Girard?" I said, eating a little ice cream, followed by a sip of water.

"Yes, the church with the white preacher," Jackson said through a mouthful of grilled cheese. I wrote myself a quick note.

"I hate to bring this up, Miss Jackson, but when did you first notice Kareem starting to get into trouble?" Eli asked hesitantly.

She looked so sad I thought she might cry but she soldiered on after taking a spoonful of hot soup, which must have strengthened her resolve.

"It was . . . it was," she started, as if searching her memories or for the words to describe them. "I think in middle school, seventh or eighth grade. No, it was seventh. He was, I think, thirteen. They wanted to hold him back a grade but I refused, so Kareem went to the eighth grade," she said. "Looking back now, maybe I should have held him back."

We were now getting to the crux of the matter, and I was hanging on Jackson's every word. The ice cream could wait. For several days, I had harbored doubts regarding the how and why of Kareem Adams's death and how he became the leading suspect in a young woman's murder.

Perhaps in the next couple of minutes, a clue would appear to unravel the mystery.

"That's when he started running with a bad crowd in the neighborhood. I tried to help him as much as possible but I was working so much. I did make sure he went to church every week. That white preacher was trying to help him but it was hard," she said.

"Did he get into any trouble with the law during his time in school?" I asked.

"Some juvenile stuff," she answered. "Nothing big."

She stopped and looked at us. Tears welled in her eyes but had yet to fall as she fought back her emotions. It was a losing battle. "If he had only got straightened out as a child, it wouldn't have been so bad by the time he was eighteen."

A tear dropped into her soup.

While she was staring down at her food, I touched Eli's thigh and nodded. He took my hint and stayed silent to allow Jackson to resume eating in peace. The waitress checked on us, though after seeing Jackson crying, she started to back away.

"You can take this," I said, indicating my half-melted cup of butter pecan. But I addressed the grieving mother on the other side of the table.

"Miss Jackson, tell me about when Kareem went to prison."

"He was just a boy," she said. "He was lost. I couldn't go up there often, 'cause I had to work, but I did as much as I could. After a while, he made a friend, I guess you'd say. He was from here in Philly. He helped Kareem out a lot in prison, showed him how to survive. His name is Benny."

"What happened to this guy?" Eli asked.

"He got released before my Kareem did but they stayed in touch and Benny helped Kareem find a job when he got out," she said.

"Do you remember his last name or how to get in touch with him?" I said.

Jackson suddenly looked scared. She sat back in her seat and pushed away the remains of her meal. Her hands began to visibly shake and her eyes darted around the room as if she was searching for a way to escape. I reached across the table in an attempt to calm her. The gesture seemed to do the trick.

"Please, Miss Jackson. We're here to help you."

"I was told not to talk to the police," she said.

"By whom?" I asked. But she moved on.

"I don't know how to reach him or where he lives but Benny's name is Floyd. Benny Floyd."

The name hit me like a bolt of lightning out of the blue. It was so unexpected, and I thought my reaction was obvious to the others. I glanced quickly at Eli but the name hadn't registered with him yet. Jackson was similarly unmoved. But it was a revelation and I needed to confirm that I heard the name correctly.

Returning to Jackson I said, "Floyd? Benjamin Floyd? Kareem knew Benjamin Floyd in prison?"

"I think that's his name. They was in prison together," she said. "I saw him a few times with his brother. His clothes was always too small. Don't fit right."

Eli looked at me strangely, as if to ask whether I knew this person and why it was important. "We can talk about it in the car," I said as calmly as possible, so as not to raise any alarms with Kareem's mom.

"Benny's big and Kareem said he saw him hurt people real bad. He said he stayed on Benny's good side 'cause he didn't want Benny to hurt him one day like he did to other folks," Jackson said. "But Benny also took care of Kareem when he got out. Got him a good job for the railroad."

"Amtrak, you mean," I clarified.

"That's right. Amtrak. Benny introduced Kareem to the head porter and got him onto long trips out West," she said. "His boss was a little, slick-haired hustler named, ah, Penderton or Pennyman. Something like that."

"You mean Pennypacker?" I asked, my tone neutral. My heart, however, threatened to leap out of my chest.

"That's him, I think. How'd you know?"

I thought fast for a plausible lie to satisfy her without drawing too much attention to the answer. "I did some security work for Amtrak a while back."

It must have worked. She didn't probe.

"He be in charge of all the porters," she said. But then she started to look fearful again. "He started having Kareem smuggle things back to Philly from California. Small stuff, mostly, at first. Easy to conceal."

"Was the stuff stolen?" Eli asked.

"I think so. Kareem be nervous but they forced him. Blackmailed him. Say if he don't do like they say, they'd squeal on him for breakin' parole and he get sent back to jail. I told him to get away from them but he say it was hard to do."

She was about to break down again just as the waitress came over with the check, leaving it near me.

"If that's all, you can pay me or at the register up front," she said, taking away the last of the dishes.

"Doing all that wrong stuff is why he volunteered down at the church he used to go to . . . to make up for the stuff he was doin'," Jackson said. "He told me he felt trapped, and scared. Kareem say they'd hurt him if he didn't do like they say."

"When did that start, do you know?" asked Eli.

"'Round Christmastime last year, Kareem come back from California real scared. This time, he say he wanted to quit his job."

"Why was that?" I asked.

"He say in his gear he smuggled some piece of expensive jewelry. A necklace. He knew it had to be stolen. He told me it had diamonds and green jewels in it. And they all was nervous about that necklace," Jackson said. "When he got back, Benny told him to only give it to the head porter, the old guy. Nobody else. And keep his mouth shut."

"And did he? Give it to Pennypacker?" I questioned.

"Yes."

"What happened to the necklace after that?" I asked.

"He never said. But he took time off from the job. Told them he was tired of the long trips."

"He wasn't working?" Eli said.

"He worked some, but no long trips. And when he be home, he stayed with me some but also moved around a lot. Staying with different friends."

"Why was that?" Eli said.

"Scared, I guess. But he also was helping out at the church more," Jackson said. "with all the drug situation up in North Philly."

"What did he say about helping out at the church?" I asked.

Again, Jackson looked particularly nervous but then reached into her purse that was next to her on the bench seat. From inside, she pulled out a series of pictures, looked at them one by one, and then handed them to me.

"My baby say I need to keep these safe. And he say if anything happened to him, I should go to the police," Jackson said.

"And did you? Go to the police?" I asked.

Jackson reached back into her purse and pulled out some wadded up tissues, dabbed her eyes and wiped her nose. "No. They first came to me after that girl was killed, searching for Kareem. I said I didn't know where he was staying. I don't know if they believed me. Then about a week or ten days later some detectives came to say he was dead and took me downtown to identify the body."

She broke down crying, her shoulders rising and falling as she wept. Neither Eli nor I said anything, giving her space to grieve.

I showed Eli the pictures, mostly taken at twilight or at night. There was a series of them and were time-stamped when they were developed — from mid-March to early April, all less than two months old. They showed a man and a woman in an expensive car purchasing drugs from a dealer on a street corner. Probably somewhere just off of Girard Avenue. There were pictures of the people in the car and also the back of the car as it drove off.

Though a little out of focus, the faces were recognizable.

"Look at this, Eli," I said quietly. "The woman there looks like . . . Mary Ann Tolk."

But he was more interested in the man in the picture. Pointing to him, Eli asked, "Do you know who that is?" I shook my head. "He works in City Hall. I recognize him because we . . . the Consortium . . . have dealt with him on a number of social issues. He's the Council president's son. He goes by Crocker the Fourth."

"Mrs. Jackson," I started cautiously, "What I don't understand is why you didn't go to the police with these."

Fear of going to the cops wasn't all that unfamiliar in the Black community, a remnant of decade upon decade of mutual distrust between the two. While that was neither my understanding nor experience — well, not completely — I certainly understood where she was coming from. Thank goodness for Randolph, who has a well-known presence in the community, for paving the way for me.

"I was scared," Mrs. Jackson said. "Benny's brother . . . I don't remember his name but he is mean-lookin' with two gold teeth in front . . . he came to see me at home. It was just before Kareem was found. He say he know 'bout some pictures that Kareem had and demanded them. He threatened me. I told him I didn't know nothing about no pictures," she said. She seemed to gather up her courage. "I wasn't about to give that hoodlum anything about my son."

"And why are you willing to talk to us now?"

"The reporter said you're a man with some connection and I can trust you," she said. "You could put the pictures to good use."

"And what about the guy who came to you? Benny's brother, you said. How did he threaten you?"

"He say to me, 'If you know what's good for you, you won't talk to the cops. Or I come back and do the same thing to you I did to that white bitch.'"

CHAPTER XX

I told Marie the history of The Jade Empress

Friday Saturday Sunday was on a corner on 21st Street, only a block and a half west of Rittenhouse Square. The front was small and narrow but I saw its awning before we reached it. Once inside, an attractive hostess in a smart yet simple yellow dress greeted us.

"My name is David Blaise and I called and made a reservation earlier today."

Looking down, she ran a finger down a page in a book with reservations, then looked back up at me with a satisfying smile of gleaming white teeth.

"Oh, yes, right this way, please," she said and turned to head deeper into the restaurant.

Normally, we had casual meals, but this restaurant wasn't a casual place. Marie wore a form-fitting, V-neck blue designer dress by someone I had never heard of, and, somewhat surprisingly, a string of pearls. I had redressed in the slacks, jacket, and tie I wore earlier to visit with Elise Carmichael.

A man in black pants, a white shirt, and a black bow tie appeared out of nowhere. He wore a white, knee-length apron tied around a waist that was so slim it made me wonder if this man ever ate. His hands were behind his back and he didn't appear to have a notebook.

This was the type of restaurant where, regardless of their complexity, orders were taken by memory.

"Good evening," he said in a pleasant and welcoming tone, taking a moment to address us both. "My name is Leonard and it will be my pleasure to serve you this evening. Would either of you like something from the bar? We also have an exquisite wine selection. I can provide you with a wine list and make recommendations, if you'd like."

We ordered cocktails and Leonard dutifully ran through the day's menu off the top of his head. Then he retreated as quickly and silently as he had appeared.

Marie and I made small talk until after the drinks arrived and Leonard had taken our dinner order.

"I'm likely going to do some things tomorrow that people aren't going to like. The intention is to shake the bushes a little and see what comes out," I said.

"You don't hunt, David, and so your hunting metaphor sounds dumb," Marie said.

My shoulders slumped a bit. I wasn't sure if she was being serious or was making a joke. What was certain, however, was that she wasn't going to make this an easy conversation. But I plowed ahead.

"Maybe. But still, I need to make sure you're protected and safe when I do."

A remarkably prepared dinner arrived. Marie had a herring pasta dish and, since my palate has always been limited, I went for a New York strip. At least our wines paired well with our dishes thanks, of course, to Leonard's suggestions.

I barely noticed the prices when I ordered. They were mostly irrelevant. I was willing to sweeten the pot if it meant I could get Marie into a safe place for a couple of days.

Marie seemed to greedily savor every bite, while I consumed my steak without taking much note of its taste. As we ate, I avoided any discussion of The Jade Empress, and the fact that we'd have to return the necklace to someone.

"Would either of you like some coffee, or some dessert? We have an excellent selection made fresh daily in our kitchen," Leonard asked as he cleared the table. He used a small metal scraper to collect the crumbs and scoop them into his free hand.

I looked at Marie, who nodded, and Leonard rattled off a list of the desserts of the day. We ordered two coffees and a large chocolate brownie topped with a scoop of vanilla ice cream, a dollop of whipped cream, and a cherry.

"Very well, sir," Leonard said and headed off.

Finally, I told Marie the history of The Jade Empress.

"I was walking around New York City with a priceless piece of jewelry around my neck that was once a gift to Jean Harlow?" she said, sounding shocked. "What are you going to do?"

"Your safety is my first priority. Nothing else is more important than that," I said.

Marie reached for my hand across the table. With the full story, she seemed much more understanding.

"Thanks, Boo. Of course, we have to give it back. It's stolen," she said, but leaned back somewhat though she still held my hand. "Why didn't you just explain everything to me on the phone? You were so vague."

"Just saying that much over the telephone was more than I should have. There's likely a tap on the phone by now. Could be the FBI or someone else. Who knows? But I couldn't risk it."

I took a sip of coffee. Much better than the swill I often get at a Wawa or McDonald's.

"When I got the necklace, what I saw was just a nice, pretty piece of jewelry that I thought would be a great gift for you, which is why I bought it," I said. "But now . . . the world is falling down around us and I've endangered you once again."

Marie's eyes were bright — smiling, caring, loving — and reinforced the assurance she offered. She tightened her hold on my hand.

"Don't worry about that. After the shooting in the cemetery last year, I've always felt safe with you. And you'll figure out everything. You have a sharp mind and you're the smartest guy I know. You're quite analytical . . . when you allow yourself to think outside the box. It's why I have so much confidence in you."

Leonard delivered the dessert, with a spoon for each of us, and placed it near the middle of the table, thus allowing relatively easy access to both of us. We charged into the delicious dessert with gusto. Given that many women are continually conscious of their weight and over their physical appearance — and Marie was no exception to this — I was a little surprised that she matched my pace of consumption, spoonful by spoonful.

"I originally thought of you going to spend a few nights with Grammy Taylor," I said. Marie indicated that I had a little whipped cream on the edge of my lip, which she reached over to dab off with her napkin. "Allen would be there, and Renee, and my grandmother, of course. And her gentleman friend, Mr. Dennis. . . ."

"Who?" she interrupted. Shocked.

I laughed to myself. "With so much going on, I forgot to mention it to you. It just slipped my mind. My sweet grandmother has a boyfriend . . . of sorts."

"Really?" Marie looked delighted. "Good for her."

"Are you kiddin' me? At her age? Has the world gone mad?"

"Oh, David, calm down. It sounds wonderful. And I'm sure it's totally innocent."

"That's what Renee told me and Valerie reaffirmed it when I talked to her."

We were finishing dessert. I looked over to Leonard, who had just delivered plates to a nearby table, and I indicated I wanted the check. He acknowledged me and headed toward the back to complete the work.

"Grammy Taylor knows Mr. Dennis from church. He's a former police detective, and he gave me some tips on handling the jewelry investigation. And he persuaded one of his former colleagues in the department to park a patrol car outside the house."

"Sounds like he's a helpful guy all around."

Leonard came and handed me a small black folder containing the check. I looked at it and hoped my face didn't display what I was thinking.

The waiter was turning to leave when I reached into my jacket pocket for my wallet and credit card. I had only recently started carrying an American Express card, in part because of their advertising tagline: Never leave home without it.

And now, I don't.

"Very well, sir. Thank you," Leonard said as he took the card and scurried off.

"Instead of staying at your grandmother's place in North Philadelphia," said Marie, seductively, "I could just stay with you in your place. You could protect me there."

My eyebrows went up. "That was my first thought," I said. "But Mr. Dennis reminded me that my place may not be much safer than you staying at home."

"Where, then?" she asked, just as Leonard handed me the receipt, which I signed and added a good tip.

"I've figured that out, too," I said, rising from my chair. Marie rose, as well. "Come along."

~*~

We held hands like love birds as we walked in the direction of Rittenhouse Square, where earlier I had been lucky to find an open parking space on the street on the south side of the park. Despite the comfortable place we were in at the moment, there was still the open question of where our relationship was headed.

"I won't stand in the way of your career, even if it means you moving out of town . . . to New York," I said as I opened the door to the car. She didn't get in, just turned toward me and looked up.

"I know that. And that's why it's so hard. It's a tremendous opportunity I can't just pass up. What would *you* do?" she said. "If I turned that down, I could end up resenting you and neither of us wants that."

"No."

"Then we'll just have to find a way to work it out."

She got in the car and I walked around to the driver's side. Deep in our own thoughts, we said little as I drove around the park and exited onto Locust, where I continued down toward 7th. Just before 7th, I reached into one of the cup holders between our seats, retrieved a clicker, and pushed the center button. As I turned left into a short, narrow, one-car driveway, a garage door slowly rose and I entered.

"David," Marie said in awe. "Whose place is this?"

I didn't answer as I closed the garage door and we got out of the car. Up a few short steps, I unlocked and opened the door into a small mud room just off the kitchen. Beside a bench along the wall was a row of shoes, mostly men's and women's sneakers, and several pairs of shoes for a little child.

The kitchen was large for a house of its age. Given its location in Society Hill, the house could be close to two hundred years old. But of course, it would have been redecorated numerous times since then. The cabinets were a slate blue with frosted glass fronts, and pale gray and white ceramic tiles were on the walls. It had a modern gas stove with six burners and a wall-mounted microwave above it. Clearly, the owners liked to cook.

But the place also looked lived in. In one corner was a small table and next to it was a box of toys.

"David, who lives here?" Marie said, admiring it all.

"My friend Raymond."

"Your frat brother from college? The one who works at. . . ."

"Strawbridge's, yeah," I finished for her. "He's getting married this fall and he, his fiancée, and their baby girl are off to Boston to tell her parents, whom I'm sure will be overjoyed. The baby is already about two years old."

"Wow. That's exciting! When is it and where? In Boston?"

"No, it'll be here in a couple of months. Mid-August."

"I'm so happy for them. Make sure you congratulate them for me," Marie said.

"I will do that the next time I talk to Raymond. I got him on the phone before he left and they agreed that you could stay here. I can go get some clothes for you for a couple of days."

"But David, are you sure? This place is just so incredible, I'd be afraid of messing up something. I should stay somewhere else."

"No. It's best that you keep as low a profile as possible if anyone thinks you might know about or have the Empress. In the intelligence game, this is what we'd call a safe house. Just a very nice one. It's safe because no one will know you're here," I said. "I can pick up some things for you tomorrow. Just give me a list of what to look for."

"So, you want to look through all my things, I see," she said with a twinkle of amusement. I wish I was more in the mood for it.

"I just want to keep you out of trouble," I said seriously.

The subject was dropped.

I took her upstairs along a wall lined with pricey art, mostly by Black artists. A nursery was on the second floor, down a long hall to the left of a two-room guestroom suite, with windows that opened onto Washington Square. The master bedroom was on the third floor.

But we didn't discuss any of that until later.

I lifted Marie into my arms and carried her to the bed in the guest room. We hadn't made love in months, since we officially "broke up." So now, the longing for each other threatened to consume us both.

"I love you so much. I can't imagine a life without you in it," I said.

"Listen to you, the serial monogamist," she said with a smile. Kissing me, she added, "And I don't know what I'd do without you."

We explored each other's bodies in a rush of built-up passion, but savoring each kiss, each touch, and the ecstasy of our joining.

"I love you more than I can say," I said.

"I know. I love you, too," she said. "I want this moment to last forever."

When we finished — sweaty and satisfied, and all too soon — we fell asleep in each other's arms.

CHAPTER XXI

"If you move a muscle, I'll shoot you dead."

Since returning from Manhattan and with her college work completed, Marie resumed working at the newsstand where we had met last year in the Sheraton Hotel on JFK. She even picked up more hours. We were up early and she put on the same outfit as the night before but without the pearls, and I got her to work by seven. By arrangement, either Eli or Allen agreed to pick her up and take her to Ray's place if I was unavailable.

Marie gave me a list of items to get from her apartment, which I promised to do later in the day.

Once more, it was time for me to greet Thompson in his office early in the morning. In his normal work attire, his suit looked like it needed to be pressed, his pants were wrinkled, and a stop at a shoeshine stand would do wonders to his shoes.

But today, his suit was neat, the pants sported a sharp crease, and his black shoes were buffed and polished to a nearly blinding shine. He really must have put some work into it.

"Why, detective, look at you. Don't you look nice?" I said as I walked up. "You going to the monthly meeting of the Smartly Dressed Police Officers Club?"

"Why do you keep doing this, Blaise, this early morning stop by my office?" Thompson said. He was standing and had been reading a file but closed it quickly as I approached. "I do have other cases. And I'm due in court at 10:30 to testify in a case."

It was half-past eight.

"Yes, yes, yes. You're busy. I know that, but this won't take long," I said. "Last night, I was going over my notes and I figured out something in the Adams case. It'll change everything and I know you're gonna want to know."

A smile appeared on his face. It was unexpected.

"He was left-handed," Thompson said, and my jaw dropped to the floor.

"You know that?"

"We're not stupid," Thompson said, although he added contritely, "most the time. And you are sometimes useful." The acknowledgment made me smile.

"When did you figure out that Kareem was left-handed? And why didn't you mention it to me?"

"First of all, I don't answer to you. I am under no legal obligation to share *any* police information outside this office," he said, letting it hang in the air for effect. "And second, I told you I do have other cases. While the Adams case is still technically open, quiet as we're keeping that fact, it isn't a high priority. I only just started re-examining the file. You told me you went up to Girard Avenue to ask around and talked to some people, like that church pastor. You mentioned that he said Adams was left-handed. I checked our records, which confirmed what I remembered at the scene. I saw the heroin needle in his arm. His left arm."

"A left-handed person shooting up would use his right arm for the drug," I said.

He put the file on his desk, face down. "Yes, that's right. Someone stuck the needle into his arm after he was already dead."

I looked around the room as I thought, not focusing on anything in particular. "That means there's a killer out there, and you might want to check the video of her stabbing again."

"It's scary that we're thinking alike," Thompson said. "I did that today, just after I got in an hour ago."

"And?"

"The perp who killed her used a knife in his right hand," he said. "You were right all along."

"And speaking of me being right, you might want to check out these pictures. I got them from Kareem's mother last night."

~*~

Marie told me her roommates would certainly be at work when I stopped by to pack a few things for her. But she also said I should knock on the door ahead of time so as not to shock anyone if they were home. Therefore, imagine my surprise when I walked up to her door and it was already open.

Quietly pushing the door further open, I listened for the sound of the occupants. What I heard was the loud crashing of things upstairs in the area of Marie's bedroom.

Reflecting on it later, I shouldn't have called out her roommate's name. "Heather. Are you up there?"

That's when the crashing sounds stopped, which meant whoever it was upstairs knew I was inside.

I raced up the stairs two at a time without having a clear plan of what to do when I got there. As I reached the top, I was hit with a body blow that was harder than any I had ever felt before. I was knocked back up against a wall and somehow managed to keep from falling only to have a big man come at me with both arms outstretched. I ducked into an open bedroom just in time and tried to shut the door as he pushed against it. Then I let it go and stepped back, allowing him to lose his footing and fall forward into the room and onto the floor.

I grabbed a table lamp, yanking it out of the electrical socket, and smashed it into his thick head. He stumbled onto the bed as I ran from the room. I turned back just as the man came out of the bedroom. He was only a few feet away and would be on me before I had a chance to reach for my gun.

From my military training, I could tell this guy was undisciplined as a fighter and I could use that knowledge to my advantage. He snarled with anger, displaying two gold front teeth. I knew at that moment that I might kill this man.

He charged me and I ducked a blow but hit him with my entire body into his mid-section. His reaction was to grab me and place me in a head lock, just as I hoped. He had me on his right side and I struggled a little to reassure him that he was in control. But then I lowered my left shoulder so that I could slide my left arm under his body and up between his legs. I raised both arms up as I stood, lifting his entire body. The air rushed out of his lungs when I slammed his body back down onto the floor. I made sure his head hit first, leaving him completely dazed as he tried to catch his breath.

I backed away, undid my belt and pulled it out of my pants in one swift movement. Before he was aware of it, I was behind him and had looped the belt around his thick neck. I pulled it tight and yanked backwards and up.

His reaction was immediate. He gagged and tried to reach back at my arms. But I only pulled tighter until he grabbed at his neck. The harder he struggled, the harder I pulled. Tighter and tighter. He would die soon if I kept pulling. It was an option. After all, he was here to harm Marie. But, I needed answers and I intended to get them from this monstrous thug.

The guy's arms finally dropped to the side and soon afterwards his body went limp. He was unconscious. I kept the pressure on his neck as I counted to 10 to insure he was definitely out, then let him go and he hit the floor, face down, with a mighty thud.

In another context, I would have found it humorous seeing him fall forward, as if in slow motion, but I didn't have time to contemplate that. I only had seconds, perhaps a minute, before enough oxygen reached his brain and he'd regain consciousness. At that point, the dynamics of the situation could dramatically shift. My only viable option then would probably be to shoot him.

I pulled both his arms behind his back and used my belt to tightly tie his wrists. Having been in the Navy, I know how to tie a quick, secure knot. Took less than 12 seconds. I rushed back into the bedroom and grabbed the lamp I struck him with. I used as much of the lamp's electrical cord as possible to bind his feet.

He had been out for a little more than 30 seconds and time was ticking away fast. For one or two seconds, I considered leaving him unconscious, hog-tied, face down on the floor but decided I'd risk moving him with what little time I had left.

I hauled him up to a wall and partially sat him up.

Still facing him, I stepped back and pulled out my gun just as his head suddenly snapped up and his eyes fluttered open as he took a huge gasp of air. He tried to move and quickly realized that he was tied. He looked up at me, anger burning in his dark brown eyes, as his brain suddenly filled his mind with his last conscious thoughts before he blacked out — he was fighting me.

In a voice loud enough for him to hear and understand, I said, "If you move a muscle, I'll shoot you dead and throw your ass down the stairs. I . . . will . . . kill . . . you, and claim it was self-defense."

Still gasping for air and struggling to get his hands free, his eyes settled on my gun and then he stopped moving.

"Before I call the cops, we're going to have a little talk," I said, my gun pointed directly at his body. I was breathing heavily, but the aim was steady. "Your brother came to my office and threatened me and my secretary. I showed him restraint. I only shot him in the leg. He'll walk again. But . . . YOU . . .

came here for my girlfriend. To harm her. The . . . woman . . . I . . . love."

I intended to drive the point home.

"Look into my eyes. Right now. Look. I will not show you the same restraint. If you don't tell me what I want to know, I'll kill you. Right here. Right now. I promise you that."

I raised the gun and pointed it between his eyes. Gone now was the defiance, replaced with worry and the fear of death.

"I'm glad I have your attention. Now we talk. Who hired you?"

~*~

"You're a magnet for trouble, aren't you, Blaise? Why is it that I get a call all the time involving you?" said Thompson, who was still wearing the clothes for his court appearance. I was sitting in the living room on an old sofa with bad springs and the man was sitting on the floor just inside the front door, his hands cuffed behind his back.

"You're just lucky or cursed, would be my guess," Gregory said to his partner.

"Let me see if I have this straight. You came to pick up some clothes for someone," said Thompson, notebook in hand.

"Yes, Marie. I didn't want her staying here alone with the likes of him out there. She's gonna stay somewhere else for a few nights or until this all gets sorted out," I said.

"Marie. Your '*girlfriend*,'" Gregory remarked in a snarky way, and using his fingers to make quote marks. "We met her last year . . . at the end of one of your escapades, right?"

Was there no end to his condescension?

"You like putting your friends in harm's way?" he asked.

I barely managed not to take the bait.

"Where is she now and where will she be staying?" Thompson said. I looked at him with a questioning expression, then back over to the assailant against the wall. "Never mind,"

Thompson said.

"When you arrived, you found this man. . . ," Gregory said, stopping to check his notes, "Bradley Floyd, according to his ID . . . Floyd was in her room, going through her things. That right?"

"That captures the essence."

"And you attacked him?" Thompson asked.

"No, he first attacked me. I fought back."

"And you got the upper hand in hand-to-hand combat," Thompson said.

"Again, that captures the essence."

Gregory walked over to stand next to Floyd, who was being guarded by uniformed officers. "He claims you tried to strangle him to death and then threatened to shoot and kill him."

I looked up at Gregory, never a person I cared for. But his tone and body movement told me he wouldn't have been bothered if I had succeeded. "He's still alive, isn't he?" I said.

Gregory grunted. Was that a bit of admiration I saw? "Let's get him out of here," he said to the officers.

"Marie wasn't here and she's all right?" asked Thompson.

"She's fine and doesn't know anything about this," I said.

Thompson flipped his notebook closed. "Thanks for the pictures today. We'll be looking into that situation."

"Thanks."

"Seems this perp is related to the guy you put in the hospital with a hole in his knee," he said. "We'll put the squeeze on Bradley to get to the bottom of things. But the Feds are really gonna wanta talk to you. In depth. Hope you're ready for that."

Thompson departed and left me to contemplate the fact that I had been ready to kill that man with my bare hands, if need be. It wasn't as hard a reality to accept as I might have thought.

Using the list Marie had given me, I gathered the things she wanted and packed them in an overnight bag. I straightened a little in Marie's room and closed her door, and made sure the downstairs door was secure. Then I dropped off Marie's bag at Raymond's house before heading back to my office on the west side.

Mae rose from her desk and rushed over to hug me when I walked in. I wasn't sure which nearly overwhelmed me — the hug or her perfume.

"You okay?"

I exited her embrace before the scent could give me a headache. "I'm fine. They have the guy and took him downtown."

Mae blinked several times quickly and I noticed her eyes were red and she appeared puzzled.

"What guy?" she asked.

Now I was puzzled but then remembered she did not yet know about my most recent confrontation with a killer. "I went to Marie's place to gather some clothes for her. When I got there, a guy was already there searching her room. When he saw me, he attacked me."

Astonished, she said, "Oh, David. Are you okay? What happened? You didn't . . . kill him, did you?"

That made me smile. I did not, however, want to go into great detail about the fight. "No. But I was able to subdue him until the police arrived." It was then that it occurred to me that Mae had been crying before I arrived in the office and told her about the fight at Marie's place.

"Mae, are you okay?"

She went to a chair near a filing cabinet and sat. A despair I had never seen in her before seem to cover her like a shroud. I went over and kneeled in front of her. And I asked again, “Mae, are you okay?”

She looked tired when her eyes met mine.

“I guess you haven’t heard,” she said, holding her emotions in check as much as possible.

“Heard what?” I tried to keep worry at bay.

“It’s all on da radio. I thought you listened to KYW. The guy I told you about. The guy who called me and threatened me. Mr. Charlie. He was shot and killed downtown today in broad daylight.”

I stood as a flood of questions filled my brain and I tried to focus on what I needed to know most. Looking down at Mae, I started with confirmation.

“Are you sure?”

Mae rubbed her forehead with her left hand as if doing so would fight back a forming migraine. She didn’t immediately look up at first when she answered.

“I had the news on, listenin’ to KYW. It was background noise while I was workin’,” she said. “They was just reportin’ on a shootin’ downtown in Center City. In broad daylight.”

“Okay,” I said, not wanting to distract her but needing for her to get to the specifics. “What else?”

“Shootin’s don’t happen much in Center City but I still didn’t think much ’bout it,” she continued. “But then Rita called me. Here in the office.”

The mention of Rita raised the hair on my arms as I worked to come to terms with what Mae might tell me next. “Rita? Is she okay?”

Mae didn’t answer the question directly. “She say Mr. Charlie came in today and saw one of the girls. He stay the normal time.” Mae stopped, as if to gather the nerve to finish. “She say after he was gone, right after that, she heard shots outside, at the corner. She say she knows she shouldn’t be lookin' outside but she went to the door to look out and saw Mr. Charlie on the ground, bleedin' bad."

I turned on the radio and dialed the AM station to 1060 KYW. It was just at the bottom of the hour and the Center City shooting was the top story.

Mae and I stood, staring at the radio on a cabinet as if doing so would somehow entice more details from the reporter.

According to the reporter, witnesses said the older Black man had just reached a corner when another man, a nondescript white man, approached him. The men spoke briefly before the older guy started to back away and the assailant pulled out a gun and shot him several times, including after the victim was on the ground.

The assailant then turned, pushed several startled people out of the way and headed to the stairs to the subway, where he ran down and disappeared.

When police arrived at the scene, they checked the victim, but he died before medical assistance arrived.

"The name of the victim is being withheld pending notification of the next of kin. The police investigation into the shooting is ongoing. Christopher Clark reporting from the scene for KYW News radio."

I sat down in the nearest chair, looked up at Mae standing close by, and asked the question she had already confirmed. "Rita is sure the victim was Charles Pennypacker?"

"Yes. She say it was Mr. Charlie."

I considered what this all meant.

Pennypacker was a direct link between the fencing operation and the search for The Jade Empress. Whoever was running things must have decided to cut their losses, and I had to find that person. That necessity was becoming more urgent by the minute.

I got up and headed to my office. Mae, having regained her composure, was on my heels. "What's our next move?"

That brought a smile to my face but she was right. We were a team. It would be "our" move.

"The guy in Marie's apartment was named Bradley Floyd and he's the brother of the guy who came to the office."

"The guy you shot?" Mae said with a comical smile.

"Yes, well, anyway, Bradley and Benjamin Floyd are local thugs with some serious connections. Bradley told me that Mr. Charlie, whose real name is Charles Pennypacker, was under extreme pressure and that he had to recover the necklace soon, or there'd be hell to pay. And now, it appears, he was right. He paid with his life," I said.

Mae nodded.

"I've been just reacting to what's been happening but that's going to change, right now," I said. "I'm going on the offense. I want some answers and I know where to start."

I walked around my desk but didn't sit down before I picked up the telephone. I didn't dial anything, just listened to the dial tone for a couple of heartbeats, and then spoke into the mouthpiece.

"I know you're there, listening. If you want to know where The Jade Empress might be, meet me tonight at Mont Serrat, the restaurant on South Street just below 7th. Eight o'clock. This is your only opportunity, so don't be late. And bring your credit card. You're paying for dinner."

With that, I hung up.

"You can go home, Mae. I'll fill you in in the morning."
She shook her head. "I can stay. I'd like to wait and see what happens next. We're a team."

CHAPTER XXII

"Don't forget to leave a good tip."

"That was a stupid move, Blaise," De Luca said just after he sat down. A waitress came past but he waved her away.

"And you're an ass, ANGIE," I said, pointedly. "You thought I wouldn't figure out you were bugging me? The cops have no reason to, so it had to be you. And it was too heavy-handed."

The site was neutral ground, unlike during our last encounter in his office. I arrived at the restaurant first and picked a table near the back and took the seat facing the front, meaning De Luca's back would be toward the front door. Knowing his desire to control every situation, this might unnerve him, at least a little.

"On the phone, you said you knew something about The Jade Empress. I knew my source couldn't be wrong about you. He's too good and he's never wrong. So where is it?" he said. "Do you have it?"

"All in good time," I said, signaling for the waitress. I was stalling but didn't want to appear obvious. "Why don't we order a little something first? I don't know about you, but I'm hungry."

"Surely you didn't invite me here to waste my time," he said, and pressed his hands on the table as if to get up. But the sudden appearance of the waitress blocked him.

"She's waiting, Angie. What'll you have?"

He relented. "A bottle of water, still, not sparkling, and some fried mushrooms," he said to her. To me, he snapped, "Satisfied?"

"Quite. Now, let me see," I said, studying the menu as if for the first time, "Bring me a Coke and a house salad as an appetizer. Blue cheese dressing. On the side. We'll order a main course in a few minutes."

She took it all down and walked away.

"I told you I don't have the necklace and I don't. But I know where it is and I think . . . well, I'm pretty sure . . . I can get my hands on it quickly," I said. "There's just one . . . two, really . . . matters to resolve first."

I could hear his foot lightly tap the floor and stop. I wasn't sure if it was nervousness or impatience.

"What matters?" he said.

"Let's talk about my reward, or finder's fee, which is more appropriately what it is," I said.

"You're going to try a shakedown?"

"No, this is a negotiation. I have something you want and we both know you're willing to pay to get it. The question is: How much?" I said. The waitress returned and placed a glass with a brown soda in front of me and an empty glass next to a bottle of water in front of De Luca.

"A negotiation," he said, appraising me closely.

"You wouldn't expect anything less," I said calmly.

He opened the bottle and poured the entire contents into the glass, never taking his eyes off me. "Mr. Blaise, you're an amateur playing with professionals. There are seriously dangerous people out there. This is an adult game, and a deadly one, too. You should get out before you get yourself hurt . . . or someone else hurt, someone you care about."

"Are you threatening me, Angie?" His eyebrow twitched each time I call him Angie. I was getting under his skin.

Good.

"I never threaten. I act. It's just a word to the wise. Be careful."

"Word taken," I said, sipping the Coke. "Now, back to business."

I told him I had researched The Jade Empress and knew it was valuable and that his client, the person paying him to recover it, wasn't the true owner.

The appetizers arrived but we didn't order dinner yet. I took a fork and stabbed my salad. Angelo didn't touch the mushrooms.

"How much are you getting paid for procuring it, huh? Must be a lot . . . for a Big Time operator like you," I said between bites. Pointing the prongs of my fork at his bowl of mushrooms, "You better get started on those before they get cold. Or maybe you're just going to take home some leftovers for Mrs. Angie."

"Damnit, Blaise. What do you want?" he said, pounding the table, drawing attention to us.

"Shhh. Quiet down, quiet down," I said and waited until the people at nearby tables went back to what they were doing. "I know you have expenses. It costs a lot to cover all your bets. There's the Floyd brothers. You covering Ben's hospital bills? Doesn't matter. I have a source, a retired police detective who still has contacts, who says the Floyds are the West Philadelphia muscle for a South Philadelphia mobster. After all, can't have white Italian South Philly guys coming into a Black area and busting heads without the authorities noticing. You still with me?"

De Luca didn't say anything but hung on my words.

"They're connected with Mario 'Pearly Whites' Martino, who got popped last week inside Rubinstein's jewelry store. And as you know from reading the papers, the body of his partner, Joey 'Buttons,' was found in the trunk of a car in South Jersey two days later. He was wounded in the jewelry store but what killed him was a single gunshot to the back of the head. Difficult to survive an execution-style shot like that.

"And, of course, Joey Buttons is tied back to you. Off the books, of course," I said, stretching what I actually knew but knowing it made sense.

I waited. Nothing came. He didn't breathe a word. Probably for the best, so I continued.

"Anyway, this is the deal. I want one-fifty for the necklace."

"Thousand?" He almost spit out the water he was drinking.

"You got it. One-hundred-fifty big ones. And you leave me and anyone connected to me alone. That's the deal."

"You're insane." And now he was genuinely smiling. "No one would ever pay you that much for that necklace."

I considered my negotiating position. "Maybe, but I'm guessing, given the effort and expense you've expended so far, your client is willing to spend more than the fifty-thou I'll have in my hands tomorrow after I call the attorney for William Powell's estate and hand it over to them."

The smile disappeared. Now we were getting down to business.

"Sixty-five thousand."

I shook my head no. "Better but not close. One-twenty-five."

"You . . . are . . . insane," he said again, stressing each word. He looked down at the mushrooms, took one and popped it in his mouth and chewed. "Seventy-five."

"How badly do you want the necklace? Obviously, not badly enough because I know I can get fifty legit for it, and probably more than that if I fenced it through someone other than you. I know there's other people who want it. A good source told me it's the most sought after piece of jewelry in the country right now. But I'm willing to do business with you. One-hundred thousand dollars and that's my last offer or I walk."

"It may be difficult to come up with that sort of cash quickly."

"Then it's a deal?"

He cracked his knuckles. I imagined he wanted to crack me in the same way. "I have to talk to my guy first . . . but I think we can swing that."

I sat back. "Good. But I have to hear from you in the morning or there's no deal. I'll call Powell's widow at noon."

He started to get up but I stopped him.

"You forgot. Part of the deal is that you leave me, my family and my friends alone. If anyone as much as gets a hangnail, I have an insurance policy. And I will flush you down the toilet. I mean it."

"Insurance? I don't give a flyin' fuck about your damned insurance," he said viciously. "You wanta know who thought he had an insurance policy for protection? That nigger Amtrak porter. Surely, you've heard what's happened to him? Same could happen to you. At any time."

I kept my tone straight and serious. "It's you who should be worried if we don't have a deal."

"You gonna shoot me?" he said with a snide expression. "You ain't got the nuts for that, Blaise, and we both know it."

"I was an intelligence officer in our military and was stationed in the Middle East. I recruited agents and sent men into situations I knew they weren't likely to return from. I know death. It's best that you don't test me on this," I said, getting up and dropping my napkin on the table. "Thanks for the salad and Coke. Don't forget to leave a good tip."

~*~

It wasn't late yet and I walked a block-and-a-half east on South Street until I reached the used bookstore on the corner at Fifth. I went in and browsed in the mystery section.

I love mysteries. If only I had more time to read them.

The classic writers of the genre, Hammett, Chandler, Christie, even Conan Doyle, are all great reads but I found myself more recently drawn to Chester Himes, whose African American characters and locations speak to me in ways many of the white authors do not. After all, who couldn't love a writer who created characters like Coffin Ed Johnson and Grave Digger Jones?

The mystery section in the bookstore, however, served an additional purpose. It was over to the side and toward the back of the store, and provided a perfect peek out the front window. Yet, the view from the street into that section of the store was somewhat limited.

As I looked out the front window, I saw Freddie the Pickpocket loitering across the street crowded with passersby. It was the perfect location for petty crime.

I busied myself checking out book titles on the shelf but kept a watchful eye on Freddie, who wore what I assumed was his favorite outfit for his work — a loose-fitting dark jacket, black pants with extra pockets, and soft-soled black sneakers.

I picked up a book, an old noir classic mystery by Dashiell Hammett, and flipped through casually, then looked up again at Freddie.

Stealthy, unobtrusive, and extraordinarily observant, Freddie took a quick glance at people as they passed. Must have been how he chose his targets and successfully picked so many pockets. His casual intensity was a pleasure to watch because his observation skills were so keen.

Until recently, when I became too busy, I had a contract with the city transit authority to patrol stops on the Broad Street subway to keep an eye out for people like Freddie. On a platform at the Pattison subway stop in South Philly is where I first encountered him. He was picking the pockets of fans headed to a Sixers game.

Some fifteen minutes after I entered the bookstore, Freddie crossed the street and wandered in. I moved over to the end of a long bookshelf, so that no one from the outside could see me.

"De Luca came with only one guy, a driver, who stayed outside the restaurant. He didn't have any other backup. Neither of them followed you here," Freddie said.

"And?"

Freddie pulled a book off the shelf and opened it, as if looking inside. "Placed it under the right front bumper. It's on and it's working." He put the book back and continued talking. "She's amazing, you know. Mae, your secretary. Just amazing. Dressed up like that, she had him totally distracted while I placed it."

"He didn't go with her, did he?" I asked.

"Stop worrying. That was never part of the plan. She did her part and I did mine. That's it."

CHAPTER XXIII

C. Jonathan Morton-Brown. Blue blood.
Old Philadelphia money. The idle rich.

The tracking device has a considerable range and so I waited a short time before slipping out a side door. Freddie met me at my car and we switched on the tracker. The *beep, beep, beep* was strong, though fading, and indicated he was heading through the city and toward the Schuylkill Expressway. He exited the expressway at City Line and ultimately turned toward Montgomery County. I drove, with Freddie giving me turn-by-turn instructions.

There were several false turns but we ultimately followed the signal into Wynnewood, the home of the wealthy. The signal was the loudest when we reached a large, well-lit, brick and stone multi-story house with sweeping lawns and mature trees on roughly five acres. It had a circular driveway, and De Luca's car was directly in front of the door. It seemed like every light in the house was on, although I detected no movement inside when we passed.

A way up, the street curved and had a wooded area on the left next to another large house. We drove until we were out of sight of De Luca's car and then turned the car around and switched off the lights. I parked near the wooded area. With difficulty, we could still see the house through the trees and the leaves.

Thank goodness it was dark out.

"When I saw him enter the restaurant, I could have picked his pockets," Freddie said. "For a man in his position, he was very personally vulnerable. He was begging to be a victim."

"I'm glad you showed some restraint," I said into the darkness. "If you want, put on some music while we wait. But it's been a long day for me. I'm going to close my eyes for a few."

I leaned back and closed my eyes and thought about Marie.

My eyes almost immediately snapped open when Freddie's voice pierced the darkness. "He's leaving."

I glanced at the digital clock on the dashboard as I pulled my seat back into an upright position. I was shocked. I had been asleep for thirty minutes.

Giving him a chance to get out of sight before we started, I fired the engine and drove slowly past the house again, making sure we got the correct address.

"First thing tomorrow, we need to find out who lives in that house."

"You think it's related to the necklace?" Freddie asked.

"Probably. Makes sense. I made him an offer and he said he'd have to check with someone about the price. He knows I need an answer fast. And clearly, it's not the sort of thing he'd want to discuss over the phone."

~*~

I was pouring a bowl of cereal in my kitchen before heading up to bed when the telephone rang. It was Marie.

"How did it go?" she asked.

"Quite well, I think. Should be over soon," I answered.

"Are you safe?"

"For the moment, yes. At least I think so. I have something he wants and he knows he'll never get it if he hurts me," I said, though I didn't voice what De Luca was likely to try to do to me once he had what he wanted.

Marie either hadn't thought that far ahead or didn't want to.

"I have some good news for you, though," she said with

a burst of sudden excitement. "After everything calmed down, my housemate gave me a note that said to call Willi Smith's assistant when I get in. Said to call at any time. Before I headed over here with Allen, I called and got her. They want to hire me, AND because he's moving some of his operation here, she wanted to know if I was interested in working out of Philadelphia. David, do you know what that means? I won't have to move to New York this summer."

"Congratulations. That's excellent news, Marie."

"He's opening a small design studio here for a new line of men's sportswear. It's what I'll be working on," she said. "I'll still have to travel up to Manhattan on a regular basis . . . at least a couple of days every month . . . but I'll be based here and working here most of the time."

"I always hoped everything would work out in the end," I said, and meant it. "I want you in my life. I need you in my life. But I wouldn't want to stand the way of a great opportunity for you."

"I wanted things to work out, too," she said. "I love you."

"I love you, too," I said. I paused and smiled as an amusing thought raced through my mind. "Since I'm going to be the Best Man, maybe Mr. Smith will design a tuxedo for me to wear to the wedding," I joked. "Like with Caroline Kennedy."

"You can't afford Willi Smith." She said, but then added, "But. . . ."

"I was only playing, Marie," I corrected. "It was a joke."

"I know. I know. I got that," she said. "But you could afford one of his newly acquired apprentices."

"Really? You'd do that? For me?" I said, getting serious.

"Of course I would. I'd have to measure you to get your precise body measurements to get the right fit. I could see if they'll let me use one of their shops to do the work. On my own time, of course."

"They would let you do that?"

"I'm sure they would. Besides, there'd be no harm in asking. After all, Willi Smith was quite taken by the necklace you gave me. You genuinely impressed him."

"You'll be my Plus-one, of course," I said. "That goes without saying."

"I'll make sure to bring a heavy purse to beat off all the hot babes who'll be after you once they see you in the new tux I'll design."

At that, we both laughed. It felt good after a long day.

~*~

I slept well, though it was with my gun beside the bed. I knew I could trust De Luca to an extent but there was still a limit. I had mapped out my morning the night before but things took a turn for the worse as I was leaving the house. Two large, dark sedans pulled up behind my garage. I calmly turned around and headed back into the house, locking the door, and heading for the front. When I opened it, two men in dark suits were standing there. And behind them was FBI Special Agent Darcy Hayes.

"Let's talk," she said.

The trip down to the federal building downtown where the FBI office is located was uneventful. They took my gun, of course, but I wasn't cuffed for the ride in the back seat with another agent beside me. There wasn't any chit-chat, either. It was all business-like.

We entered the garage through an underground entrance on 8th and parked in a space near the elevator. The ride up was also in silence. I didn't know what they wanted, but Thompson had warned me they'd want something.

I was ushered into a conference room that looked out toward Independence Mall. On the paneled wall was a seal for the Department of Justice and a framed picture of Ronald Reagan. I didn't vote for him in 1980 nor two years ago in 1984. I tend to ignore his picture when I see it.

I was alone for a moment until Hayes walked in holding a

file in one hand and a cup of coffee in the other. The file landed with a splat on the table and Hayes was about to sit when she looked at me.

"Did anyone offer you any coffee?"

"No, they didn't."

"There's a pot right outside the door. The cups are to the right."

I went out for a cup of coffee and returned to the room, stirring the brew as I sat down again. "Why am I here?"

"Because you lied to me when we first met. Or at the very least, you omitted some information," she said. "From the picture you gave me, I knew you might have some knowledge or involvement in a major merchandising fencing operation we're investigating. But now it appears there's more.

"It's recently come to my attention that you were involved in a fatal shooting at a store on Jeweler's Row about thirty minutes after we first spoke in the park. That store is the focus of an on-going investigation here at The Bureau. And it appears you were there when it occurred or right afterwards and then fled the scene."

You can't lie to federal law enforcement. It's a felony. I could lose my license. I wasn't going to do that.

"I was there."

"Why did you flee?"

"I really didn't know anything, and I thought you'd get everything you needed from the owner and his sons."

"I could hold you as an accessory to a crime," she said, brushing her hair off her face.

"You've had several days to do that and you haven't," I said. "What is it you really want to know?"

"What is your connection to the illegal fencing operation we've been investigating this year? You must know something. You gave me the picture you took of me in Fairmount Park during a sting operation to get to the bottom of who's behind it."

I stared at her for a moment. Dumbfounded. But the pieces of the puzzle were coming together.

"I was in the park on behalf of a retail client here in the city. They believed someone . . . an employee . . . was stealing merchandise and selling it," I said, looking at my coffee before taking a sip. It was getting cold. "I just happened to be in the jewelry store on Sansom when two guys walked in with guns."

"That's quite a story, Mr. Blaise."

"It's true," I said, hoping to reassure her. "They appeared interested in the younger son of the owner. As the shorter of the two assailants was about to turn violent, shots were fired from the back of the store. The shorter assailant was hit badly and the other man was hit in the back . . . likely in the leg . . . but he escaped. The older son of the owner, who was holding a gun, told me to get out, so I got out. End of story."

"Detective Thompson, your friend in the Philly police department, tells us you draw a lot of trouble," Hayes said. "I hope you aren't lying to me. Or that you aren't in over your head."

She closed the file. I thought the meeting was over but I was wrong.

"I have one more question," she said, reaching behind her for that day's copy of the Philadelphia Inquirer. The top story shocked me, which was the point. It was a story of the shooting death the previous night of Joseph Rubinstein in an alley behind the store. "Where were you yesterday afternoon at around five?"

"You're kidding me, right? You know where I was."

"I know where you were when the police responded to the call at the home of Marie Toussaint. Your girlfriend. The one you just stated you were thinking of buying a gift for," Hayes said. "We checked, and the timing is about right. You had time to stop by Rubinstein's store and shoot him before you went to your girlfriend's house."

"And do you believe that?" I said.

"Doesn't matter much what I believe. It's what the facts will reveal," she said.

"I doubt they'll reveal I was involved in his death. Otherwise, we wouldn't be sitting here casually talking over cups of cold coffee."

Hayes said nothing for what seemed hours but was only a few seconds, then stood, as did I.

"Don't leave town, Mr. Blaise. I'm sure we'll have more questions."

I flagged down a cab on Market Street and rode home to get my car. With Rubinstein's murder, I needed to take a more aggressive approach to that case. But I couldn't risk talking on my phone at home or work. I considered heading to Grammy Taylor's house but didn't want to put her at risk. Plus, her phone could be bugged, too.

I knew where I'd go. It offered a degree of privacy but was public enough to provide some protection, as well. If only I could use the phone.

The bar was on 13th Street, just north of City Hall. I knew the bartender, who seemed to work all day and all night.

"Imanu, how's it going?" I asked as I walked in. Being early in the day, well before lunchtime, the place was mostly empty. He was keeping himself busy behind the bar but was ready in case a customer entered.

"Well, David Blaise. It's good."

I walked up and took a stool. I looked around and saw only one other person in the place — a guy nursing a beer alone in one of the booths. I took a twenty out of my wallet and slid it across the bar to him. "I need to use the phone in back, in private."

He looked at the money and back to me, then discreetly took it, putting it into his pants pocket. "How long?"

"Just a couple of calls. Not long, I don't think. I won't tie up the line."

He nodded his head to the right for me to follow him to the end of the bar and then toward the back. "No long-distance calling."

"Of course not. All local," I said.

He said nothing and I went into the small, crowded office. The desk with the telephone held stacks of papers — invoices, payments, inventory sheets. It was a wonder anyone got anything done back there.

I took the phone and first dialed the office.

"Mae, it's David."

"Are you okay, boss? The phone's been ringing off the hook this morning."

"Yeah, I'm good. Who called? And only the really important ones right now. I don't have a lot of time."

"Angelo De Luca asked you to return his call ASAP."

I'll bet he did, I thought to myself.

"Now listen to me, Mae. I'm going to be away from the office a little today, so I need you to hold down the fort. I'll call and check in when I have the chance."

"Okay, boss, but how will I reach you?"

"I'll just check back with you. But I have got to go now." And before she could say another word, I hung up.

It took me a couple of calls before I learned who lived in that Wynnewood mansion. It was C. Jonathan Morton-Brown. Blue blood. Old Philadelphia money dating back nearly two hundred years. The idle rich.

It took a few more calls before I learned he currently headed the Film, TV and Entertainment Office of Philadelphia, which worked with film and television production companies wanting to work in the Philadelphia area. But more importantly, he had one of the largest private collections of Hollywood film memorabilia in the country.

Jackpot!

It was going to take some doing, but I knew what my next move would be.

CHAPTER XXIV

"He told me no one would get hurt." "He lied."

The film office wasn't downtown, as I expected, but was located in a building near the Penn campus on the west side. I parked on 34th Street, near Locust, and walked the two blocks to the office.

For an enterprise with little city or state funding, the Philadelphia film office had very comfortable digs. It looked like what I imagined the office of a top Hollywood producer would look like. The walls were painted a muted red and were covered with numerous posters of movies or television shows shot in or around Philadelphia. Oddly, there was one movie poster directly behind the reception desk for a film that wasn't shot in Philadelphia but fit both the office and undoubtedly the personal tastes of Morton-Brown.

In the center of the color poster, set against a red background roughly the same color as the office's walls, was Katharine Hepburn, with Cary Grant kissing her right cheek and James Stewart kissing the left. It was the quintessential movie about the city's idle rich — *The Philadelphia Story*.

Before I arrived at the office, I had contemplated how to play this, and I had decided to lie. Couldn't let him know too much too soon. I rehearsed the story in my head once more as I approached the receptionist.

I hoped I had dressed the part.

"Hi. Brandon Alderson. I'm a film producer from New York," I said in just a slightly effeminate way. "I hate to just drop in on you like this but I was in the area and just fell in love with so many locations in Philly. And I thought, this is where I need to shoot my next picture. So, if it's not too much of a bother, is Mr. Morton-Brown in?"

"It's no bother at all," said the pretty receptionist, probably a film major somewhere. "But he's not in at the moment. He's on location on a shoot. But if you don't mind, I could take your number and have him call you as soon as he gets in. I know he'd love to talk to you. You have a business card on you?"

"Aren't you such a precious thing?" I said as I patted myself down. "Oh! I think I must have left my cards behind."

"It's no problem. I'll just take your name."

"It's Brandon Alderson. And let me give you my office and home numbers." I rattled off a couple of random numbers with New York area codes. "I'll be going. Oh, by the way, what's shooting in Philadelphia at the moment? I loved *Witness* with Harrison Ford last year. Breathtaking."

She batted her eyes a little and said, "I know I shouldn't tell you this, but they're shooting scenes for a sequel to the George Washington mini-series we had two years ago. They're on location down in Society Hill. On Pine, near 7th. That's where everyone is."

"Why, thank you, darlin'," I said and headed out before she realized what she'd just told me.

Traffic on eastbound Pine Street was backed up west to Broad because the street was closed from 8th down to 6th because of the filming. I went over to South Street and headed down, and the only open parking space I could find was near 10th. I fed the meter enough change for two hours and walked the half mile to the film set.

They were shooting an exterior scene, and I was amazed how they were able to cover most of the street with dirt, hide the curbing and make the townhouses appear to be from the eighteenth century. It perhaps wasn't that difficult. Most of the houses in the area were more than one hundred and fifty years old.

I walked to the nearest person who seemed associated with the shoot. She was a thin young woman in jeans, and carried ID around her neck.

"I'm from the city and I was told Jonathan Morton-Brown from the film office was here on the set today. Can you show me where?"

"I don't really know him, but you can try one of the production assistants up there," she said, pointing to a small gaggle of people milling around.

"Thanks," I said and headed off.

A PA told me Morton-Brown was talking to the film's director and executive producer in one of the production trailers while the next shot was being set up. I walked over to the trailer, knocked once, then opened the door and stuck my head in.

Three men were standing behind a table with a TV monitor, watching a replay of something that had already been shot. Two of them were casually dressed, one was in a gray suit and a tie.

The film director was a familiar face, though I didn't recall the name.

"May we help you?" asked a man I didn't recognize, but I assumed was the producer. And then there was Jonathan Morton-Brown, the man in the suit and tie.

A distinguished man, he was about fifty, with a full head of gray hair. The thickness of his body was partially hidden by his well-tailored gray suit. He wore a shirt that Marie would describe as robin's egg blue, with a white collar and cuffs. His silver cuff links matched the tie pin in his red tie. His attire was meant to display his taste, wealth, and power.

"I'm Irving Washington from downtown and was sent here to have a word with Mr. Morton-Brown."

"And this can't wait? What's this about? We're in a middle of something, here," he said in a voice with a pitch that was higher than I expected.

I stepped inside and the door closed with a click. The other two men, though silent, appeared to support Morton-Brown. "I'm sorry," I said, "but it's private."

All three men looked confused and I moved closer, reaching into my jacket and pulling out an envelope and handing it to Morton-Brown. He opened it, pulled out a paper, and looked at it. His skin, which was already a pale white, turned whiter, and his gray eyes widened. But he put the paper back into the envelope and managed to recover a bit of his dignity.

"Uh, gentlemen, you will have to excuse me while I handle this urgent matter. I shouldn't be long," he said. Then he and I stepped outside. He directed me away from the set and onto a closed side street.

As we walked, he held the envelope tightly in his hand, as if to let it go would release its secret. "Who are you and where did you get this?" he said, holding it up higher so that it was near eye level. "And why should I care?"

"Come, now. It's obvious, isn't it? That's a picture of The Jade Empress beside a copy of today's Daily News," I said. "And as for me, I'm sure De Luca told you about me last night during a meeting he held at your house in Wynnewood."

He stopped walking and became so unsteady that, for an instant, I thought he was going to fall to his knees.

"You don't have to say anything. Let's just keep walking," I said.

When we were once again on our way, he regained use of his vocal cords. "What do you want from me?"

"I want to cut a deal directly with you. There's no need for a middleman like De Luca. And given that people he's worked with keep showing up dead. . . ," I said. Morton-Brown stopped again. "That guy killed last night in back of the jewelry store. Rubinstein's. That was De Luca's doing. And that kid, Kareem Adams, who was wanted in the killing of Mary Ann Tolk in Center City. Police said Adams overdosed. But they're wrong. That, too, is De Luca's doing. It's all connected to a fencing operation that De Luca controls."

"He told me no one would get hurt."

I nearly laughed because the statement was so naïve. Surely he wasn't deluding himself to the point where he believed that.

"He lied," I said, getting him moving again. "Now, as I was saying, since people connected with De Luca keep showing up dead, I think I'd rather deal with you. I can get you the piece if you can get me the money. Otherwise, I'll return it to its rightful owner, the estate of the late actor William Powell."

"The entire one hundred fifty thousand dollars? I told Angelo last night to inform . . . you . . . that I'd need a little time to get that much together," Morton-Brown said. We had reached a shiny black Mercedes.

Hmm. Angie apparently planned to skim fifty-thou off the top.

"Okay, then. If we have a deal, I'll give you extra time. Otherwise, I go to the Powell estate attorney," I said, sounding as menacing as I could. "And don't talk to anyone about this . . . and I mean anyone. Or you won't get the necklace and you'll be very, very sorry. I'll call you later today with the details for the exchange."

I slapped him hard on the back and left him standing next to the Mercedes.

I rushed back to my Honda and put some distance between me and the movie set as quickly as possible. I assumed Morton-Brown would call De Luca. After all, the High Society man wasn't used to dealing with a low-life like me. He would leave that to the likes of De Luca. And while De Luca was a concern, he wouldn't be a big problem if he couldn't find me. And I planned to be scarce, at least until I called back to make the drop, which was going to take some planning.

CHAPTER XXV

"You didn't see this coming?"

I generally have a fit body, but part of that is genetics — my dad was thin — and part is a regular exercise routine. Battling both was my grandmother's cake. She made a delicious lemon cake with lemon icing that was to die for and I was in desperate need of cake and the company of my grandmother.

No one was there except Grammy when I arrived. Though, somewhat conspicuously, a police patrol car was parked outside near the front of the house, thanks to Mr. Dennis and his contacts in the department.

I think I like this guy.

It was much too late for lunch and much too early for dinner. My brother and his wife were at work. But that was okay. I loved time alone with my grandmother.

I sat on a little step ladder, which my tiny grandmother needed to reach the cabinets, holding a plate with a large slice of cake in one hand and a fork in the other, as she busied herself with kitchen housework. A glass of milk was on the counter nearby. She was wiping down the stove, having finished cleaning out the fridge.

The cake, of course, was moist and each bite melted in my mouth. It was like a dream of what dessert must be like in heaven.

Once she was finished, she turned to face me. And what she said next caught me totally off guard. "You and your friend Marie. When are you two going to get married?"

I suddenly couldn't swallow and nearly dropped the plate. Reaching for the milk, I gulped some and put the glass back.

"Grammy, it's not that simple," I started.

She stopped wiping the stove and came to stand beside me. With me sitting on the little step ladder, we were at nearly the same eye level. But in reality, she definitely held the superior ground.

"What's not simple? You love her, don't you? She loves you, doesn't she?" I nodded yes to both questions. "Then it's simple. You get married."

"But Grammy," I said, getting up. She looked at me in a way that made me sit back down. "It's not that simple. Our lives are not totally in sync right now. She's just finished school and she'll be starting a new job soon. And then there's my job. It takes a lot of hours. I barely have time enough just for myself."

She put down her cleaning rag and took off her yellow rubber gloves. "Your grandpa and I married when we were young and always lived here. It was a good life. A happy life."

She placed her hand on the side of my face. It was a tender moment. "You can go anywhere. Do anything. Don't close the door on love and happiness."

She went back to work without saying another word. I finished the cake, thanked her for the advice, and left.

~*~

There was still much to do, though I was tired. Getting caught up in a murder investigation can do that to you. I wanted to head straight to Raymond's house, take a hot shower, then jump into bed with Marie and watch late night television. But there were plans to be made for tomorrow. Sometimes, work seems unending, but not with the case of The Jade Empress. It was coming to an ending soon, and hopefully a happy and safe ending.

I had contacted a friend in the telephone company earlier in the day. It didn't take much to learn Morton-Brown's home telephone number, although it was unlisted. I didn't want a trace when I called him, so I used a payphone off the lobby of the hotel at 18th and Market streets. Still, I intended to give the instructions quickly and hang up.

"Mr. Morton-Brown, this is the man you spoke with earlier today on the movie set," I said.

"How did you find this number?"

"How I got the number is just as unimportant as how I found you to begin with. I have the number and the address, so can we move on?"

"Yes. I have your money."

"Okay, this is what we're going to do. I'll meet you tomorrow at noon in the production trailer on the movie set," I said.

"It's not my trailer," he said.

"Make it work. It's on a crowded movie set and, while our business dealings will be private, I want people around nearby in case there's a double-cross."

"There will be no double-cross."

"Then there shouldn't be a problem. I want the money in a blue canvas gym bag. Something people on the street won't take much notice of. And I'll give you the necklace in a small blue bag."

"I want to inspect the necklace before you leave," he said.

"And I'll look through the money, just so we're both on the level."

"I agree."

"But we do it quick. Understand? No monkey business." He said nothing in reply. "And, listen, it's only me and you. Nobody else. We do our business and I'm out of there and out of your hair in only minutes," I said. "But know, if you don't follow my instructions, there will be a lot of trouble for you. Got it?"

"Yes. I got it."

"Good. Bring the money, blue canvas bag, come alone and I'll see you at noon tomorrow."

~*~

Marie and I were at the bank at nine the next morning when it opened. After retrieving the Jade Empress from the safety deposit box, we put it in a small blue bag that Marie got once when she bought something at Tiffany's. Then we gathered together in Valerie's office. The door was closed.

"You sure you want to handle it this way, Davey?" asked my sister, concern in her eyes. I hugged her, forever grateful.

"It's the way it's got to be," I said, rubbing my hands together. Valerie sat in a chair beside the wall next to Marie. "It's going to be fine, ladies. I promise."

"There's no way you can possibly know that, David," Marie said. Her legs were crossed at the knees, making her appear calmer and more relaxed than she was. The nervous bobbing of her right foot betrayed that.

I was leaning with my butt up against Valerie's desk.

"We've talked about this. We talked it out last night. I go in at noon, do what I have to do, and I'm out. I call you by one. That's all there is."

It was a little after ten. Time to get moving.

"Let's go, Marie," I said and she got up, walking over to me and taking my hand.

"Where will you be?" Valerie asked Marie.

"Shopping around, trying to take my mind off things. I'll probably stay in Bonwit's most of the time, then come back over here at noon." She waved and we left the office.

For some reason, unless I'm working, I rarely notice security in the bank. But today I was working, so they seemed ever-present.

"Be careful, Boo," Marie said.

~*~

I got a pass to enter onto the set when I told the guard that I was there to meet the head of the city film office in the production trailer. Few people seemed to take notice of me as I walked through — most people were busily going about their jobs — and the few who did take note merely nodded as I passed. It was as if I somehow belonged there. I didn't see either the director or the executive producer, which was good. I wanted to get this over with quickly, and the fewer people involved, the better.

At precisely noon, I knocked on the production trailer door but didn't wait for a reply before opening it and entering. Morton-Brown, impeccably dressed as ever, was standing at the far end next to a blue gym bag. He looked anxious.

"I see you're on time," he said, reaching down to touch the bag as if to reassure himself of its presence. "Let me see the necklace."

I took the little bag out of my pocket and handed it to him. He opened it and took out the necklace. Holding it up, examining it, a joy came over him that was visible throughout his entire body. He was a kid on Christmas morning.

"Magnificent. Exquisite. More beautiful than I ever imagined," he said.

"Yeah, yeah, yeah. I'm in a hurry here. The money. Hand me the money."

Again, that anxious look.

I reached for the bag just as a door behind Morton-Brown opened and out stepped Angelo De Luca. Snatching the bag from my hand, he shoved me backward and I fell onto a couch along the wall. I tried to regain both my dignity and my balance as I tried to get up. But De Luca pushed me down again and opened the bag, dumping its contents onto my lap. It was nothing but paper cut to the size of dollar bills and bundled together.

"What is this? I said come alone."

"You didn't see this coming, Blaise? I warned you. I said this was a situation for professionals and you, sir, you are an amateur. And a stupid one. An idiot," he barked. "Look at you. You thought you could do an end-run around me with a private deal. You're an idiot. And you'll pay dearly for your stupidity. Get up."

I got up and he patted me down, taking my gun. He looked at it and laughed.

"Look at you. Walking in here without any backup, trying to make the Big Score," he said. He hadn't pulled out his gun yet but I got a glance of it on his hip. "It's no wonder little guys like you end up dead."

"You can't get away with this," I protested. "There are people outside. And I have an insurance plan in place in case of a double-cross."

"Ain't nobody worried about your fucking insurance," De Luca said, pushing me toward the door.

"I'm worried about it," Morton-Brown said. "What about me?"

"He's probably going to kill you, too," I said.

Morton-Brown's pale skin turned paler, as if all the blood in his body was being drained out. He was almost ghostly now in appearance.

"Shut the fuck up, the both of you," De Luca barked. To me, he said, "Balcombe should have killed you last year. You're only alive today by mistake. But it's a mistake that won't be repeated this year."

"Wait a minute," Morton-Brown said, taking De Luca's arm. "You said there wouldn't be any violence. You promised me last night."

"He lied. Again," I said.

"Don't be stupid like him," De Luca said, indicating me

as he faced Morton-Brown. "And don't you ever touch me again."

I held my ground and De Luca reached in and took out his gun. "How did you think it was going to go down once you told him I contacted you?" I said to Morton-Brown. "He's going to do to me what he did to Joseph Rubinstein."

"He double-crossed me so, of course, I had to kill him. And that Negro porter, too. They tried to work around me and fence something that wasn't theirs. They got what was coming to them," De Luca said, not taking his eyes off me.

"I didn't bargain on this," Morton-Brown said. He was then standing next to the man with a gun.

De Luca looked at him with such anger I thought he was about to shoot the man.

"Listen to me, Jon. You've got what you wanted and it hasn't cost you as much as you thought. Of course, I had to hurt some people to get it. I hurt people to get all that other stuff for you, like that Oscar from 1939. Do you think that came easy? Hell, no. But I got it, all that stuff you treasure so much down in your basement," De Luca said. "You go hang up your new pretty little piece and jerk off to all that other stuff I got for you that no one cares about. And let me handle this."

"Someone's expecting my call by one o'clock," I said as he pushed me toward the door.

"Miss Toussaint? Don't you worry about her. I'm having someone pick her up. And after that, you two will be together. Forever. In a landfill in New Jersey. Now, move," he said. "Don't try anything stupid. I've got the gun. My car is over on 8th Street. Head over that way. Slowly. I'll be right behind you with a gun pointed at your back."

I opened the door and paused briefly, squinting because of the sudden bright light from the sun. Then I walked down the four metal stairs, followed by both De Luca and Morton-Brown.

"FBI. FBI," several people shouted from different directions as a large group of people descended on us. "Hands up, hands up, and get on the ground,. On the ground. NOW. All of you. On the ground."

We were surrounded by armed officers in dark pants and blue jackets. It seemed like there were hundreds of guns, and all pointed at us. I sensed De Luca freeze for an instant, undecided, but then he was forced onto the ground.

He might kill people. But he didn't do the dirty deed himself.

"Hands behind your head."

My face on the ground and turned to the right, I saw a nice pair of women's shoes coming my way as the three of us were patted down, and arms forced to our backs.

"Help him up," Darcy Hayes said to the agent closest to me. When I was facing her, she said, "Well done, Mr. Blaise. Thompson said you could handle it."

Amidst the federal agents, I noticed Thompson and Gregory off to the side. And just beyond them was Mr. Dennis, beaming widely.

"Did you get it all?" I asked.

"Oh, yeah. We got it all," the film director said as he walked up. "Sound. On camera. Everything."

De Luca and Morton-Brown were handcuffed and pulled to their feet. One of the FBI agents pulled the bag with the necklace out of Morton-Brown's pocket.

"We have you on theft, possession of stolen merchandise, extortion, terroristic threats, kidnapping and murder," Hayes said to De Luca. "And, yeah, we got it all."

"Marie. Is she okay?" I asked.

"The same agents with you this morning at the bank stayed with her and haven't left her side. She's safe. You don't have to worry." Hayes said.

"I'll go call her now and let her know it worked out . . . and that I'm okay," I said.

"Sounds good," said Hayes. "You go do that."

As the FBI moved the two men away, I turned to De Luca. "And you didn't see this coming?"

~*~

Marie ran up and threw her arms around me as soon as I reached the bank. "Oh, thank God, you're okay. I was so worried," she said as she kissed my face.

Valerie, as well as Allen and Eli, both of whom had also arrived for some reason, came over and hugged me and patted my back.

"Well done, big brother," Allen said. "You make me proud."

"We're all proud," Eli said. And with a smile, he added, "When I grow up, I want to be just like you."

"You're already all grown up," I said, chuckling. "And are doing a great job with what you're already doing."

Eli gave me a light tap on my mid-section with the back of his hand. "You know what I mean, big brother. You get things done, bring order and justice to life." He paused briefly, looking down at his feet, then back up at me. "Just like when you went back to McDonald's and got me another cheeseburger when I was a kid."

We hugged again before I went over to sit down on a sofa. The last twenty-four hours had been exhausting. Marie came to sit next to me.

"How did you figure it all out?" Allen said.

"I knew Angelo De Luca was involved as soon as I talked to him and then learned my phones were bugged," I said, then looked up at Eli.

"But Kareem Adams's murder is what linked everything together. Kareem brought the necklace to Philly and, thus, he knew about the fencing operation. As long as he was cooperative, everything was okay," I said. "But his having a moral center created a problem, especially once he discovered the Council president's son was dealing drugs. By framing him in Mary Ann Tolk's death and then quickly killing him, it focused any attention related to Kareem on Tolk's case and away from The Jade Empress and De Luca's fencing operation."

"When will you know about the reward for the recovery of the necklace?" Valerie asked.

"I'm not sure. The FBI contacted the attorneys for the Powell estate for me last night to let them know that we had it and it would be in their custody today. The attorneys planned to send someone today to get it but I haven't heard yet about when it will be," I said. "And I'm sure there will be lots of paperwork involved."

"What will you do with all that money?" Eli asked.

"I don't know," I said as I reached for Marie's hand. "But half of it is Marie's anyway. I did give the necklace to her, after all."

"I know what I'll be doing with some of it. Paying on some student loans."

~*~

We were sitting in the living room of my grandmother's house when the local evening news came on.

The screen showed a white man and a black woman sitting behind a desk with a station logo in the background, which suddenly changed to a fast-moving graphic that said, "Breaking News."

"We are just getting new information on an arrest this morning of a prominent Philadelphia man on the set of the new George Washington movie being shot in Society Hill," the man said. "I'm Marc Howard of Action News."

"And I'm Lisa Thomas-Laury." She turned to her left as another camera focused entirely on her. "The FBI recovered a priceless piece of Hollywood history this afternoon when they arrested C. Jonathan Morton-Brown and another man on charges of having possession of a jade necklace that once belonged to the actress Jean Harlow.

"Morton-Brown, seen here being taken away in handcuffs, is the head of the Philadelphia film office. He and Angelo De Luca, also seen here, were arrested on the set of the new film. The pair are charged with theft, receiving stolen property, extortion and a host of other charges related to the case.

"The FBI says the necklace, known as The Jade Empress, was made in 1937 for the late actor William Powell who planned to give it to Harlow, his fiancé at the time. But she died before he was able to give it to her. Powell, who played Nick Charles in the famous Thin Man movie series in the thirties and forties, held on to the necklace until his death at age ninety-one two years ago. It was then supposed to be donated to charity but went missing last year and was thought to be stolen. FBI spokesman Benton Colfax."

The shot changed to show a man standing in front of the federal building with a couple of microphones being shoved into his face.

"We recovered the priceless necklace in an operation that took place on the movie set. We have contacted the rightful owners who are coming to get it. In addition to the theft and extortion charges, Angelo De Luca also faces murder, attempted murder and kidnapping charges related to the case," Colfax said. "Local police are also investigating his possible involvement in what was once considered the accidental overdose of Kareem Adams. Adams had been wanted in connection with the murder of a Center City woman last month."

The voice of an unseen reporter asked, "We heard there's a reward for the recovery of the necklace."

"Yes. The estate of William Powell offered a reward for the necklace's return. I'm not sure of the amount. You'll have to ask attorneys for the estate that question. At present, I'm unable to say who will get the reward, other than it's not to a federal employee. It's a private person."

The shot switched back to Howard and Thomas-Laury behind the desk. "Morton-Brown and De Luca, the head of a local security firm, are expected to be arraigned in the morning. Filming of the movie is set to resume tomorrow," she said.

CHAPTER XXVI

"She talked to me, too, last week."

Marie was glad to be back in her own bed and I was glad I knew she was safe. I was sitting on the bed, my back up against the headboard, as she went through her nightly preparations for sleep. She'd already taken her vitamins downstairs so now she was washing and pat-drying her face before moisturizing it. We had long since become comfortable with seeing the routine aspects of each other's daily life. She probably didn't give any thought to walking around in a worn, loosely fitting white sleeveless t-shirt and less-than-flattering blue PJ pants that should have been retired a year or two before we met.

Standing before a full-length mirror on the door to her closet, Marie brushed and brushed her hair as she looked at me reflected in the mirror. I was reading a book, an enjoyment I wished I took more time for.

"You did good work today. It was so dangerous and yet, you did it," she said. "I was very worried, more than when you told me about the guy who came into your office. And it made me stop. And think."

I put down the book, unsure of where she was going. The tenor of her voice didn't bode well.

Marie put the brush on her dresser as she came to the bed. She climbed on top of me and laid her head on my shoulder. Her arms were wrapped around me. I put my left arm around her and stroked her head with my right hand.

"For a long time, I didn't know if I could cope with what you do. Long term, that is. At first it was just fun, even after that woman nearly killed us both last year. It was thrilling. And I knew how much you love what you do and do so well," she said.

I didn't dare stop her at this point. I was sure it must be a turning point in our relationship but I would just have to wait and see which way it would go. Marie pulled away and sat up, crossing her legs and leaving her hands on her lap.

"As I waited to hear from you today, knowing if something went wrong, the entire thing could go very bad. It was so hard knowing there was nothing I could do." She took my hands in hers. "And it was in that moment, when I could barely breathe, barely see, barely do anything . . . that I found the strength to carry on. I put my faith in you, all my faith, knowing that you were doing everything you could to be safe and do your job. After that, I was at ease, for the first time since you walked into the lobby of the Sheraton Hotel last year. I was totally at ease."

She took my face in both hands and gently kissed me.

"I want to be with you, King-David Anderson Blaise. Even if we're living in separate cities, I want to be with you."

Surprised, I pulled back a little. "Who told you my full name? No one calls me that. Well, almost nobody. I don't even have it on my driver's license."

"Everyone in your family knows it. You're named after your great-uncle, Grammy Taylor's brother. The one who survived, just like you today," she said. "When Valerie told me your full name, that was when I knew they thought of me as part of the family."

"I want to be with you, too, Marie Toussaint," I said and kissed her again. "And just for the record, Grammy Taylor wants us to get married."

She pulled back and a wide grin spread across her face. "I know. She talked to me, too, last week."

We got a laugh out of that, then got under the covers and cuddled up. I reached over to turn out the light on my side, finally casting the room into darkness. Within a couple of minutes, the only sounds in the room were of Marie's soft snoring.

~*~

I lay awake in bed in the dark thinking, long after Marie detached herself from me and unconsciously moved over to her side of the bed. I stared into the night and thought about the possibilities of life. I slept fitfully when I slept at all.

I gave up trying at around six in the morning. Getting out of bed, I went out to a convenience store and bought a copy of both the Inquirer and the Daily News, a tabloid newspaper.

The front cover page in the Inky, with copy and pictures, was on Morton-Brown and the recovery of The Jade Empress, which most people had never heard of. And an accompanying story just below the fold detailed the FBI taking down a major stolen merchandise fencing operation operated by De Luca. Calls to The Henderson Group, De Luca's security firm, went unanswered throughout the day and the long-term fate of the company was uncertain.

The Daily News also had a story on the necklace on the inside. But on the front page was a large picture of Council President Crocker Smithson III and his son, Crocker the Fourth, with a headline blaring: **Council prez, son face inquiry**

The story, which started on Page Three, involved a new police and district attorney's investigation into the Council president's son regarding the death of Kareem Adams and the reopening of the Mary Ann Tolk murder case.

Nowhere in any of the stories were the names David Blaise or Marie Toussaint mentioned.

However, when the Philadelphia Tribune story written by Randolph Williams hit the streets on Friday, he would quote unnamed sources involved in the investigations that neither The Philadelphia Inquirer nor the Daily News had.

There'd also be a sidebar story on the life of Kareem Adams written by Lynn McCullough.

CHAPTER XXVII

"David, I think you be ready for this."

I was in my office, finishing up the paperwork from my two latest cases, when Mae walked in. She stood over my desk but didn't immediately say anything.

"May I . . . help you?" I ventured.

"You're not done yet, you know."

"With what? These cases are done. I got a call from Powell's estate thanking me profusely. The attorney said after the necklace is authenticated, they'll send me the reward. And I even got my money back from Rubinstein's for having bought stolen merchandise there," I said. "All is good."

"I'm gettin' a raise?" she said cheerfully, as if daring me to say no.

Some sort of financial reward had been on my mind, because Mae had been a tremendous help in the cases. But I could tell that wasn't the reason she invaded my office. "What do you want, Mae?"

She struck a pose, her right hip cocked and her hand on that hip. "You're such a dummy, aren't you? Do I have to spell it out? You've got to get Marie another necklace or something else equally as impressive. After all, you gave her a necklace that was for some blonde bombshell and then took it back."

She was right, of course, but it was going to be a hard thing to top that necklace.

"Okay. What do I do?"

"We could lock up and go shopping," she said.

Ten minutes later, we were in my car heading toward Center City. It was a nice spring day. With the car windows open, a breeze filled the interior of the car.

"Marie. You love her?" Mae asked.

"Of course."

"Then you have to show her you're serious," she said over the wind coming through the open window. "Go to 16th and Walnut. Bailey, Banks and Biddle."

"You serious?"

"Absolutely," she said. "The question is: Are you?"

We parked on the street only a block from the future site of Liberty Place, which would break a decades-old Gentleman's Agreement in very provincial Philadelphia not to construct a building taller than the top of William Penn statue on the tower at City Hall. It's why there were no buildings in the city higher than around forty stories.

Just like that old, unwritten Gentleman's Agreement, Bailey, Banks and Biddle represented something very old and very serious.

I stopped at the revolving door and gestured for her to go first. Just before pushing through the door, Mae looked back at me and said, "David, I think you be ready for this."

I smiled at the thought.

"So do I. I know I be ready."

And with that, I went through the door and into one of the oldest jewelry stores in the United States.

THE END

About the Author

Photo by Jay Alley

MB Dabney is a retired award-winning journalist whose writing has appeared in numerous local and national publications, including Indianapolis Monthly, the Indianapolis Business Journal, Ebony magazine, and Black Enterprise.com. He has co-edited three anthologies for the Speed City chapter of Sisters in Crime — *Scenic and Sinister*; *Decades of Dirt: Murder, Mystery and Mayhem from the Crossroads of Crime*; and *MURDER 20/20* — and has published numerous short mystery stories. He was a co-writer and co-producer of *Deadbeat*, a one-act play produced by the chapter that debuted at the Indianapolis Fringe Festival in 2018.

Pursuit of the Jade Empress is the third novel in the David Blaise mystery series, which includes *A Deadly Game, A David Blaise Mystery* (2023), and it's 2021 prequel, *An Untidy Affair.*

The father of two adult daughters (and a son-in-law), Michael lives in Indianapolis with his wife, Angela.

www.ingramcontent.com/pod-product-compliance
Lightning Source LLC
LaVergne TN
LVHW020042110826
845155LV00029B/601